TROUBLE IN ATLANTIC CITY

J.L.FLANNERY

BLACK PUMPKIN BOOKS

To Dad,

Who loved books and whiskey, but hated parties.

This one's for you.

CONTENTS

1

PART ONE: MILTON'S CONFESSION

✦ ⅱ•————•••————ⅲ ✦

'It's not like I went looking for trouble. It's just that somehow trouble always has a way of finding me.'

Milton Costello,
The Atlantic City Tribune, Sept 10th, 1927

CHAPTER ONE

❧⊱━━━━━━⊰❧

By the time they dragged George O Malley's body out of the sand, it was already too late for me. The cops had already taken me for a murderer.

When I got the news about George, I was lay sprawled on my back like a starfish, a hospital drip in one arm and a bullet wound in the other.

Consciousness drifted in and out, ebbing and flowing like the tide, while some young fry, keen to impress the captain of the force, sat at the foot of the bed keeping watch, in case I made a run for it.

I didn't catch the rookie's name, but he took great pleasure in breaking the news, tossing the latest copy of the gazette on my lap, the news of George's death screaming out in black and white at the top of the page.

'Looks like they finally found your old buddy. You're gonna fry for this Milton.'

I opened my eyes just enough to take in the headline before passing out again:

BODY OF MISSING MAN FOUND UNDER THE ATLANTIC CITY BOARDWALK.

CHAPTER TWO

✤ ▪▪─────▪●▪─────▪▪ ✤

I 'm sure you've heard the story more than a million times by now. How one day in August, my good friend, George O Malley got up and drove to Kelly & Son's, the drugstore where he worked.

He never arrived there. Never returned home neither.

The law tried to find him but they'd no leads, no evidence, no nothing on George. The case had them scratching their heads for weeks, wondering how it was that a standup guy like George could disappear without trace?

Then, in September, on the weekend of the Fall Frolic, some guy is standing in his backyard with a cup of joe in one hand, cigarette in the other. Story goes, that a seagull flies down and perches on his garden table, a chunk of bread sticking out of its beak.

The guy doesn't think much of it at first. Sea birds being scavengers take any scraps they can, so he just stands there sipping his coffee and smoking his cigarette.

When the bird squawks and the 'bread' drops out, the guy realizes it wasn't a piece of bread in its beak after all: it was a severed finger.

And around the middle of the finger, sitting like a lifebuoy, is George O Malley's gold sovereign ring.

Well, the guy pukes like anyone would, but once he gets himself together, he calls the law to come take a look for themselves. Wedged under the fingernail they find a line of sand and a couple of hours later, they finally find George half-buried under the Atlantic City boardwalk, the body missing a finger on his right hand. The very same finger the seagull had dropped earlier that morning.

The cops tell me he was still wearing his pharmacist's apron when they found him. Ribs crushed. His face purple and bloated. Marble eyes looking up at the sky.

And as for the sovereign ring?

Well, turns out its embossed with the crest of Clarence Kelly, local businessman and mine and George's boss. As fate has it, Clarence Kelly was gunned down months before and as we all know, no one, not even someone as powerful as Clarence Kelly, can order a hit from beyond the grave.

The law can't have a killer on the loose in a tourist town - they've got to pin George's murder on someone. And given that almost everyone else involved in this sorry tale is dead, and my ex-girl Pearl has skipped town, it looks like the poor sap taking the heat is going to end up being me.

They say I could fry in the chair for this. Telling you everything could be my only hope.

And we both know everyone believes what they read in the papers. Even the jury.

So here it is, for what it's worth: the truth about what really happened to me, Milton Costello and my friend George O Malley.

4

CHAPTER THREE

It was the Summer of twenty-five and I knew as soon as I met George that he was a standup guy. There I was, all tin ribs and nylon suit, while George in comparison was real spiffy with his slicked back hair and brogue shoes polished to such a sheen you could almost see your reflection in them.

When I first saw him, he was standing under the candy-striped awning of Kelly & Sons wearing a pharmacist's apron, staring at the bottles in the window so intently that you'd think he was trying to memorize their names.

Of course, I now know that George always looked this intently at things; like he was drinking in the details in case he needed to recall them later in case anyone asked.

He may have only been twenty, but his face was lined with the grief and experience of a much older fella. Some of which, I was glad I'd no experience of. You see, even when George smiled, as he did when he saw me, there was this profound sadness ever present behind his brown eyes. Six months down the line he spouted the truth that it was on account of the tragic death of his wife, a few years back. Just nineteen years old and run down by an automobile in New York, leaving him and his three-year-old son Lou behind.

'You must be the Anti-Saloon League kid.' He gestured towards me with his lit cigarette. There was an air of reassurance and confidence about him that I didn't possess yet.

I nodded. 'Yeah, that's me. I'm Milton Costello. Mr Kelly sent me. About the job.' I pointed to the advert in the window: Help wanted.

He blunted the end of his cigarette against the wall, sending sparks flying and placed it behind his ear for later. He stretched out his hand for me to shake.

'I'm George,' he said. 'George O Malley. It's good to meet you, Milton.'

He had a firm, warm handshake and I liked him straight away.

Even on that first meeting it felt like me and him drank out of the same bottle. Were cut from the same cloth. Whatever you want to call it, there was something that bonded us right from the start.

Breaks my heart to think that within two years of that meeting, he'd be dead already.

5

CHAPTER FOUR

❖ ▬▬▬▬ ••• ▬▬▬▬ ❖

I heard about mine and George's Boss, Clarence Kelly, long before I met him in person.

Under the boardwalk where local boys met to smoke cigarettes and drink their father's moonshine, he was a folk hero: someone who lent families money so they could put food on the table. Who bought children their coats for Christmas, so they didn't go cold during the Winter. He was the King of Atlantic City.

Clarence Kelly's Atlantic City was sugar-scented with candy floss and soda and the smell of a good time. On the beach, the screams of seagulls competed with the excited screams of girls in bathing suits, all lining up ready to take part in the Fall Frolic beauty pageant. These weren't the sort of girls you saw at church. These were girls with New York haircuts and rouged lips. The sort of girls you saw leaping over the waves hand in hand with a sweetheart newly met that same day on the train ride there.

It wasn't just candy Clarence Kelly could sell you. If the price was right, he could get you anything you wanted: a pretty girl to spend the night with, an illicit game of cards (if you're willing to have a substantial sum riding on the outcome, of course) and better yet, he could get you all the illegal hooch you could ask for, and more to take back home.

When me and Ma first arrived, I'd never seen anything like it. I wanted so badly to get a piece but of course, like anything shiny and beautiful in Atlantic City, rub hard enough and you'll soon find tin beneath the gold. And just like his precious city, underneath all the sharp suits and golden words, Clarence was all tin.

With politicians and coppers wrapped round his plump fingers, Clarence Kelly ran every racket there was and the law unapologetically turned a blind eye to every law he broke. If he kept his hands clean and paid his taxes, no one cared how Clarence made his money. Especially as it brought the tourists in. Trainloads of them from all around America, longing for a sweet taste of whatever was on offer.

And Atlantic City offered it all.

At the Anti-Saloon League meetings, I went to with my Ma, Clarence was no folk hero. He was little more than a devil put on this earth to tempt those who had no willpower. Rumor was he'd ruined a good many women's lives, luring them to his speakeasy, Kings, only for them to come out again addicted to liquor, jazz and bad men who never kept their promises.

Worse than that, according to the speakers at those meetings, those loans the local kids talked about came with increased interest if you missed payments and the threat of a black eye or maybe even broken kneecaps if you couldn't pay.

I should have been scared spitless of him, but truth was, the more stories I heard about him, the more intrigued I became.

My bones ached to meet the guy I'd heard so much about and finally, one Saturday afternoon, I got to do just that.

Chapter Five

M a believed every word the Anti-Saloon League said.

So much so, that she insisted we accompany them every Saturday on their protests against the speakeasies and the bathtub gin drinkers. Come rain or shine we would walk the boardwalk, handing out leaflets about how 'Gin leads to Sin' and alcohol ruins families.

She bought me a new polyester suit with the little money we had, and I felt I'd no choice but to accompany her, although my embarrassment meant I tried to keep my face hidden and stood at the back.

Ma would proudly take the podium outside a speakeasy specifically selected for that day, and we'd shout slogans and lecture patrons on their sinful ways, hoping to shame them into abstaining and going home to their families.

Sometimes the owners got sore about it and chased us away but most of the time, they left us to it knowing that getting fried was the very reason that most people were there in the first place.

Some drinkers stood and heckled us until we felt obliged to move on. It was obvious to me that we were fighting a losing battle. Not one of the drinkers I'd seen looked unhappy, like Ma claimed they were. They were out there having a grand old time, laughing and talking to broads that were real pretty, and there was a secret part of me that longed to be stood on the other side with them.One Saturday Ma was sick and couldn't come along but insisted I went out and protested anyway. It was sheer luck that me and a few of the guys ended up stationed outside Kings.

It didn't look like the den of debauchery I'd heard about. Peering in through the doorway, it didn't look so dissimilar to the Blenheim Hotel where the Anti Saloon League had held their annual meeting.

Without Ma leading the group, I was the one made of tin. The words everyone expected to come out of my mouth stuck fast in my throat. I could see them all looking at one another wondering who should be the one to begin the chanting now that Dierdre Costello's son had lost his nerve.

Before any of us could chant anything, in the alleyway next to Kings, the back door slammed open and a guy came falling backwards, landing on his ass in the dirt. Two men stepped out after him, one wider and meaner looking than the other, with slicked back hair that was undercut. This was Jesse.

The other, Elmer, was tall and thin, dark skinned with the twitchy hands of a guy who would have preferred in that moment to have had a gun in hand.

'Next time you wanna go touching things that don't belong to you, I suggest you think again.' Jesse loomed over the guy, and he crawled backwards, whimpering like a dog.

'I said I was sorry, didn't I? How was I to know this place belonged to Clarence Kelly.'

The blood was ringing in my ears, the way it used to when Da got that look in his eye. The threat of violence hanging in the air. The group I was with scarpered away behind me, but I was fixed to the spot, unable to run. Unable to do anything but watch the scene unfold before my eyes.

Jesse stepped forward and grabbed the whimpering guy's shirt, lifting him up off the ground. The guy's legs flailed underneath him as he attempted to find some solid ground to place his feet on. Elmer looked down the alleyway and spotted me eyeballing them. He nodded and spoke loud enough so I could hear, like he was making a point of signaling his intentions to any witnesses that were around.

'C'mon Jesse, he's not worth getting into a jam over. He's small fry. Just let him go.'

Elmer stepped back inside, waiting for Jesse to let go of the guy and follow him.

Jesse grunted, disappointed, and 'let go' of him conveniently next to the garbage so that he landed right in the center of it.

'Just don't come back here again.'

Jesse spat on the floor half inch away from the guy's foot and as he turned his back, it was like time slowed down.

I saw it all: the guy getting to his feet. The guy reaching into his back pocket. The glint of sunlight on the blade.

'He's got a knife!' I shouted out.

Jesse turned to look at me, just as the guy thrust the blade towards him. Elmer turned and stepped forward to push him out of the way at the last moment, the knife narrowly missing his guts.

His balance lost, the guy fell back down onto his knees. The knife flew out of his hand and skidded across the ground. There was no time for him to reclaim his blade. Not if he wanted to get out of there alive.

The guy got back up, all the time skittish as a horse, his wild eyes homing in on Jesse.

Jesse lunged for him and missed. The guy started running like his life depended on it. Which it did.

Jesse and Elmer were running now too but they were too slow. The guy had gotten a head start and they would never catch up with him now.

The guy filtered into the holiday crowd, invisible, and Jesse and Elmer slowed to a jog. Then a walk. Then a complete stop. Jesse bent over, wheezing.

All the time, I stood there watching it all.

The two men walked back towards the alleyway, Elmer picking up the knife the guy had dropped.

'Here,' Elmer said, handing it to me. 'Take it. That could have ended differently if you hadn't warned us.' I was scared spitless of these guys, but I could hardly say no. I took the blade from him, hand trembling.

'Say, you wanna come inside? Get yourself a drink and calm your nerves?'

I needed to sit down so I nodded.

Even so, I've never felt such a scaredy cat as in that moment. Even stepping over the threshold of that place was like stepping into Hell if Ma and her friends were to be believed. And coupled with that were the rumors that Clarence Kelly was bound up with the likes of Al Capone. I held onto my leaflets so tightly that they became crumpled, sweat smudging the print. To the untrained eye, Kings looked just like any other place that sat along the boardwalk: a room of cabaret tables draped in pristine white tablecloths. Posies of flowers in vases in the center. Only the faint tang of stale hooch and cigarette smoke in the air made it feel less welcoming than the Blenheim.

On the stage, red velvet drapes hung where I'd been told vaudeville acts and scandalous women with short, bobbed hair performed night after night, the spotlight shining like the moon on their bare bodies.

At the piano next to the stage the pianist tinkled the keys amongst the raucous laughter of his band mates getting ready to rehearse.

It was the little things that I didn't know about yet that revealed Kings tin beneath the glitz: the tommy guns strapped to the underneath of the bars, manned by barmen chosen not for their pouring skills but for their instinct for sniffing out troublemakers, their quick reactions and accurate shot. Upstairs, away from the main entertainment lounge, the VIP suite was made up of bare tables, the only table dressing after dark being a fifty-two pack of cards and a stack of poker chips. There were rumors that some of the chorus girls offered more than just family entertainment to some of Clarence's VIP clients too.

Elmer walked on ahead, stopping next to the guy who looked quizzically in my direction, to whisper the tale of what had happened in his ear. The way he sat so upright, regal, making even the bar stool he sat on look like a throne, gave him away as Clarence Kelly.

I could see why those who admired him nicknamed him 'The Gent,' the fragile porcelain cup and saucer cradled in one hand as he stirred the sugar into his tea with a silver spoon, a gold ring on every finger. He'd come a long way from the cramped one bedroomed apartment in Hell's Kitchen that he'd grown up in, scrapping over the last slice of bread with his siblings. The exquisite pin-striped suit in fine Italian fabric gave no hint of his past, though he was reminded of it whenever he came to hang it up at night next to the others, suits hanging in his wardrobe like carcasses in a meat store.

And there I was, stood in my itchy polyester suit that looked two sizes too big for me, prohibition leaflets in hand and suddenly in front of him, I felt a real sap.

He beckoned me over and ordered me to sit down at the table where Elmer and Jesse now stood either side, flanking him like attack dogs. Clarence smiled and when he did, his whole face lit up. This wasn't the expression of the devil I'd been told about. This was the smile of a preacher. One that invited you in and made you feel at home.

'Can I get you a drink? A soda perhaps? A tea even?'

The fan whirring above us did nothing to cool the sticky air and the heat was made much worse by my wool suit and my nerves made much worse by the calm he exuded.

'A glass of soda please, Mr. Kelly.'

At hearing his own name being spoken he gave a half smile as if acknowledging his own infamy. The two brunos flanking him laughed openly at me, only for Clarence to flash them a look so cutting that they instantly shut up. He waved them away and ordered Jesse to bring me an ice-cold glass of coke. When they were gone, Clarence turned his attention to me.

'I heard what you did outside. That was brave of you. Most boys your age run away from danger, not get themselves caught up in it.'

He eyeballed the leaflets I still held in my hand and gestured for me to hand them over which I did. All the while I was sweating, ashamed to be protesting against a man who was being so kind to me. He took the one from the top and skim read over it, his face stony. He handed the pile back.

'What's your name, kid?'

'Milton.'

'Ah, like the great poet. You really believe in this stuff, huh?' He nodded at the leaflets I held in my hand.

For a moment, I didn't answer. All the time I'd been going out there campaigning and no one, not Ma, not anyone, had ever asked my opinion on whether or not I really believed in what I was saying. It was just a given. And now that I'd seen Clarence Kelly with my own eyes and he wasn't the monster I'd been led to believe he was, I began to ask myself the same question. How much did I really believe in what I was doing?

'My Dad was a drinker.' It was the best answer I could muster and the one that was the best justification for what I'd spent my weekends doing for the past two months.

'He was in the war?' He said it like it was a fact, not a question. The darkness in his eyes suggesting he knew all about what it was like to live as a soldier.

'Well, yeah. How did you know?'

Clarence shrugged. 'Easy guess. Happens to a lotta guys. They go out there, fight for their country, protect their fellow men and when the war ends, they come back home, and they don't know what to do with themselves. Can't go round shooting at people all day when you're a civilian. Some of them turn to drink because that's all they can do to cope. You still live with your Dad?'

I shook my head. 'With my Ma. Da's dead.'

'And your Ma is...'

'Usually with me, it's just that today she's sick.'

'Oh, that is unfortunate.'

His tone didn't sound like a man who was disappointed. He was silent a moment as Jesse returned with my glass of coke, the perspiration down the side of the glass matching the rivulets of nervous sweat down my back. I took a long gulp.

'Would you like to work for me, Milton?'

'What?' I wasn't certain I'd heard him right. 'You want me to work for you?'

'Not here, of course. Your Ma would never approve of that. I own a lotta businesses here on the boardwalk: the taffy shop, the barbers. I also own the local drugstore, and we could do with a boy about your age to help dispense the medicine. I promise I'd pay you well for it. It must be hard for just you and your Ma. I've found that it's all very well believing in God and the law, but good faith rarely pays the bills, don't you agree?'

I wanted to say no. I mean, I knew that was what I should say but there I was, a boy of sixteen and I didn't know how to. Not to a man like Clarence Kelly. No one ever said no to him.

'I dunno, my Ma...'

'Don't worry about her. I'll send someone to talk to your Ma. Explain it's in the best interest for both of you. Look, call in at the florists on the way back and give them this.'

He took out a card and a pen and he scribbled a note on it.

'They'll send her some flowers to sweeten the deal. Tell her if she lets you work for me at the drugstore, you and her'll never go hungry. Never struggle again. Won't have to worry about anything. I'll even throw in a donation to the Anti-Saloon movement. I can't say fairer than that.' It sounded more than fair – it sounded too good to be true.

I finished up my coke and walked over to the florists to pick up some gladioli, but Clarence's boys worked quickly and by the time I made it home they'd already been and gone. Ma sat waiting at the kitchen table, a hundred-dollar bills brick in front of her. Her hair was scraped back and tied up the way it always was, but she looked more tired and gaunt than usual, like she was exhausted by the weight of what it meant to be alive and poor. It was only as I got closer, I saw that she was crying.

'Ma, are you okay? I swear if anyone has so much as touched a hair on your head...'

'Oh Milton!' She got up from the table and threw her arms around me.

'Mr. Kelly's offered to pay our rent for the next six months and his men said they would ask our landlord to fix that leak in the roof.'

She wasn't crying out of fear after all, but out of relief. I knew the past few months hadn't been easy. We started our new life in Atlantic City with the clothes on our backs and what little money we had left after paying Da's debts, but I hadn't realized quite how dire the situation had become.

'Did they tell you what happened?'

I still had the knife that almost killed Jesse in my back pocket. *'Keep it,'* Clarence had said. *'You've earned it, kid.'*

'They said you'd been offered a job at the drugstore in town: Kelly & Sons.'

I didn't want to ruin everything by telling her the details of what had really happened, but I couldn't, in good conscience, stand there and let her take the money without knowing who it came from.

'Are you okay with me working there, Ma? I mean, this is Clarence Kelly we're talking about. I don't think the league will like it.'

She sat down again, her gaze falling on the piles of money on the table. She was silent a while, gently tracing the outline of the silver crucifix she wore around her neck with her index finger. She often did this when she needed comfort. The necklace had been her Ma's, given to her on her deathbed, so poor by the time she died that she had nothing else to offer her only daughter. The crucifix was the only thing she had left.

Ma lit a cigarette and took a long drag on the filter, like it was giving her the oxygen she needed to speak her mind. Still, she lowered her voice, like she was ashamed to admit it out loud.

'God owes us,' Ma said. 'For your father; for both of your brothers. Perhaps this is his way of compensating us.'

'Da used to say there's no accounting for what God wants.'

I disliked the bitter tone and blasphemy in her voice. Not because I didn't agree with what she was saying but because this was so out of character. This wasn't my Ma speaking. How could one visit from Mr. Kelly's goons have changed her mind so completely? They must have spooked her real good.

'Maybe we've been wrong about a lot of things. Those rich women, with nothing to do all day but complain about their maids and how tough it is finding a good French tutor for their children; they ain't never lifted a finger to help us pay our bills. When I told Joan Saunders we were struggling, you know what she said? That our belief in God and the cause would sustain us. That woman lives in one of the largest houses in Atlantic City. And yet you know what else I see?'

I shook my head.

'Families being bought new clothes by Clarence Kelly. Food. None of it bought by the Anti-Saloon League. It's got me wondering if maybe we were wrong about him. I'm as surprised as you Milton to find Mr. Kelly offering us help, and right now it's the only help we got coming our way, so who cares what those rich women at the league think?'

She stubbed her cigarette out in the ashtray, the embers glowing and hissing like a demon. She blew out a cloud of grey smoke that swirled up to the ceiling. She looked me straight in the eye.

'What if God *wants* us to have this? If, it's God's will then it can't be wrong, *can it?*'

I knew, having seen Kings that it wasn't God's work that Clarence Kelly did and that if I took this job, I would be newly baptized. Dragged under as deep as it was possible to go.

Ma tucked her crucifix back inside her blouse, keeping it hidden and I knew her mind was made up.

On the following Monday I started working at Kelly & Son's drugstore alongside George O Malley.

Chapter Six

I didn't see Clarence again for months. It was the way he liked to work, keeping anything that could get him behind the eight ball at arm's length.

I'd no kick about it. It was best for Ma's reputation for us not to be openly associated with him. Besides, it was George who was the respectable face of Kelly & Sons. Everyone had heard of George and not one person had anything bad to say about him. I mean, he was a real ace. On that first day as we stood in the doorway, he placed his hand between my shoulder blades and proudly introduced the drugstore as if it were his own home.

'Well, this is it. I'll show you round.'

He led me over to the mahogany cabinet that ran wall to wall filled with jars lined up like soldiers storing all manner of herbs: rosinweed, sage, comfrey root and pre-made remedies in bottles.

'You're not to touch these. If anyone wants anything outta here, you'll refer them to me, and I'll discuss it with them. The part you'll be looking after is over here.'

He pointed over to the curved counter at the center of the room. At one end was a soda fountain with a couple of stools placed in front for the punters to sit at. There was a small glass cabinet on top that housed several brands of cigarettes, as well as tobacco and paper to roll your own. At the other end of the counter was the till and a gumball machine. On the back wall were a variety of items: combs and cosmetics; magazines and toys.

He led me round the side so I could get a feel for it. Out of the corner of my eye I spied a rifle taped to the underside of the counter and my stomach flipped like one of Ma's pancakes. I knew then that this was no ordinary drugstore. Whilst I wasn't a stranger to guns, seeing them there so out of context, made my stomach queasy.

'Don't you worry none,' George said, realizing from my line of sight what I was looking at. 'I've never had to use it in all the time I've been here. It's just in case, you know. You hear about these people holding up banks and stores and you gotta be protected. Have you ever shot a gun before?'

I thought of my horse Swift at the end of his life, his sad eyes looking into mine as I raised the gun. A memory I tried to push down into my gut.

'Yeah, I know how to shoot. Just don't like doing it, is all.'

'Well hopefully you'll never have to use it. Follow me and I'll show you out back.'

I trailed behind him, out to the back room, glad to change the subject. The room was sparsely furnished with a large counter running the length of it and a telephone hanging on the wall.

'Just in case you ever need to call Clarence, the number for Kings is in here.'

George pulled out a drawer and inside was a scrap of paper with a phone number written down. Next to it was a pile of prescriptions, all blank except for the signature scribbled on the bottom.

'I thought you had to see a doctor to get one of those?' I said.

George gestured to the phone. 'Got a hotline to Dr Rothstein right here.'

I could tell by his flushed cheeks and smirk that it was a lie. I doubted very much that Dr Rothstein, whoever he was, was called by George for every blank prescription to be filled in.

Next, George showed me the scales and pill roller machine where he compounded the medicines.

'Are you a real pharmacist?'

The question was out the kisser before I'd had a chance to even think about what I was saying, but George looked too wet behind the ears to be a trained physician. Besides, after seeing the rifle and the blank prescriptions I was beginning to wonder if there was anything about the place that was legit.

The coldness of his voice said George was offended at the very suggestion, 'Well, Clarence paid for me to get my license but yeah, I'm real enough.'

'Look, I'm sorry. I didn't mean nothing by it. I've just never met someone so young that's so qualified. It must have taken some hard work to get where you are.'

George warmed then. I learned that if he had one flaw, it was that he'd flap his gums for anyone who fed him a line.

'Yeah, it did. You know, Clarence has a son called Charlie who was meant to train to do this instead but he's hoping to go to study philosophy or something at Princeton. Clarence is trying to persuade him to study Law at least – you know, something useful; but so far Charlie's refusing to be a part of the family business. Which is good news for me, of course, cause if Charlie had done what his Dad asked, who knows where I woulda ended up? Him turning it down turned out to be my lucky break.'

George suddenly aware he had spilled his guts to someone he had only just met and so added, 'of course, Clarence is real mad about the whole Princeton thing so maybe don't mention it around him. Anyway, that's everything to show you.' George cleared his throat.

I pointed to the door at the end of the room. 'What's in there?'

'Just storage,' George said.

Those first four months at the drugstore were easy. All I had to do was turn up, help the punters who came in, and collect my pay at the end of the week.

Ma warmed to me working for Clarence Kelly too after seeing how everyone treated us with respect. There was no need to wait in line at the bakery anymore, or anywhere else for that matter.

Of course, Ma couldn't keep the news that I was being employed by him quiet for long and soon enough, a bluenose broad called Ada Mae from the Anti-Saloon League heard the rumors and we were asked to leave the group. Ma was upset at first, but said she never much liked Ada Mae anyway and that me working for Clarence had opened her eyes. She wasn't even sure anymore if prohibition had been the cat's meow everyone thought it was going to be.

'People are still drinking,' she said. 'Only now families are paying three times as much for something that was made in someone's back yard.'

I don't mind saying I was relieved we'd been collared. It meant I could ease up a little with George and not care anymore about who walked in through the door of the drugstore.

George had a great sense of humor, and it was this, combined with his zip and straight talking that kept the punters coming back in, time and time again. There were even a few regulars who dropped in every week, and George would walk right up to them, put his arm around their shoulders and lead them to sit with him in the back room whilst he crushed powders and gave them various bottles of colorless liquid from the storage room.

When it was quiet, George would take the time to teach me a little about the herbs we sold. He would choose one of the glass pots at random and talk me through their applications and effects. One of the first things I learned was that a small amount of wormwood was an effective remedy for an upset stomach but get the dose wrong and you could cause seizures, paralysis and a trip to an early grave.

Sometimes, when the weather was warm, we'd close up the place for an hour and take a walk along the boardwalk and I would eat my sandwiches while George eyeballed whatever food stalls or shops were open that day. He'd end up eating eels or a whole bag of taffy for his lunch and I often ribbed him that he was greedier than the seagulls.

Even now, despite everything that has happened since, one day on the boardwalk stands out in my memory more vibrantly than any other. If we had just stayed at the store and ate our sandwiches, I'm certain everything would have been different.

We were strolling along the boardwalk when she appeared out of nowhere: the girl that was about to change everything.

Chapter Seven

The Summer crowds had arrived, train carriages bursting at the seams so that even the steam engines spat out a sigh of relief as they pulled into the station.

Tourists spilled out of the open doors, like grain from a torn burlap sack, filling every available space on the beach with a patchwork of striped towels and deckchairs.

They swarmed the boardwalk too without a care. Taking up space and sauntering so slowly that they held up the rest of us going about our daily business. Outside the salt-water taffy shop, families gathered transfixed by the machine whirring round, pulling and stretching the taffy into shape like it was some sort of illusionist's trick. On the pier couples walked arms around one another; bimbos in their sharp suits and broads in dresses so delicate that when they walked, they looked almost ethereal.

Perhaps that was why we never noticed the girl straight away.

All weekend there'd been girls dressed like her. Girls in long pleated dresses and cloche hats, each one a cookie cutter copy of others that passed by. She could have been standing there watching us for five minutes or fifty.

George, led by his grumbling stomach as usual, had been too busy perusing the food stalls to notice anything. It was only when he returned to the bench I was sitting on, paper bag of chestnuts in hand, that we became aware of her, leaning back on the pier railings. Even then she wasn't enough to draw my attention away completely.

'Go on Milton,' George kept saying, shoving the paper bag under my nose. 'Just try one. How do you know you don't like them if you don't even try them?'

I pushed his hand away, George, I just know. Don't like the stink of them. They just smell all wrong to me. Besides, you can never trust these stall-owners. I ain't never seen any of them wash their hands.'

George never gave a damn about that, and the girl gave a wry smile, watching him munch on the whole bag, stuffing chestnut after chestnut into his mouth. When he was done, he tossed the bag and sat down next to me.

'Hey, check out this broad,' George nodded towards her.

I looked up and there she was, this girl with curly red hair. Pretty. A real doll to look at, with a heavily made-up face and a beaded dress that wouldn't have looked out of place on a Friday night at Kings. It was as though everything sped up around her, people passing by just a blur whilst she remained serene despite the frenzy of activity around her. I couldn't take my eyes off of her.

'She's sure dressed up to the nines for a Monday morning,' George whistled through his teeth in approval.

I noticed the stack of flyers she held in her right hand and the air of self-righteousness she had. It was the same one I'd walked around with only a couple of months before.

'Don't be fooled George,' I said, even Anti-Saloon League janes dress like flappers now. It's how they draw you into the conversation.

I bet you a dollar those flyers are all about how we're all gonna go to Hell.'

Seeing us staring at her, the girl blushed and started walking over to us.

'Now we've gone and done it,' I said. 'She's coming over. She's gonna try and save our souls I bet.'

'Morning Gentlemen,' she said, and I was taken aback by her voice. She might have looked eighteen, but her voice didn't sound young at all. Her tones were deep and sultry, like the voice didn't really belong in her body, and in truth, I was a little unnerved by her.

She handed us both a flyer each.

George read it out aloud.

'Madame Zelda's. All fortunes told. Palmistry, tarot and communications with the other realm.' He looked at the girl. 'You Zelda?'

The girl grinned and shook her head. 'No. But I work for her. She's opening her place, right here on the boardwalk this weekend.'

She pointed at the date on the flyer, and I looked around for the shop she was talking about, but I couldn't spot it. It sounded like a load of hooey to me.

'So, you can't read fortunes then?' George said.

Despite George's heartbreak over his dead wife, he still skated round plenty, and I couldn't figure out if he was mocking her or giving her a line. Maybe both.

'I wouldn't say that exactly.'

She looked across at me and I noticed how green her eyes were. The color of absinthe. My face reddens.

'Look if you're wanting to test me to see if it's all genuine, that's fine,' she said. 'Lots of people do. I can tell you your future right now. Both of you.'

We'd only worked together a short time, but me and George already instinctively knew what the other was thinking and at that moment George looked at me as if to say, 'this girl is clearly a few tarot cards short of a full deck.' I looked away to stop myself from laughing out loud.

'Fine you can do me,' George said, and he extended his palm for her to read.

She shook her head and instead came right over to me and took my hand in hers. Her hands were soft and warm. I tried not to look at George behind her, who was stifling a laugh.

'You're a hard worker, right?' she said.

I nodded.

'Well, your boss, he knows this. He's going to give you a promotion,' she grinned.

What a load of baloney! I had a white shirt and tie on. Ain't no holiday maker wearing a penguin suit in the summer heat! Of course, I'd a boss of some sort. I nodded politely but I wasn't buying none of it.

'There's something else,' the girl said. 'One day, you're going to own that business you work for.'

'That so?' I smiled at her, disbelieving.

She looked right at me, her eyes piercing through me so that the hair on my arms prickled. I couldn't tell now if her irises were green after all. They were almost metallic under the midday sun.

'Yes. You're going to pull things towards you but be careful: there's a jewel there that could bring you trouble. I guess you could say, you'll be a 'King' of sorts.'

The way she emphasized the word King as she spoke. It was too uncanny. How did she know anything about Kings? She didn't look like the sort of doll who would drink in a joint like that.

I tried to speak but as she dropped my hand it was like the words got caught in my throat and I couldn't utter a single one. All I knew was that my hand she had held in hers was purple with cold. She shifted her attention to George.

'And you,' she said. 'You won't have great success or great riches, but you will be remembered as the greatest of the two of you.'

She dropped his hand to signal that she had finished speaking and took a step back, waiting for one of us to say something, but I was too dumbstruck to say anything. George calmly took a cigarette and a match from the case in his top pocket.

'Thank you, that was…enlightening.' He openly winked at me, thinking he was a hot sketch.

The girl was unfazed by his mocking. 'You're welcome. When it comes true you must come to see Zelda in her new place and thank her personally.'

George didn't say anything in response, but I knew he was thinking she was a fraud. The silence was getting awkward, so I reached out and took one of her flyers and I swear the weirdest thing happened. As I did so, the sun glinted off the gold rings on her finger and I swear, for a split second, one of them looked just like Clarence Kelly's sovereign, but when I looked again, it was just a normal gold ring set with a tiger's eye. I don't know how she did it. It was like an optical illusion, or trick of the light or something.

'Thanks for reading,' I said, tipping my cap to her.

George got up from the bench. 'We'd better go, or we'll be back late.'

'Of course.' The girl smiled and we both watched her head off down the pier and disappear into the crowd.

Neither of us spoke for a while on the walk back to the drugstore. Her words were a whirlwind in my head. I was glad when George finally spoke.

'So,' George said. 'You're going to own Kings apparently,' he gave a snort.

I understood why. I'd barely met Clarence, let alone was in a position to take over his business.

'Says you,' I laughed. 'The only way Clarence will be giving Kings up to anyone is if he's six feet under.'

It was meant as a wisecrack but somehow it didn't seem as funny spoken out loud. It hung in the air a moment before I quickly moved the focus back onto George. 'Well, you'll be greater than I am, apparently.'

'Yeah, but she mentioned a promotion for you,' George said. 'Now, that I *can* see happening. You've learned a lot these past few months. Who knows, you might end up taking my job.'

He laughed, but the hollowness sounded like there was resentment behind his words. I felt like I'd been left holding the bag for something I hadn't even done yet.

I laid it out straight for him.

'You know George, she just told us what she thought we wanted to hear, thinking we were a pair of saps. I'm happy as I am. The last thing I want is people thinking I'm trying to get them replaced.'

George smiled. 'I know, you'd never do that. All I'm saying is if you get the chance to rise and move to Kings then you should, palm reading be damned.'

But it didn't matter what I wanted. The cogs were already turning and there wasn't going to be anything anyone could do to stop it.

CHAPTER EIGHT

✦■————•■■•————■✦

S o, I know the law says I'm this big bootlegger, but I swear I was
so green back then I barely knew which way was up. I'd been
working at Kelly & Sons for three months before I fully got the rumble
of what was really going on.

One night as we were clearing up, George got a phone call. He's
standing in the back room, voice barely a whisper to whoever was
on the other end of the line. Still, I could sense there's some beef
happening from the way he kept raising his voice.

'Yeah, well I guess you just go on ahead and do whatever you want.'

He slammed down the receiver, the scowl on his face a mixture of
anger and frustration. I'd never seen George look so furious. I could
have kept sweeping the floor and minding my own business, but I
wanted to know what it was that had made him have such a change
in mood. I called over.

'Everything alright George?'

He sighed. 'It's nothing. Someone just let me down on an errand I
said I'd do for Clarence, that's all.'

The look on his face suggested it was more than nothing. He walked
over to the soda fountain and helped himself to a coke. He looked over
at me.

'You want anything?'

I wasn't really thirsty but I asked for a root beer anyway so I could sit down next to him while he flapped about what was on his mind. And boy, did he spill his guts. All about how hard he worked for Clarence and how he'd always been overlooked. How hard it was to be the sole parent of his little boy Lou, trying to make money to put food on the table. How Clarence's son Charlie was spoiled in comparison and was a good-for-nothing letdown who does what he wants without any repercussions.

'Wait, you mean to tell me Clarence's own son is the one who's let him down?'

George nodded and explained that Charlie was meant to drive him somewhere to go pick something up for Clarence. I mean, I couldn't believe it. What sort of guy leaves his own Pa in the lurch?

For some reason, a memory rose to the surface: my Pa slumped against the wall of his buddy's house, barely able to stand, let alone walk or drive. And me at twelve helping him into the back of the car and driving him home, feet only just able to reach the pedals.

'Well, I can drive for you,' I said. 'I ain't got nothing else to do. If you need a hand, I'll be glad to help.'

Hesitation flickered in his eyes. This was George's chance to say no. To stop me from doing something that would drag me deeper into a world I didn't need to know anything about.

I could also see him thinking it over. He was in a tight spot and there I was offering the very solution that would get him out of it.

'You know, that's mighty good of you but I gotta warn you, you can't tell anyone anything about what we're doing. You think you can manage that?'

'Sure,' I nodded.

'Thanks. You'd be doing me a real favor.'

He gave me a real friendly smile, and I finished off my soda and went back to sweeping the floor and no more was said about it until later after we closed up for the evening.

The plan was simple. We'd meet the next block down from George's house at seven. We'd take the car Clarence had lent George and drive all the way to a meeting place in Princeton. Once there, the job was to collect a few boxes, cut a deal with a couple of guys for a few thousand jacks, and drive all the way back. We'd get a couple of hours of shut eye and reopen the drugstore as usual.

At seven I was there waiting at the corner of the block, stomach aching with hunger. I'd been too nervous to eat before I left the house. I still didn't know what we were collecting or who we would be dealing with and that made my guts churn. I hated unknowns.

At five past the hour George pulled up in a muddied Ford. He must have seen the disappointment on my face. He leaned out the window.

'C'mon what are you waiting for? We'd better get going.'

'I expected something a little more...'

'Hotcha?' George laughed as I got in. 'We're trying to avoid drawing attention, not courting it, Milton. Don't you worry, I'm sure you'll get the chance to own something a little swankier yourself the way you're going.'

Princeton was pearls and apple pie in comparison to Atlantic City. Where the night air on the boardwalk was punctuated by the hiss of the sea and the holler of tourists, here the only sound was the wind blowing through the trees. Standing pious as a church, the college loomed above the rest of the town. In another life, perhaps I could have been one to study there and join the other young men on the verge of the rest of their successful lives, but fate doesn't work like that. You only have the hand you're dealt, and Princeton was for players like Charlie, not players with low stakes like me.

We pulled up outside a quaint townhouse. As we did so, the door opened, and a guy stepped out to greet us. He walked over to the car and stuck his head in through the open window.

'Well, here's your man, I see!' he said, looking over at me. 'Hi there, I'm Clyde. Clyde Wilson.'

Having been told not to say too much, I gave a smile and a nod as Clyde and George started talking like old pals. When they were done exchanging pleasantries about kids and Ruth's home runs for the Yankees, Clyde lit a cigar and got down to business. He explained to us both that he would bring the car round and lead the way to the meeting place.

I didn't say anything, but I'd assumed we were already at the meeting place! The fact he wouldn't tell us exactly where this meeting place was should have given me the shakes but there was something about Clyde's smile and calm tone of voice that instilled a certain reassurance in me that fooled me into thinking that everything would be just fine.

'He seems a standup guy,' I said to George as we watched Clyde walk to his own car.

'Sure is. Friendliest flatfoot in all of New Jersey.'

At first, I thought I'd heard wrong.

'Clyde's a copper?'

'Yeah, a damn good one too. Knows the difference between when to keep his mouth shut and when to shut other's mouths for us. He's on the payroll, of course. He doesn't believe in prohibition.'

George made it sound like prohibition was a philosophy you could take or leave.

'So does that mean he's not on the side of the law or...'

'The only side Clyde is on is Clyde's. He protects whoever pays him, but don't worry. The fact he's on the payroll means he's as much in our pocket as we are in his.'

It didn't sound particularly reassuring to me and I didn't understand how George could be so sure this guy wasn't a dry agent, but it made me wonder, which other respectable people were part of all this? Who really knew how deep the rabbit hole went if you really dug deep?

We tailed Clyde all the way through town and as we drove further away the streetlights and roads were replaced with darkness and a dirt track. We turned off to the right and headed down towards a clearing by the river. The headlamps lit up the silhouettes of a row of men, each one with a tommy gun in hand. Behind them, a stack of crates and three cars. My stomach was churning. So, this was where the rabbit hole led: to dark pathways in the middle of nowhere with bimbos packing guns.

Now I'd always known Clarence wasn't legit, but in my naivety, I hadn't really thought about what that could actually mean. I was just a kid on an adventure. I wasn't looking to get cut down. And now I became acutely aware I'd no piece to help me if I needed it and I was beginning to wish I'd taken the rifle from under the counter at the drugstore. Not that a remington would be much of a match for the tommies they had.

George looked over at my hands gripping onto the steering wheel, despite us having stopped.

Look, don't you worry none, Milton. I've done this a million times. Those goons ain't looking to use any of those guns. It's just to show you they could if they wanted to. You get what I mean?'

I nodded. I understood but it didn't make me feel any better.

We wait until Clyde gives us the go ahead,' George explained, and we both watched as Clyde got out of his car and walked over to shake the guy's hands.

'Who are they?' I said.

'Thomas and William Abel. The Abel brothers from New York. Two of the biggest Canadian whiskey importers. They reckon it's the real McCoy. They used to bring it to us on the rum row, and we'd meet them out at sea, but the dry agents caught wind of it and now it's safer to meet on the road. Princeton is halfway and let's be honest, no one's gonna be expecting this place to be a hotbed of bootlegging.'

Up ahead of us, there was a real ing-bing going on between Clyde and the brothers. The shorter of the brothers, William, kept eyeballing us and pointing towards the car. George reached for his gun in the glove box and put it in his holster.

'Wait here.'

Now my stomach was twisting like a snake in my guts. The other brother, Thomas, with his fat gut and thin pencil moustache, looked like he was about to sock someone. George held his arms up like he was surrendering as he approached them both.

All the time I was watching this and wondering if something happened to George, what the hell would I do? I was just a yellow-bellied kid doing his friend and boss a favor.

Thomas' face broke into a smile at the sight of him and George walked up and shook hands with them both and waved to me to get out of the car.

Despite his reassuring wave, it didn't stop my legs from feeling like Jello.

'Milton, grab hold of these crates will you. Do not put them in the trunk or in full view of anyone. If you lift up the back seat, you'll find a place to put them.'

I took my first crate, not making eye contact with anyone else and I carried it back to the car. Sure enough, underneath the back seats, was an empty space big enough to hold not just one, but several crates.

Once the car was full, we were ready for the drive home. George shook hands with Clyde and the Abel brothers and came back to the car.

He put the gun back in the glovebox and sighed.

'Everything okay?' I asked.

'Sure. Everything is jake. Although Clarence is not gonna be best pleased to hear they've hiked the jack up. I persuaded them we'd owe them the rest of the money. Let's get outta here before they change their minds.'

I didn't need to be told twice. I reversed out of the clearing, the line up of men and Clyde eyeballing us as we left.

'You did good tonight,' George said. 'You know, they weren't just sore that Clarence was playing dumb about the price. They were sore I'd brought you along with me when they were expecting Charlie. You being a stranger to them, you know? I thought they were gonna come and drag you outta the car at one point, but I managed to calm them down. Clyde told them you were a bare-knuckle boxer who would take them both down if they tried anything, guns or no guns.'

George started laughing but I failed to see what was so funny.

'Jesus George! What if they hadn't believed him.'

George smirked. 'But they did, so it's no bother.'

Chapter Nine

I was sore with George. Of course, I was! Him putting me in danger like that. I wasn't just some chump, but he'd certainly made me feel like one. The Abels could have turned on me at any time, but I guess George was right – they hadn't. They believed that hooey about me being a bare-knuckle boxer.

I chuckled to myself. The idea that someone like the Abels respected that made me feel tall. To have that respect. That power. It was my first taste of the honey, and I couldn't take the grin off my face.

George had been in the back room most of the morning on the phone to Clarence, explaining the importance of paying the Abel brothers the jack they'd agreed on. Clarence was refusing, saying it wasn't the amount that had been agreed and who did these bimbos think they were?

George came out onto the shop floor, exasperated.

'I need some air. Let's go out for lunch.' Out on the boardwalk, he spilled his guts.

'This can only end badly if Clarence doesn't pay up,' George said, smoking a cigarette. 'He's been in the business long enough so that he thinks everyone will bow down to him and he can get by on name alone. He doesn't realize that things are changing. Most of his acquaintances are dead. The Abel brothers are pups – they have no idea who he once was or is. And the truth is they couldn't care less about that; all they want is their money. And I swear if Clarence doesn't give in to them, he'll be bringing us a whole lotta trouble.'

We walked to the end of the pier and back. When we returned from lunch there was a guy waiting for us to open up. Skinny guy, with a pencil moustache. When he smiled, he had this Weasel look that said there was something hinky about him, though I couldn't pinpoint what.

'Can I help you?'

George came up behind him with the key and weasel-face stepped aside to let him open up.

'You own this place?' the guy asked.

'I run the place if that's what you mean.'

George opened the door and walked in, the weasel slipped in behind him and followed him in, his beady little eyes taking in everything.

'I heard you sold hooch here,' he said loudly.

'Medicinal we do,' George said, unlocking the door to his workspace.

I took my place behind the soda counter only an arm's length away from the rifle that was taped underneath.

The guy kept on grilling him.

'Oh, c'mon. I heard you have more than medicinal,' he snorted.

He was bordering on disrespectful the way he wouldn't let up and I could see by the way George kept clenching his fist at his side that he really wanted to give this guy the gate.

'Like I said we have medicinal...'

The guy pulled out a wallet full of notes before George had a chance to finish what he was saying.

'...if you have a prescription from your doctor.'

'Oh c'mon!' Weasel-face leaned in and said something to George that I couldn't hear.

George held his ground, his face not giving anything away.

'Like I said, if you get a prescription from your doctor, I'll be able to help.'

Weasel-face laughed. I stepped closer to the rifle. Just in case. He looked from George to me and back to George again but seeing that neither of us were about to break, he shrugged and put his money back in his wallet.

'Fine,' he said. 'I'll be back with a prescription.'

When he was gone, George let out a sigh.

'Jeez! Who the hell did that chump think he was, getting up in your face like that? He would just not let up!' I said.

George shrugged, 'I'm guessing he's a dry agent. You'd think he'd be more subtle about it, but I guess he wants us to know he's here in town. It's funny, Atlantic City has always been openly above the law but since the papers have been talking about it, it seems they're determined to take us down. I'd better warn Clarence the prohis are in town.'

The bell above the door tinkled and two old women came in. We both straightened ourselves up and George disappeared into the back room, while I came round the front of the counter to talk with them. The weasel faced guy was forgotten about.

***

T

hat evening, I was sweeping up while George was in the back
room when there was a rapping at the door. The blind was
pulled down and all I could see was a guy's silhouette behind it.

'We're closed!' I yelled and carried on sweeping, but the gentle
knocking turned to hammering.

In the end, George poked his head round the door and shouted,
'For goodness' sake, Milton, go and see what they want.'

I opened the door a crack to see the weasel was back. He was waving
a piece of paper that looked like a doctor's prescription.

'I know you're closed but do you think you could do a guy a favor
and help me out. Doc took so long I thought I'd never get here at all!'

He still gave me the feeling he was trying to chisel us, so I looked
over at George, but George gave the nod to let him in and walked back
into his workshop.

I sighed at him. 'Yeah sure.'

As I unhooked the chain from the door, I felt the full force of his
kick, the door bursting wide open, knocking me backwards.

'Hey, what's the big idea!'

I was still on my feet, just about but before I knew it, weasel's fist
came hurtling towards me.

It happened so quickly: the searing pain in my nose as the blood
gushed from it down my white shirt. The sharp chop in the back of
my knees, as Weasel pulled off the head of the broom I'd been using
and swung it like he was going for a home run. The fall to the ground
as my legs gave way beneath me.

'You ain't no bareknuckle boxer,' he scoffed as he raised the broom
handle above him and bought it crashing down on me.

Chapter Ten

My head throbbed and I'd the copper taste of blood on my tongue. I sat up slowly, unsure where I was at first. The broom that had done the damage to me lay snapped in half on the floor.

Weasel hadn't even bothered to tie me up or guard me; that's how much of a sap he thought I was. For some reason, this made me sorer than the hit itself. I could hear him snapping a cap at George in the distance somewhere and despite still bleeding, the adrenaline and anger fueled me enough to rise up and tear the rifle from its hiding place.

I'd no intention of shooting weasel-face but I knew a rifle would give me the upper hand. He hadn't had a gun himself so hopefully just pointing this one at him would have him surrendering pretty damn quickly.

I waited a moment behind the door in the back room, just listening in.

'I told you there's nothing in there. I swear it.'

'Oh, c'mon George. Everyone knows this is Clarence Kelly's joint. He owes the Abels, and they've told me that if he's not gonna pay up, then I'll just have to take back what's rightfully theirs. Trust me, you don't wanna get in the way of that.'

'Alright, alright. I just need my key to unlock the door.'

'Hurry up!'

A jangling of keys. The creaking of a door opening. Footsteps echoing as they walked away.

My hands holding the rifle were trembling, but I had to do something. Rifle poised ready to shoot, I burst through the doorway, but there was no sign of either of them. It was like they'd just disappeared.

At the end of the storage room, underneath the desk I spotted it: a trapdoor.

And its mouth was wide open.

CHAPTER ELEVEN

It was difficult to see where the steps led to. The one lantern screwed to the wall only illuminated to where the wooden steps changed to ones cut out of grey rock. Wherever they led, it didn't look like your usual basement. A cold breeze blew upwards from out of the darkness and whilst I couldn't see him yet, I could hear Weasel's angry voice, so loud that it echoed above the rhythmic hiss of the sea.

'Don't play smart. Take me to the shine he collected from us last night.'

My heart was beating a drum. I took slow, careful steps, barely making a sound. As I neared the bottom step the cave came into view, a rope of lanterns strung up like bunting, lighting the way. In the cave were hundreds of wooden crates, like the ones we'd picked up the night before, stretching back as far as I could see. One of the crates had fallen into the water; the glass bottles inside rattled as the tide ebbed and flowed into the spaces around them.

Towards the mouth of the cave, there were two silhouettes: the skinny outline of Weasel-face, and George next to him, arm twisted behind his back, walking stiffly along like he was scared to make the wrong move. George wasn't even attempting to fight or flap his gums, which could only mean that Weasel had a weapon in his other hand poking into George's ribs.

I hesitated. I wasn't no weakling but contrary to the rumor George had started, I wasn't a natural fighter either. Shooting to put a lame horse out of its misery wasn't the same as shooting a fully grown guy. Still at least I could shoot. I had that in my favor.

As I checked the rifle was loaded with shells, I looked back up to see a speedboat entering the mouth of the cave with two passengers. So, Weasel-face was smarter than he looked, and had accomplices. And now the odds were definitely against me. I was scared enough at the thought of fighting one goon. Now I realized there could be more, I don't mind admitting I was scared spitless. I pulled back the bolt lever, ready to shoot.

Stepping down off the final step, I crouched down behind the first tower of crates I came to. Through the gaps between crates, I could see George being forced down onto his knees and weasel pulling a rope from out of his pocket to bind his hands behind his back.

The speedboat moored up and the first goon, the one with red hair, went right up to Weasel to tell him to hurry up as he fumbled around tying the rope around George's wrists.

'C'mon Joe,' The red-haired guy waved him off the boat. 'What are you waiting for?'

It was difficult to see them clearly from a distance, but I was pretty certain they were two of the guys with shotguns from the pickup the night before.

Joe nodded towards George. 'What about him, Danny? We were supposed to just get what's owed and go. We can't do that now. He's seen our face. Knows who we are.'

Danny looked at Weasel.

Weasel shrugged. 'I guess you're right. I just wish someone had said that before I started tying this darn rope.'

He reached inside his coat, pulling out a revolver and casually, like he was about to shoot tins off a wall he raised the gun to the back of George's head. 'He can't tell no one if we fill him with daylight.'

I didn't even have time to think it through. If I didn't act quickly, George would be dead. I aimed the rifle right at Weasel's chest and pulled the trigger.

Not ready for the kickback from a gun I'd never used before, my shoulder snapped back, and the shot ricocheted off the cave walls, making my ears ring.

Weasel bent over clutching his bicep. The goons froze momentarily, not fully aware yet of quite what had happened.

With a smoking shell case at my foot, I pulled back the bolt handle and shot again. My aim wasn't much better, hitting him in the thigh instead of the chest but at least this time I got lucky and hit him. The blood sprayed out of him like a shaken cherry soda.

Weasel crumpled to the ground, howling like a hurt dog. He's pleading to God, his mother, anyone who might be able to end the pain and his life.

'Please,' he whimpered. 'Show some mercy.'

But I was fresh out of mercy, and I wasn't restocking. Besides, I figured by the way the blood was spurting out of him like a fountain, that he'd only got minutes left to live anyway.

George shook off the rope Weasel hadn't finished tying and stepped round Weasel's body to prize the pistol out of his hand to take for himself. He aimed it right between Weasel's eyes and pulled the trigger.

The shot echoed off the cave walls, deafening. Danny pulled out his own pistol and aimed it at George with the safety off. Joe though, isn't so brave, bolting like a panicked deer, clambering back into the speedboat.

'Come on Danny! Forget it!' he yelled.Danny can't, now he's made his move. Now he and George are eyeballing one another, guns aimed, ready to fire. Question is, who will be the first to pull the trigger, knowing that I'm waiting in the dark, ready to open fire?

'If you put the gun down, we could both just walk away from this,' George says.'And get taken out by the Abels instead?' Danny shakes his head. 'I'd rather take my chances.'

I only had three shells left. I kept still and thought about what my Da taught me. Breathe deeply. Keep your hand steady. I aimed the gun at Danny's heart, whilst out of the corner of my eye I could see Joe scrambling to get to the boat.

This time when I pull the trigger it lands exactly where I want it to. Danny clutches at the rose of red blossoming across his chest and stumbles a few steps before dropping to the ground.

Joe was no bother, too much of a scaredy cat to fight back, so I stepped out of the shadows to track him.

I could see him cursing his own hands as he struggled to start the ignition whilst me and George moved in closer and closer. Just as we were about to take him out, the speedboat engine coughed into life, and Joe pulled away, a grin of relief all over his face. No doubt he really believed he would escape but every chump knows even the fastest boat can't outrun a bullet.

When I pulled the trigger, the bullet shattered the lantern Joe had placed next to him. He yelped and jumped back as the light went out.

He didn't know that the shot was a deliberate miss, and I was just playing with him.

George shot two more times into the darkness just for emphasis; a reminder never to return.

Joe sped off out towards the horizon. I had no kick about it. I didn't enjoy killing people and Joe seemed like he was even less cut out for violence than I was. He could go and do something else with his life now. If the Abels didn't get to him first.

I ran down to George, and he embraced me as a brother; Weasel's blood spattered against his right cheek.

'Darn it, George! We almost got them all. Are you okay?'

George nodded but I noticed his trousers were soaked through at the front.

'Jeez Milton, you just saved my life. I swear I thought they were gonna kill me. I was thinking what'd happen to my Lou if they did.' He dropped down to the floor, exhausted.

'They weren't dry agents after all, were they?' I said, sitting down next to him.

George shook his head. We both knew who'd sent them.

'I guess we'd better call the law. Clyde...' I said.

George shook his head. 'No. Not Clyde. It's best we keep him outta this one completely. We'll go back upstairs, and I'll call Clarence.'

'But I've just shot two people dead... it was self-defense though.' I really wanted to believe the words I was spouting out of my own mouth.

'Well, that's exactly why we call Clarence first before anyone else,' George said. 'You don't wanna go to jail for this, do you?'

'Course, not.' I hadn't even thought about that but now that I was, the thought of prison food wasn't too appealing.

'Good. Well, Clarence'll make sure that you don't. He'll help us. Besides, he'll wanna know what happened and find out who these two chumps were.' George gestured towards the two bodies of Weasel and Danny.

He reached out into the water and took one of the floating whiskey bottles. He unscrewed the cap and took a swig, before offering it to me.

'Here. Take it for the shock. It's medicinal,' he smirked.

'If that was meant to be some sort of attempt at drugstore humor, it wasn't funny.'

I snatched the bottle from him anyway and took a swig. I wanted to feel something. Have something to warm the numbness. The warmth burned up from my belly and into my chest.

'Urgh! It's like drinking fire!' I handed the bottle back to him.

George chuckled and took the bottle back off me for another swig.

'Well, now you're in the bootlegging business, no point you holding out and sticking to soda anymore. Ain't no place in heaven for either of us now. Only the fiery depths.

The two of us sat there a while trying to calm our pounding hearts and shaking hands.

I've often thought about the events of that night and what could have happened if I hadn't taken the shot. What if I'd taken the coward's way out and stayed in the drugstore until it was all over? What if I'd stayed hidden behind the tower of crates and never shot that rifle? What if poor George had died there and then, instead of disappearing and leaving me to get the blame all those months later?

What if?

Chapter Twelve

❧ ⸺ ••• ⸺ ❧

Of course, Clarence Kelly never came to help us.

Being the big cheese that he was, he sat in his warm plush office barking his orders to George over the phone. I was too absorbed in my own shock to listen in, but I was vaguely aware of George's voice floating in and out, giving answers to Clarence in code.

'There's been a spillage at the drugstore...no I haven't touched anything...' George glanced across at me. 'Yes, the apprentice is working late.'

When he finally got off the phone and called my name, I realized I'd been staring into thin air for the past; well, I didn't know how long. George walked right up and sat on the stool next to me.

'You sure you're okay?'

Of course I wasn't, but how could I possibly put into words how it felt to have killed not one, but two men in one night. As I was rearranging the thoughts in my head George answered for me.

'Look, you did the right thing. Without you, they'd not only have cleared us out, they'd have killed me too. You're a hero for what you did.'

No matter how true it was, it didn't make me feel any better.

There were voices outside. Deep voices. And when the silhouettes of the two men grew larger behind the blind as they drew closer to the door, I gulped the air in and held my breath. What if Joe had returned with the rest of the mob to finish the job?

George put his finger to his lip, signaling for me to stay silent while he picked up the rifle and aimed it at the shadows behind the door.

We waited for them to knock.

George signaled to stay still, and we sat there silent, rifle pointing towards the two silhouettes moving behind the blind.

'George, it's us. Open up.'

George shook his head at me. How could we possibly know who it was?

We waited, my heart thumping in my throat.

A different voice. This one more impatient.

'C'mon George, you goddam boob! It's us, Jesse and Elmer. Hurry up and let us in, you little sap!'

It definitely sounded like Jesse but still, after what had happened with weasel-face, I didn't quite trust my own ears.

George though, satisfied they were who they said they were, got up and walked to the door. As he reached to unlock it, I closed my eyes and held my breath, scared my heart was going to explode at any moment.

The key turned and the door burst open. Jesse pushed his way in, huffing away like a bull terrier at a dogfight.

'What took you so long?'

The sigh I hadn't even realized I'd been holding in, came out of me and I flopped down on the chair like a marionette whose tangled strings had finally been cut. I never thought I'd say it was a relief to see the two goons, but it was.

Elmer followed in after Jesse and nodded towards me.

'You okay kid? You look like you've seen a whole houseful of ghosts.'

I jumped down from my stool and pushed past them to get to the door. Once outside, the bile pushed itself up from my guts and sprayed out onto the boardwalk.

***

When I went back inside, Jesse and Elmer were nowhere to be seen. George stepped out of the back room.

'Feel better?'

I shrugged. 'Yeah, thanks. You?'

'Oh yeah, I'm fine.'

He sounded like he was trying to convince himself but the shakiness in his voice gave him away. He nodded in the direction of the office.

'Jesse and Elmer have gone to get started on the clean up.'

He made it sound like it was a messy room the day after a party, not a bloodbath that they were cleaning up.

'Look, you should go home. Clarence's orders.'

I shook my head. I couldn't take a bunk leaving them to clean up my mess or they would see me as weak, but as I tried to sidestep him to go and help, George stopped me and pushed a bottle of pills into my hand.

'Look, the first is always the hardest. Everyone knows it. So, go home, take one of these and get some sleep. Clarence said to take a couple of days off and when you're ready swing by and see him over at Kings. He wants to show his gratitude for what you did here tonight.'

I wasn't sure I needed the pills. Now that my adrenaline levels had lowered, my body ached all over. All I wanted to do was lie down and sleep. I put the pills in my pocket.

'Okay, I'll go home but I'll be back here as soon as I can. What about you?'

'Trust me, I'm fine. We can handle this here.' George walked me to the door, and we said our goodbyes.

You know, the one thing that struck me as I was walking home was George's words: *The first is always the hardest.*

This might have been my first murder, but something told me it couldn't possibly have been George's.

14

Chapter Thirteen

❖━━━━━━━━━❖

A s I arrived home, Ma was at the window with her housecoat on, hair in rags. I could see her pacing up and down behind the lace curtains. She came out onto the front step, shrieking about filling out a missing person's report and how close she was to calling the law as I walked up the yard.

'Ma for goodness' sake,' I hissed. 'Keep your voice down, you'll wake the neighbors.' I glanced around to check none of them were peeking through their blinds. 'I was working late, that's all. You didn't actually call the law, did you?'

'No, but I was about to...'

'Well don't. Never call the cops.'

Perhaps I spoke a little harshly, but I was tired and stressed by the day's events and the very last thing I needed was the law sniffing around the place. I pushed past her to take my shoes off in the hallway, but she stood over me, flapping her gums about what a crook Clarence Kelly was and how she never should have agreed to me working for him.

It was because of Clarence Kelly I'd been able to afford to buy the kewpie lamp on the shelf behind her, but she happily turned a blind eye when it benefited her. I swallowed my irritation and forced a softened voice.

'Look, I'm sorry you were worried Ma, but you don't have to be. I'm not some soft-headed boy anymore who hands out flyers on the boardwalk.'

'No. No, you're not. My boy Milton wouldn't turn up with a bloodied nose and tell me not to worry about it.'

I could tell by the sound of her voice that she didn't approve of this new version of me. The one that didn't take orders from his Ma anymore. I wasn't going to stand there for her to give me the third degree.

'I'm going up to bed.' I started up the stairs, but she followed two steps behind me.

'What about your dinner? It's been kept warm in the oven?'

'I'm not hungry.'

***

I was so grateful to strip off my clothes soaked with sweat and terror and just lay flat on the mattress. Every time I closed my eyes Weasel's grinning face swam into my consciousness. Maybe those pills George gave me were a good idea after all. So, I took one and hid the rest behind the Bible in my bedside drawer.

And I tell you; it was the best night's sleep I ever had. No dreams. No nothing. Just sweet oblivion. I would never sleep that deeply, or that soundly, ever again.

For the next few weeks my nights were spent lying wide awake on that mattress, expecting Clyde to knock at the door at any moment.

I would stop at newsstands and flick through the papers looking for the story of the two men who disappeared or worse, were shot down in cold blood, but there was nothing. It was like they'd never existed in the first place. I found out later that Clarence had everyone paid off: the newshawks, the cops. Only ones that hadn't been paid were the Abels.

Not that Clarence was worried about that. To him, everyone owed him something. He had the whole of Atlantic City in the palm of his hand.

But now that he'd made the trouble I could have been in go away, that unfortunately also included me.

Chapter Fourteen

❖·•·························•·························•·❖

'**M**ilton, you need to get up. There's a man here, asking for you.'

It wasn't so much the panicked whisper that woke me, so much as the violent way Ma yanked back the drapes, revealing the early morning sunshine. I let out a groan, her words barely registering at first.

'Didn't you hear me. I said, there's a man downstairs.'

The memory of the previous week's events played across my mind like a picture at the movie theatre. Weasel-face's grin as he brought the broom handle down onto my skull. Aiming the gun, heart pounding. Weasel-face's dull stare as he sighed out his last breath.

Momentarily forgetting where I was, I reached out for the rifle that was taped to the underside of the counter at Kelly & Sons but found it had gone. I remembered where I was. I was safe in my bed at home. Well, at least I hoped I was safe.

'What man?' I sat up, shielding my eyes from the fierce sunlight.

'How would I know, what man? He said Mr. Kelly sent him.'

My nervous affliction was rising in me again. We had no rifle here at home. No pistol even. If the Abels had tracked me and sent someone to finish the job weasel-face had started, all I had was the knife Elmer had given me the first time we met.

Ma made to leave the room.

'No, wait! Wait for me to come with you.'

I pulled on my pants and a clean vest and shirt while Ma eyed me suspiciously.

'What's going on Milton? If you're in trouble...'

'No trouble. I just need you to start asking a few more questions before inviting someone into the house from now on. In fact, if someone comes knocking that you don't know. Don't open the door.'

'I'm not sure I like this Milt,' she lowered her voice again. 'Mr. Kelly promised me he'd look after us.'

'And he has, hasn't he?'

She had no answer. She knew she couldn't complain about the rent being paid and the landlord suddenly fixing the leak in the ceiling she'd been complaining about for the past year. It was on account of Clarence that she could afford new dresses and never had to wait in the queue at the bakery.

'Look, Ma. Just trust me, okay?'

She nodded.

'Okay, get behind me.'

I opened the drawer of my bedside table and took out the knife.

Ma's eyes widened.

It was one thing *thinking* that your son was caught up in something he shouldn't have been, but another entirely, actually seeing the evidence in front of your own eyes.

Chapter Fifteen

'Jesse?'

Seeing Jesse there with his fat fingers curled around a dainty teacup sipping tea my Ma had made for him, was like seeing a dog dancing on its hind legs.

He nodded in my direction, 'Take a seat, Milton.'

Was this guy actually asking me to take a seat in my own home, like he owned the place? Yeah, he was. I paused for a moment, and all two hundred pounds of Jesse rose from his seat to tower over me.

I fingered the knife handle I had cautiously placed in my back pocket. I couldn't sit down, even if I had wanted to. Not if I wanted to avoid stabbing myself in the buttocks.

'I'd rather stand,' I said coldly.

Jesse shrugged. 'Suit yourself.' He looked over to Ma who excused herself from the room.

'I'll leave you boys to talk.'

When she was out of earshot, Jesse stepped closer.

'Look here, Mama's boy. What I did for you the other night, I didn't do because I like you. I cleaned up because Clarence told me to. If it had been up to me, I'd have left you and George to clean up your own mess.' The great bear of a man growled the words. 'But for some reason the Boss has taken a shine to you. And now it's time for you to say thank you.'

I shrugged back at him. 'Thank you, Jesse.'

He laughed. 'You sap! Not to me. To Clarence. He wants you to go on a little trip away and sort something out for him.'

That didn't sound so bad.

'What sort of something.'

He handed me a handwritten note with a New York address on it. I couldn't believe my luck. Ma had promised we'd go one day and now this was my chance. If it was anything like the pickups I'd done before, it wouldn't be so bad. I might even get time to take a trip over to Coney Island.

Jesse grinned in a way that made me feel uneasy.

'You'll need to get going straight away,' he said.

'But what about George? He needs me at the drugstore.'

Don't worry none. This is more important. We'll tell George you won't be at work for the next couple of days. Here. Take this. You'll need it for the train fare.' He handed me an envelope stacked full of money.

I stuffed the money into my wallet.

'And you'll need these too.' He gave me a small hessian bag.

I took a peek inside to see a small bottle of moonshine, a rag and a box of matches.

CHAPTER SIXTEEN

❖▪━━━━▪▪━━━━▪❖

My stay in New York was hot and sultry, the ceiling fan in my room doing little except pushing the warm air around. I lay on the bed in my underwear, putting off the inevitable task I was going to have to do to pay my debt to Clarence.

I thought of Jesse's words to me before I'd left for the station.

'All you need to know is that that boy you let escape the other night in the cave, Joe, will be there. Room at the back of the building, bottom floor, on the left.'

I hadn't questioned why, if they'd already gathered this information, they hadn't already taken care of the situation, but I guessed they saw it as my unfinished business to clean up.

Besides, something told me this was a test orchestrated by Clarence to see how loyal I was and just how far I could go when asked. Sure, I could handle a situation like weasel-face when thrown in the deep end but what about a situation that's planned. Could I act methodically, unemotionally, soldier-like?

The grandfather clock in the hallway chimed eight. Time to go. I washed the sweat off my face and picked up my kit bag. I'd paid for three nights but I wouldn't be coming back. And if the law checked the guest book at the main desk for any reason, they wouldn't see the name of Milton Costello, only the name of my alias Dennis Walton.

I left quietly down the fire escape and walked the maze of alleyways that led between the buildings until I reached the one, I'd checked out earlier that day. I stood for a moment under the moonlight, taking in the scene.

In the room to the left of the back door, a cream scalloped blind with beaded tassels was pulled down. Inside the room, the warm glow of a lamp flickered, illuminating the two figures inside. One on them, down on their knees in front of the other like they were praying. The other stood tall, head thrown back, looking up to the ceiling.

I hadn't had much chance to get a look at Joe when he had been manning the speedboat. How could I be certain that either of these figures behind the blind was him?

I looked for something to throw and found half a brick lay next to the trash. It was risky but also the only way to be sure. Ducking down beside the trash cans I launched the brick at the window, hearing the glass shatter and a dog barking as I ducked back down again.

A woman screamed and a moment later the back door opened, and Joe stood there in his underwear, aiming a gun into the darkness yelling back into the room.

'Champ! Delores! Will you both quit your whining for a moment!'

This was quite unlike the Joe I had seen down in the cave. This one had bravado, trying to impress the woman he was with. He looked such a sap I had to stifle a laugh. I sat as still as I could. Eventually, satisfied, there was no one there, Joe eventually went back indoors pulling the door to. It wasn't quite on the latch but that wouldn't matter in a few minutes' time.

I gave it ten minutes or so for everything to settle down again before doing what I'd really been sent there to do.

I took the bottle out of my bag and unscrewed the lid. The scent of ethanol stung my nostrils and the tiny drip I'd got on my fingers when unscrewing the lid, immediately evaporated. This was going to go up like a firecracker.

Next, I dipped the piece of rag in it and stuffed it down into the bottle like a cloth wick. I struck the match and touched it gently to the edge of the rag which flared up, almost scorching my eyebrows. There wasn't much time to think. Grasping the bottle, I threw it towards the broken window and the smash and whoosh of flames as it landed on the floor and set fire to whatever cheap rug was laid down in the room.

This time, I wasn't going to wait around to see what happened. I got up from behind the garbage bins and was about to make a run for it when I realized the door was ajar and, in the gap between the door frame and the door, a dog's head appeared, eyes wide, whimpering and barking to be set free.

I could have walked away but I just couldn't do it. It was one thing getting rid of Joe. He and his buddies tried to kill me, but this dog, Champ, couldn't have been no more than a year old. A german shepherd pup, he hadn't done anything to deserve being burned.

It's okay, I'm coming,' I called up to him.

The flames had eaten away at the blinds now, the window full of flames and smoke. I covered my mouth with my hand and dashed up the steps to set Champ free.

I pulled open the door and Champ burst out.

'That's it. Come on boy!' I slapped my thigh for him to follow. 'You're safe now. Come with me.'

The two of us ran into the night as glass exploded and the orange flame and smoke engulfed the building.

18

CHAPTER SEVENTEEN

When I went back to Kings, I wasn't expecting a bull's session but that's exactly what I got. Jesse thumped me on the back like I was his buddy and led me over to the table where Elmer was sitting. Champ hadn't left my side since I'd got back from New York and when I sat down, Champ did so too, letting Elmer stroke his muzzle and around his ears.

'You did good boy,' Elmer said, and at first, I thought he was talking to Champ, not me.

'Jesse said you didn't have it in you to go through with it, but I never doubted it. Uh huh, not once. Ain't that right Jesse?'

Jesse grunted and gave a nod of recognition. He was distracted by the photographs on the table in front of him.

There were three piles; all of them showing broads in their bathing suits, legs on display; smiles oozing desperation. The need to be noticed. Recognized. My pants felt tight, and I shifted uncomfortably in my seat.

'What do you think of her?'

Jesse handed me a photo of some girl with dark hair wearing a one piece. A doll, like all the others. Same haircut. Same cookie cutter smile. This one stirred nothing in me.

I shrugged. 'I dunno. Never met her.'

Jesse started laughing. 'You know you're funny Milton. Never met her indeed!'

Elmer leaned over to pour me a glass of bourbon despite it being two o clock in the afternoon and the joint empty, except for one couple having a petting party in the corner.

I knocked it back. It was disgusting but I wasn't the sort of guy who drank soda anymore. While I did, Elmer contemplated what to do with the photograph of the broad he had in his hand.

'Well, I guess she should go in this pile.' Elmer's hand hovered over the one on the left. The discard pile. 'But I think she looks like fun so she's gonna get through.' He placed the card on the right card pile and picked up the next in line.

'What's this all for anyway?'

'Clarence is judging the beauty pageant on Labor Day weekend.' Elmer explained. 'These are all the entrants for the first round and what with Clarence being so busy an all, he asked us to sort through them.'

'Yeah,' Jesse leered. 'And I cannot wait to personally congratulate all of them.'

I'd heard Da talk like that about dames with his buddies sometimes after one too many shots. Made me feel a little uncomfortable.

'Works every time,' Jesse said. 'All women want is your attention. You give a broad a compliment. Something about their hair or their dress and they'll eat it up like a horse eats sugar lumps.'

'I told you before, this ain't no flop house.'

We all turned to see Clarence approaching the table with a furrowed brow. He jabbed his finger towards Jesse.

'I won't have you harassing any of my contestants, you hear me?'

Jesse held his hands up and pushed his chair away from the table to show he wasn't meddling with the photographs. The power Clarence had in just his voice had me in awe. Jesse stood back to offer him his seat.

Before he sat down, Clarence turned his attention to me and took hold of my hand. His handshake was firm but not so firm that he crushed your fingers, the way some men think they need to assert themselves. He didn't need to. His authority was clear.

'I'm so sorry about all this. I called you here to congratulate you, not for you to have to listen to tweedle-dum and tweedle-dee here.' He gestured to Elmer and Jesse. 'Don't you two have something else to get on with?'

Elmer leapt up off his chair so quickly it was like his chair was on fire. The two of them walked away leaving me alone with Clarence. With them gone, the atmosphere settled. With Clarence came a sense of calm.

He sat down opposite me, swiped the photographs to one side, uninterested, and clicked his fingers for the waitress to bring him a coffee.

'So, Milton, I brought you here to thank you in person for what you did the other night.'

'It was no bother,' I started to say but Clarence held his hand up to quieten me, the sovereign rings on his fingers shining. No one interrupted him.

'What you've been doing is showing loyalty and bravery and I like that,' he said. 'You not only saved George's life, but you also helped eliminate the associates employed by my rivals from New York as well as taking out one of their business ventures while you were at it. I hear there was nothing left of that building once you were done. Just ashes.'

Champ nuzzled his head against his leg and Clarence stroked him; unaware the dog was the only thing that survived me burning down that building.

'The Abels been throwing their weight around for weeks, thinking that because I'm an old man now and a nice guy, that they can just walk right in and lay down the law around here. Of course, we will need to still be on our guard, but I think we can say that our operations are safe for now. What I really need to ask you, now that you know the truth about the drugstore and the ways I do business is, if you and your Ma have a problem with it?'

Looking back, I can see he was offering me a way out.

I nodded. 'Of course, I'm good with it. Everything's jake.'

'Good.' Clarence smiled, pleased with the answer. 'Because you've really proved yourself, kid. And you could be very useful to me. Very useful indeed. I want you to do all the pickups with George from now on. And every Monday, you come and drop them off here. That jake with you?'

'More than jake.'

Pride swelled in my chest and as I looked down at the metallic light glistening in Champ's eyes, I thought of the girl at the boardwalk who'd read our fortunes.

'Your Boss is going to give you a promotion...I guess you could say, you'll be a 'King' of sorts.'

Chapter Eighteen

T wenty-five was the Summer that made me. It took me from being a boy of wax, melted me down and remolded me into the man I am now. And I had a swell time.

I spent my days with George at the drugstore, helping old ladies get their cough medicine and at night I helped shift medicine of a different sort. George and I drove through states to pick up crates of shine or whatever else Clarence wanted us to pick up.

You had an idea of what type of pickup it was depending on where it was delivered to. Homegrown moonshine, the sort punters keep stashed under the floorboards tended to be delivered to the cave under Kelly & Sons. Anything that might be too hot went here too. Once I had a crate bust open on the journey and I was delighted to find it was a whole crate of tommy guns and that we were finally going to replace those old rifles under the counters with something that could do some damage.

The stuff reserved for Kings had an air about it. It was all imported Canadian whiskey and champagne from Paris. The sort of giggle juice tourists would pay through the nose for.

And when I wasn't working for Kings, I was either walking the boardwalk, picking up broads or drinking there myself.

Kings was a different place at night; under the full moon the pup became a wolf. It grew teeth. So did its punters who paced the board-walk, already fried after drinking all day, looking for the next place to tip a few. As the crowds swayed from joint to joint, you could taste the danger in the air. A pressure you could feel building at the base of your skull, which could be the excitement boiling in your own blood, or the violent heartbeat of the hungry city. It needed to be fed and Kings, with its doors wide open, was the mouth that would feed it.

I had a table practically reserved for me next to the bar. I'd get myself an old fashioned with a twist and watch the jazz band up on the stage. The singers changed and even the members of the band, but the pianist never did. His name was Booker, and he was the best pianist I'd ever heard.

I'd stay well into the night, sometimes often by myself but some-times with Jesse and Elmer, the two of them taking it in turns to approach the pretty women from out of town and persuade them to sit with us. Sometimes, if things went really well, they could persuade them into something more. That was fine for Elmer, who lived by himself. Jesse did it just for kicks, having his old lady waiting for him back home. I could never quite manage to take it further than the usual introductions back and forth. Those women were pretty an all, but they just didn't stir anything in me.

One night all three of us were there, just drinking and listening to Booker play between acts when a guy walked right up to Jesse and punched him out.

'That's for messing with my wife!' the guy said, walking off.

Me and Elmer were so stunned we did nothing. Just watched the guy leave while Jesse lay sparked out on the floor like it was a boxer's canvas.

Sometimes, we'd end up in scuffles ourselves after one too many but mostly we just enjoyed the entertainment.

Whilst I was enjoying myself working for Clarence, Ma was becoming more and more disgruntled by it. She'd nurse the cuts on my face, all the time cursing his name.

'I never should have let you work for that devil,' she said. 'Look at the state of you.'

'Ma, I'm fine. Please stop fussing over me. I can take care of myself.'

'Evidently. I don't know what's got into you. You're never at home. You stink of booze. You're becoming just like your father.'

I shrugged. 'Ain't never hit you the way Pa did.'

That was it. The hit that was below the belt.

She stopped pressing the rag to my cut brow and spoke as calmly as she could manage without the waver in her voice giving way to anger.

'Get out. And you can take that dog of yours with you too.'

Chapter Nineteen

❖❖━━━━━━━❖❖

Ma was never sore for long.

I'd just go down to Kings and lay low for a few hours then sneak back in while she was asleep. Next morning, she'd be cooking me pancakes, just like always.

That night when she kicked me out, I almost didn't come back home at all. I was sitting at my usual table with Clarence when a girl walked in with long fair hair, wearing a blue sequin dress that glittered under the lights.

She waved over to Clarence and the sweet smile she gave...I swear I almost fell off my seat. Cancel the fall pageant, I thought, because she was, hands down, the most beautiful girl I'd ever seen. She was literally dazzling under the lights.

She walked right over to Booker who bought her over to our table.

'Mr. Kelly, Sir, this is the singer I was telling you about.'

She held her hand out and Clarence took it and kissed it.

She smiled.

'Name's Pearl,' she said.

I don't recall any of the rest of the conversation with Clarence, I was so mesmerized by the siren that had just walked in. She moved so confidently when she walked, giving orders to the band about where they should stand on the stage and yet there was a waver in her voice that suggested she didn't have complete conviction in what she was saying. If you looked at her closely, you could see she was just pretending to have the self-assurance of a much older woman and there was something about that I found endearing.

I nodded my way through the conversation with Clarence, stealing a covert glance at her every now and then, desperate for him to stop talking to her for one moment so I could fully concentrate on her. My head was lost in the fog and Clarence, oblivious, carried on flapping his gums.

'So, do we have an agreement?' Clarence's words broke in and he held out his hand for her to shake.

She walked away with Booker and when Clarence was gone, Jesse and Elmer came sauntering back over with Champ and I took the chance to crane my neck and get a real good look at Pearl, her curves soft like a ripe pear.

'Yeah, I wouldn't even bother,' Jesse said, catching me stealing a glance at her. 'Women like her's jailbait.'

'Who is she? Why have I never seen her before?'

'Ain't she a ring dinger? Jesse's just got sour grapes because she turned him down.' Elmer chuckled. She's already got her eye on Clarence's son Charlie, though. Bad luck kid.'

They didn't understand. I needed to have her. If I could get a girl like Pearl to be my moll, well everyone would start to take me seriously. And I'd heard about this sap Charlie already. The son who let down his father. He wasn't a man in my eyes. He was behaving like a boy who should have known better than to be so inconsistent and cowardly.

I stood up. 'Just going to the bathroom' I said as casually as I could.

As I walked past the stage and caught Pearl's gaze, I held it just long enough for her to notice me. I gave her a smile and looked away, feeling her eyes follow me.

21

CHAPTER TWENTY

I walked the long way around, so it didn't look so obvious, past the crowd of flappers in fur coats who crowded round the front door. I felt their eyes on me as I walked past them, but I didn't bother to turn my head to look. Quaffs like that were easy. Getting Pearl's attention, however, would be more of a challenge.

I snuck down the back corridor that was parallel to the stage. Her dressing room was here, and I hoped to surprise her and wish her luck with her performance. Halfway along, a door sat ajar, light on. From inside I heard voices. One of them hers, the other that spoke to her was male. Booker maybe.

Sore with myself for not getting there earlier, I tried to sneak a look through the gap and saw Pearl sitting on a chair in front of a mirror, wearing that same sparkling topaz dress I'd seen her in that afternoon. I hadn't noticed how much of her slim shoulders it revealed earlier on. But I did now. So much soft pink flesh. Booker was out of eyeline, but I bet he was looking at them too.

I could hear the two talking, discordant, like something wasn't quite in tune between them.

'You know, I don't think your dad is going to be best pleased when he finds out what you've been up to behind his back.'

This couldn't have been Booker she was talking to. The guy walked over and placed his hands on her bare shoulders so I could see both their reflections in the mirror. A spiffy looking guy with a $100 suit and freshly polished shoes bought with Clarence's money. This was Charlie Kelly.

'You might be right, but I'm sure he'll come round to the idea eventually. You sure you won't come with me?'

She didn't even look at him. Just sat watching her own reflection as she rubbed rouge on the apples of her cheeks.

'To sit around all day darning socks? I already told you Charlie, I ain't that sorta girl. I ain't no homemaker. I got plans for myself.'

'What, that old baloney about Hollywoodland?'

In the mirror, I saw her freeze and her expression sour. I couldn't decide if she was angry or disappointed. Maybe both. Either way, this Charlie guy was becoming more and more unlikable every moment.

'You go ahead and laugh but you can forget about meeting up tonight after the show.'

She shrugged him off her shoulders and he realized, too late, the mistake he'd made in belittling her ambition. And to make it worse, he carried on flapping his gums.

'C'mon, don't be like that, Pearl.'

'Oh please, save it! I've heard it all before.'

She stood abruptly and headed towards the door I was standing behind, Charlie trotting behind her, getting himself in a lather as he spouted apologies that fell on deaf ears.

I'm not usually a man to run but I didn't want her thinking I was some dapper dan sort, waiting outside her door. I moved quickly along the corridor and up the steps of the back of the stage, turning off to the right to hide myself behind the heavy red drapes.

A few moments later Pearl mounted the steps to the stage. When she bent down to adjust her stockings, revealing a flash of her slim pins, I imagined the frustration Charlie must have felt standing at the bottom of the stairs, watching her do it but unable to follow after her.

She took a deep breath and stepped through to the floodlit stage to rapturous applause from the audience. Walking with grace to the front, a painted smile on her face, no one would know she had just been having a disagreement with someone only moments before. Her topaz sequins glistened under the lights like the scales of a mermaid. She took up the microphone and began to sing. Uncaged, and away from Charlie she was a songbird getting ready to fly.

When she launched into the chorus the flappers and their beaus erupted into dancing, leaving their tables to dance the Charleston in the aisles.

She sang song after song and with each one her confidence seemed to swell. This wasn't the fake confidence she had during rehearsal. This was the real deal. Like she knew her place was meant to be under that spotlight. And for me, still waiting behind the drapes, with her only steps away, it was like having my own private performance.

When the set came to an end, she waved at the audience but as she turned from them, her smile dropped almost instantly. She was looking for Charlie; the only audience she'd wanted. And he'd long gone.

I stepped from the darkness into her light. She took a step back, the lights dazzling her. She shielded her eyes with her hand, squinting to see, her face breaking into a smile.

'Hey Charlie! Is that you?'

I took a step closer. 'I'm sorry, I wasn't snooping or nothing, I just wanted to see the show up close. I'm Milton.'

Her smile evaporated. 'Yeah, I heard all about you. I saw you here earlier.'

I was proud of her saying that. It meant she had noticed me and that others had spoken of me. I was getting myself a reputation.

'Well, you were the bee's knees out there. Quite something. That dress of yours is quite something too.'

Now she blushed and I wondered how long it had been since Charlie had given her a compliment. It was clear I was hitting on all eight and seeing her reaction made me stand that little bit taller. We both stood for a moment, the silence hanging between us, electric.

I held out my arm and she took it, looping her arm through mine. The band were playing a quieter jazz set, whilst the cabaret dancers lined up behind the curtain, ready to go out and we edged past them, Pearl saying hello to each and every one of them.

Out on the floor people turned in their seats to compliment her on her performance and my chest swelled at the thought that people assumed we were together, but as she stood talking, up at the main bar Charlie was eyeballing me. He had inherited his father's ritz but not his composure. You could see the rage simmering in him.

Now I'd got a good look at him, I could see he wasn't all that much taller than me. I doubted he had much of a reach on him. I wasn't no bare-knuckle boxer but I could hold my own.

But then Pearl saw him too and he locked eyes with her.

'So, I think you're tooting the wrong ringer,' I whispered in her ear. 'You already have someone who wants to buy you a drink.'

I dropped her arm and walked away without looking back. I guess some guys might think that meant Charlie and Pearl were a done deal and that I'd given her up too easily.

But sometimes things just aren't as straightforward as all that.

Chapter Twenty-One

✦❯━━━━━━❯◦❯━━━◦❯━━◦❯✦

George's silhouette moved like a shadow puppet behind the blind. I rapped on the door for him to let me in and the blind snapped up, revealing George's swollen face and black eye. It was the first time I'd seen him since the night in the cave, and I involuntarily flinched back at the sight of him as he opened the door.

'Jeez George, your face...'

'Yeah, I know. I seen it. Got in a little scuffle last night. Dunno what you're staring at. Judging by those sunglasses, I'm guessing you're a little bruised yourself.'

'Nah. Just one too many bourbons.'

'What are you doing here so early?'

'Couldn't sleep.'

I followed him in and put my apron on. I didn't want to tell him how even though every time I closed my eyes, I still smelled smoke from that night I set fire to the house in Brooklyn. And if I wasn't lying awake thinking of that, I was thinking of Pearl instead. And of Charlie's smug face that made me want to paste him in the kisser.

George locked the door behind us.

'Well, see this is how it all starts, with you helping out with bootleg-ging. In six months', time you'll be lying back on a four-poster bed, in a mansion just like Clarence's counting dollars instead of sheep. He's chosen you, you know. To raise up. I can feel it.'

He spat the word 'chosen' so bitterly you'd have thought he'd been sucking lemons. I didn't know if he'd hoped to be chosen one day but I didn't want him feeling bad, so I told him.

'Look George, I'd never step on anyone's toes...'

'Well, why the hell not?' George stared hard at me and once again I saw that there was more to George than first meets the eye. It occurred to me that 'nice guy' George was a vaudeville act. A mask he wore to gain people's trust. 'There's nothing wrong with a little ambition, Milton.'

As quickly as it slipped, the mask was back on, and he gave me a friendly slap on the back.

'You know, in this business if you play too nice, you'll never get anywhere. So, if Clarence is going to give you the opportunity to make it big then you should grab it with both hands cause he doesn't offer that kind of opportunity to just anyone.'

I didn't say anything but in my chest pride blossomed. My Da had said I'd never amount to anything and yet here I was proving him wrong.

Once the drugstore was open, George hid out back, partly because he said he had plenty of prescriptions to fulfil and partly because he didn't want his swollen face to scare the punters away.

I was standing behind the soda counter reading the funnies in the paper when the doorbell tinkled and someone stood over me, blocking the light.

'Can I help you?' I said without even looking up.

'You sure can.' Her voice was low and sultry, and I knew straight away who it belonged to. The sequin dress of last night had been replaced with a floral dress and white cardigan. She had sunglasses on and a smile on her face. She looked so different to how she had on stage, all the false confidence and make-up stripped away.

I was still sore at her for the night before, but that didn't stop the way my heart beat a tune at the sight of her.

I turned to look for George, but he was still out back, and I had no choice but to talk to her. I sighed like she was an inconvenience. I wanted her to know she couldn't just treat me the way she had the night before.

'What do you want?

She glanced at the shelves. 'I'm looking for some menthol pastilles for my throat.'

'Seems like you're talking just fine to me.' I looked away from her.

Her voice shook, the firecracker in her about to go off.

'Is this how you talk to everyone? Look, Milton, I'm sorry about last night. I honestly thought Charlie had gone.'

'So, if he hadn't been there, that would've made it alright, would it? To have another man buy you a drink?' I kept my voice calm; unemotional.

'Charlie doesn't own me,' she said. 'No one does. Sometimes you meet people and...' Her voice drifted off like she'd already said too much and now regretted it. She sighed. This was an argument she wasn't going to win.

Look, I'm sorry we got off on the wrong foot. You got me all wrong.' Her voice was softer. Less defensive. She sounded like she meant it.

I put down the paper I'd been reading and found the menthol pastilles she wanted. I didn't know what to feel. I was glad she had come in to see me. To apologize. But Ma had warned me about girls like her. Girls like Pearl were trouble. They planted their seed and let their tendrils reach up around your heart until it squeezed the very life out of you.

I rang up the till and took her money. As she handed it over, I noticed how her nails were nibbled to the quick. A sign she wasn't so sure of herself after all.

'I'm going for a walk along the pier,' she said. 'You could come with me if you wanted?'

I wasn't about to be taken for a chump like Charlie. I handed her the pastilles in a paper bag.

'Maybe some other time.'

Her cheeks flushed, embarrassed. It must have taken guts for her to ask me. A broad asking a guy like that was unheard of. Looked like a guy turning her down was unheard of too, judging by the forced smile she gave.

'Okay, well, thanks for the pastilles. Guess I'll see you around.' She walked out without looking back.

I looked over at George. He'd been watching the whole time and now he shook his head at me.

'Hey what?' I shrugged back at him.

'Are you some sorta imbecile, or what? You think trying to be tough and pretending you don't care about her is going to make her like you?'

'I dunno. Maybe.'

'Well, it won't. Go after her you dingbat.'

I took off my apron and threw it down on the counter.

'Thanks George. I'll be ten minutes.'

'Just go!'

23

CHAPTER TWENTY-TWO

Out on the boardwalk, tourists flooded the place. I pushed through the waves of them the way a salmon leaps upstream, practically barging people out of the way looking for her. George had been right. Pearl was long gone.

Heading for the pier I inspected the crowd, looking for her blonde head. Just when I was about to give up, I spotted her up ahead.

'Pearl!' I called out.

She didn't hear me. I dashed out, narrowly missing a rolling chair transporting two dames, who squealed and covered their eyes as I dodged around it and carried on after her.

'Pearl!' I called to her.

She turned, and upon seeing me, broke into a beaming smile.

'I thought you weren't going to come.'

'Ahh, forget what I said about that.'

Most flappers I'd met were lookers, but when it came to talking, they were bores with little to say for themselves. Pearl had their ritz and was a wise head. Rare as her namesake. She took the reins of the conversation the whole way along the pier. I could hardly get a word in.

'So, you've heard about that flyboy Charles Lindbergh?' She gestured towards a flyer pinned up on the telegraph pole. 'He's planning to fly from America to Paris without stopping.'

I looked at his humorless face staring out at us.

'Imagine if he does do it,' I said. 'It could change everything. In the future we could be flying to Paris, or Ireland. Even paying the King of England a visit.'

She shook her head.

'Not me. It's like Grandma says, if we were meant to fly then we'd have been born with wings. Flying one of those machines in the air. It's just not natural.'

She changed the subject. 'You like reading?'

'Some.' It wasn't exactly a lie. Sure, I liked the funnies in the paper, but I'd never call myself a reader.

She didn't seem to notice how vague my answer was. Just kept on talking.

'I just love Scott F. Fitzgerald. Jay Gatsby just might be one of the most tragic figures I've ever read about. You can borrow my copy if you like.'

'Well, I'm more of a pictures man...'

This really made her light up.

'Oh, me too! Did you hear they're bringing out a picture that actually has someone singing in it? What a dream that would be! Singing in Hollywoodland.' She made it sound like it was some faraway place. I didn't see why she wouldn't make it there. She had the pipes for it.

As abruptly as the pier came to an end, so did our conversation. An awkwardness hung in the air, that in the pictures she talked about would have been filled with me stepping forward and kissing her hard on the lips. But this was real life and if I dared go near her, I knew I would feel the sting of her flat palm across my cheek. Out at sea, a steamboat drifted past, sunbathers on the top deck. She moved closer to me and lowered her voice.

'You know I heard about what you did the other night at the drugstore. That was real brave of you, fighting off those two guys like that.'

It sounded more heroic than it was when she said it. She didn't know about the nightmares I had every time I closed my eyes.

'Well, you know. I did what I had to do…'

'Don't be so modest. No wonder Clarence has his eye on you.'

She was so close to me I could smell the Lux soap on her skin. Before I had time to ask if I could kiss her, her warm lips were already pressed against mine.

I pulled back. 'What about Charlie?'

She looked away, like she didn't want to talk about it, and I wished I hadn't brought it up.

'Things are complicated between me and him.'

She stepped in towards me for another kiss. This one wetter, more passionate. The sort of kiss that made people look away and whisper, but I didn't give a damn what anyone else thought about seeing us. She had me spellbound. She could have asked anything of me, and I would have done it. Even murder.

The clock chimed two and she pulled away from me.

'I'd better get back,' she said. 'I'm late for rehearsals. Thank you for the walk. And the pastilles.'

'Yeah, looks like you got your voice back.' I smiled, the imprint of her kiss still on my lips.

I would have offered to walk her back to Kings, but she was already walking away from me like she was in a hurry to get back.

'Pearl wait!' I called after her. 'When will I see you again?'

She turned and smiled.

'Who knows?'

***

Turns out Pearl was wrong when it came to Charles Lindbergh. That May, he landed his plane, The Spirit of St Louis, right in the center of Paris. In the weeks that followed he travelled across all of America, a hero. He came right here in the Fall, to Atlantic City.

Meanwhile, that Summer I was busy building my own reputation doing errands for Clarence Kelly. Most of it was driving to the pickup as I'd done before. I'd sit in the car and wait while Jesse and Elmer did business and then I'd move the liquor back to the cove. Sometimes, if things got a little tough; if someone was trying to chisel Clarence or goons started acting like punks, well I didn't have any choice but to become involved and take a poke at a few of them.

By the start of the Summer season, I was called on by Clarence so often that I stopped working at the drugstore altogether. Most I saw of George was when I was making the drop to the store in the rocks below. Of course, there were no hard feelings about it. Once Clarence has his eye on you and chooses to raise you out of the dirt, you'd be a fool to say no.

But where George had encouraged my new way of life, my own Ma was sore as a bear. Where she had once tried to kid herself that working at the drugstore was just that, it became clear by my new spiffy suits and the occasional bruise on my face that she had had the wool pulled over her eyes. One night, it all came to blows and she wound up throwing me out.

After sleeping on George's sofa for a couple of nights Clarence twisted a few arms and found me my own apartment across town. It wasn't nothing special, but it was home, and my favorite thing was the garden out back. I'd sit out there with a cup of joe, surrounded by the ivy growing up the wall of the building and I'd think of that first time George, and I went to Princeton.

As the magnolia buds bloomed and the nights grew warmer, I stepped into Summer, a grown man, raised up and on the cusp of being part of Clarence's inner circle.

But everyone knew that once you stepped inside that circle, it closed up. Engulfed you until there was no way out.

24

Chapter Twenty-Three

❖ ▬▬▬▬▬▬ ❖

I 'd heard about Clarence Kelly's parties long before I was invited to one. Everyone had heard about them. On hot summer nights the whoopie could be heard for miles.

There were stories about sozzled flappers in petting parties in dark corners. Glasses of fizz and gin rickey that never seemed to run dry. Silver platters piled high with roasted hams, devilled eggs and oysters. Jazz bands on the patio, couples dancing the charleston and jumping into the swimming pool, fully clothed. Even when bluenose neighbors got sore and complained to the law, Clarence had no kick about it. He simply invited them over to join the party. Sometimes they did. And even if they didn't, they never complained again on account of Clarence being such a standup guy.

My invite came that July as the nights got warmer and the parties wilder. I was dropping some crates off at Kings when Clarence walked right up and just came right out with it, easy as if he was asking me to a ball game. And some ball game that party turned out to be.

Walking up the driveway that night, I must have readjusted my trilby fifty times wanting to make the right impression. I'd paid enough jack to be able to buy another suit. Made to measure. Matching spats and shoes too. Real hotcha.

Truth was, I was hoping I'd bump into Pearl there. Since our little walk along the pier, I'd only seen her in passing at Kings. Word was that she'd made up with Charlie. Although Jesse claimed he'd heard some beef between them backstage only two nights before. I didn't know why I wanted to see her so badly again, but I did. I felt it in my gut, that instinct, that she would be there at the party. And if she was, I was determined to talk to her again, Charlie be damned.

Jesse stood at the door, Bud in hand, eyeballing everyone who walked in. As I walked up to him, he looked confused.

'You the entertainment tonight?' he snorted.

I shook my head. 'Nah, I'm invited.'

'Funny, Clarence never mentioned you were coming.'

There were guests coming up behind me now. Two pairs of couples. Girls with feathers in their hair and too much rouge. Guys in suits that looked a lot more hotcha than mine. My face was getting hot, a raging furnace burning inside of me. Jesse waved the others right in without a second glance.

I wasn't sure what had caused this change in him but him not letting me in was bordering on disrespectful.

'Look Jesse. Clarence invited me.'

'Oh, c'mon Jesse, let him in.'

I turned to see Pearl standing there in her fur coat and blue sequin dress.

'Now, I know *you're* the entertainment,' Jesse whistled through his teeth at her, and I swear her fists clenched like she wanted to sock him one, a real bearcat. Instead, she faked a smile and grabbed hold of my hand.

'Milton's with me. Now quit being a flat tire and let us in.'

Still, he stood blocking our way and I could feel my rage rising higher and higher. I'd overheard the girls behind the bar complaining about him. How he was always sniffing around backstage while the dancers got dressed and making snide comments about Pearl's blonde hair and she was only blonde from the neck upwards. And now there was this.

We had our eyes locked on one another and I was just about to sock him one myself when Charlie sidled up behind him.

'Jeez, what are you waiting for Jesse? Christmas? Let em in for god's sake.' He looked straight past me to Pearl who quickly dropped my hand.

Jesse stepped aside and as we walked through, Charlie put his arm around Pearl's shoulders. I didn't know if I should be grateful to him for getting us in or annoyed that he'd stolen my thunder. I eyeballed Jesse as I walked past, stepping over the threshold and into a hallway like nothing I'd ever seen before.

The black and white mosaic floor beneath my feet sparkled. Crystal chandeliers lined the hallway above my head, each glittering teardrop refracting rainbows of light against pristine white walls. The place was so hotcha it made my own shabby apartment look like a donkey's stable.

'Wow! I guess we'd better wipe our feet.' I said. I turned to Pearl, but she'd already gone. I turned back to see her up ahead, arm linked through Charlie's.

The party had already begun. A flapper with a martini glass in hand ran down the stairs and past us, barefoot, the pile of the carpet so thick her footsteps were silent. Behind her, her friend, already sozzled, slipped on the stairs, her glass falling from her hand and bouncing down each step.

Charlie and Pearl stopped and to my surprise, Charlie wasn't annoyed by this at all. He waved a maid over to clean up the mess and helped the broad to her feet before turning to the both of us.

'I guess I'd better get you a drink,' Charlie smiled.

I swear, the kitchen was as big as my whole apartment. The work-tops were pure marble although they were mostly covered up by the crates of shine and fizz stacked in towers. Charlie walked over to the french doors that led to the solarium where other spiffy bimbos and their broads sat sipping cocktails and eyeballing the garden. Lawns were manicured with topiary and roses and beyond that the splashes and cheers of guests in their bathing suits jumping into the swimming pool. The smell of barbecued meat wafted on the air and on the horizon, if you looked closely, you could just make out the wrought iron gate that led to the coastal path and Clarence's private beach.

I don't mind admitting that on that first visit to the Kelly Mansion I was so overcome with a mix of envy and awe that it made me queasy. That Charlie was behaving like such a standup guy, made me feel even worse.

I hoped there might be soda in the fridge. I turned to offer one to Pearl but she and Charlie had already left and were walking across the patio. I hadn't even had a chance to strike up a conversation with her.

Clarence stood in the doorway, Elmer whispering in his ear. He looked over at me.

'Help yourself to drink Milton. Make yourself at home.'

But I never felt at home anywhere, even less so in a place like this. I found a bottle of coke in the fridge and took it outside.

I walked past the topiary garden where a petting party was happening on a bench. The girl slumped drunk, the guy with his hand up her skirt. In the bushes next to them, a guy was bent over, puking into the hedges. It was early and yet it was already getting to be that part of the night where people began to forget themselves.

Up by the pool, I heard the tinkle of piano keys. I recognized the song straight away as 'it's a sin to tell a lie.' And the voice singing it as Pearl's. I walked over and smiled at her, her sparkling dress like the scales of a mermaid, her voice luring me in like the honeytrap she was.

I stood sipping my coke, watching her while people all around stretched out on sun loungers with cocktails, chatting happily with one another, paying no attention to the beautiful songbird performing for them. At first, I felt sore for her, singing her heart out with no one paying attention but when she noticed me and smiled and it was like everyone else faded into the background. When the song ended, I clapped and whistled, and she smiled coyly.

I felt a hand on my shoulder.

'Well, I could certainly get used to this. I mean, look at this place. Pool, private beach. If you ask me, we ain't getting paid anywhere near enough.'

I turned to face George, clutching a beef sandwich in one hand and a bottle of Bud in the other. I shook his hand vigorously, honestly so pleased to see a familiar face and one as friendly.

'Good to see you, Milton. Shall we grab a seat?'

The two of us sat at one of the patio tables, a stone's throw from the band so I could keep a watch on Pearl, but far enough away to be able to hold a proper conversation without being overheard.

'So, how's things at the drugstore?' I said.

'Yeah, you know. It's fine. I guess but you, I mean how are you? I hear you're quite the guy now. I told you he had his eye on you right from the very start.'

George gave a forced smile.

I smiled right back, but inside of me, snakes had settled in my guts.

'Look George, I never asked for this you know...'

'I know. Besides, after that...,' he lowered his voice so no one could hear. 'Since that night in the cave I haven't been able to sleep properly since. Every time, a guy I don't recognize enters the place I wonder if it's going to happen again, you know. I keep on thinking, if something ever happened to me, what would poor Lou do?'

'It's best not to think about it,' I said to him, but I wasn't thinking about that night. I was thinking about what happened afterwards in New York. I knew I shouldn't really speak of it, but George looked so troubled, and I knew I could trust him.

I checked around to make sure there wasn't anyone else listening.

'Look, if it helps put your mind at rest, that guy Joe who got away, didn't get away for long.'

'What do you mean?'

'I don't want to go into details here. Another time maybe. All you need to know is that you and Lou are safe. And don't feel too bad about it. We had no choice other than to take them out.'

George took another sip of his beer. 'You know what else I think about? That girl we met on the boardwalk.'

In my mind's eye I saw a flash of her silver eyes. The air around me grew colder. The hair on my arms prickled at the thought of her.

'Which girl?' I said, playing dumb.

'You know. That girl we met on the boardwalk. The one who reads palms at Zeldas. She said this would happen. That you would be promoted.'

I took a gulp of my coke. 'George, we were both in penguin suits that day. It was obvious we had bosses. She just grasped at the first thing she thought of.'

I knew the words coming out of my mouth were as hollow as they sounded.

George shrugged. 'She said you'd end up owning Kings too. And I wouldn't be surprised if that happened.'

But I just wanted him to stop talking. The whole thing gave me the heebie jeebies.

I snapped. 'Look, let's just forget about it. That girl was doing a parlor trick, that's all. She had us marked as a pair of chumps who didn't know no better.'

The band finished playing and I stood up to whoop and clap. As I sat down, I saw Charlie at the sidelines calling over Pearl. I drained my bottle of coke.

'I'm gonna go and get another of these. You want anything?'

George shook his head. 'Nah, I'm not staying much longer. I wanna be home to put Lou to bed.'

'Well, it's good to see you. Maybe I'll swing by the drugstore soon. We could go for a walk along the pier like we used to.'

'Yeah, maybe. You know I take Lou to that Monsters of the Deep show most weekends. You should come along.'

I shook his hand. 'Yeah, I just might do that.'

I stood for a while watching the rest of the partygoers jumping into the pool. After a while, I walked back to the kitchen but when I got there, there were no cokes left.

'You looking for something?' It was Jesse. He was pouring a glass of champagne for the pretty redhead he was with.

'Just a coke.'

'Try the cellar.' He gestured to the door next to the stove. Surprised he was being helpful after the incident at the door; I nodded thanks as he and his girl stumbled off into the garden.

I opened the door and started walking down the stone steps when I realized if I continued in, I wouldn't be alone. Two voices echoed up. One of them, Clarence's. I stopped where I was and listened.

'Well, someone has to go and sort it out. We can't have these Abel brothers pushing us around. I mean, who would you send?'

'Not your only son, that's for sure. You may as well put a goddam target on my back.'

The other voice had to be Charlie.

'I don't understand why it has to be me. Why can't you send Milton to do it? He was there when it all happened, wasn't he? He'd recognize them. Know exactly who it is we're dealing with.'

That yellow-bellied snake. He was trying to send me to do the dirty work he didn't want to do.

There was a voice in the kitchen.

'Well, this party really died.'

Pearl.

I went back up the steps and there she was sitting on the kitchen worktop, barefoot, swigging a half empty bottle of fizz, her cheeks streaked with mascara.

I poured her a glass of water.

'Here.'

She gulped the water down, eyes closed, barely able to keep balance. All the time, I had my eye on the cellar door, waiting for Charlie to reappear. Maybe it was wrong me skirting round his girl, but it didn't look like he was taking very good care of her, the way she looked. Besides, the guy was trying to stitch me up.

'Say you wanna get outta here Princess?'

She opened her eyes. 'Sure. Let's go for a walk along the beach. I could do with some fresh air.'

25

CHAPTER TWENTY-FOUR

We walked through the garden. The girls had kicked off their shoes and were dancing the charleston barefoot on the patio. The redhead Jesse had bought with him, jumped into the pool, fully clothed, her white dress clinging wet to her skin. In the next moment, Jesse was taking his shirt off, making it look like he was about to jump in after her.

Pearl said a bit too loudly, 'Turns out, she's not his wife after all.'

'What Eveline? Of course, she's not,' I said.

'It seems to me that no one is anyone's wife here. Is that what happens when you make it to the top? You begin collecting mistresses instead.'

The sounds of the party grew quieter, more distant as we walked down the sand path to the beach. The wind was rising and so were the waves. Pearl supped the last of her fizz, dropped the bottle in the sand and took off in the direction of the sea.

'Race you!'

She had caught me unawares and while I tried to follow after her, she was too far ahead. Her dress fluttered up around her head in the wind like a bird's feathers, but then the songbird disappeared from sight.

'Oh, Jesus Christ Pearl!'

Her head bobbed up and down, dipping under the water like she was fighting against the current. The waves rumbled as they washed in over the pebbles and there was a flash of her dress screwed up on the sand out of the corner of my eye as I reached the shore.

There was no time to lose. I stripped down to my briefs, and ran in, heart pounding as the ice water cut through my bones. I gasped involuntarily, barely able to breathe. I managed to call out her name but of course, there was no answer. I spotted her blonde hair spread out across the water like seaweed.

'Oh god, Pearl. No!'

I swam out to her, and as I reached out to grab her, she popped up out of the water, buoyant as a cork.

'What took you so long? 'She giggled.

'Jesus Christ Pearl! Are you trying to kill us both out here?'

I was so sore at her. I was half naked and freezing cold feeling like a chump. She gave a fizz-soaked giggle.

'Why would I do that?'

She swam up to me and planted the biggest, coldest kiss on my lips, her naked body up against me. Someone needs to tame this bearcat.

I didn't react to her, and she stopped kissing me and started rubbing her hands over my bare chest and stomach.

'God, you're freezing, 'she slurred. 'We should get out.'

My mood thawed a little, I thought you'd never ask.'

I grabbed her hand and led her out of the water, and we stood for a moment dripping wet on the sand, arms around one another, shivering.

'So, what happened between you and Charlie at the party?'

'Oh, you know,' she says. 'It's at that point in the evening when couples start arguing and girls start crying, glasses get smashed, and everyone is way too sozzled.'

'That good, eh?' I smiled at her. 'Look, how about we blow this joint? I'll drive you home if you like?'

She hesitated for a moment, and I could see her thinking it over.

'Yeah sure,' she said. 'Take me home.'

The night air was warm and by the time we arrived back at my car my clothes were mostly dry. Pearl's so sozzled that she dozes off on the drive to her apartment. When we got there, she woke up and stretched out, curving her spine like a cat.

'Thanks for jumping in after me,' she says, and she leant over and kissed me. 'You can come up and get dry if you like.' She gestured to her apartment.

I shook my head. 'Sorry baby, bank's closed. I'm almost dry and you're too fried.'

'Well, how bout you come up anyway? I won't be fried when we wake up in the morning. Then we can both decide if this is a mistake we want to make.'

She gives me that sweet smile that gets my blood pumping and of course I say yes because how could I say anything else?

Pearl and I were fated to be together.

Fated to cause one another's downfall.

26

Chapter Twenty-Five

We decided not to spout to anyone about 'us.' Charlie was rumored to be the jealous type, which is usually a euphemism for being the violent type, so we both thought it best in everyone's interests to keep hushed.

Days at Kings were full of secret glances and kisses up against the wall backstage when no one else was around. Pearl's love had me stuck on her the way a dope peddler lures a fiend. No matter how much of her I had, it was never enough. Every day, at the end of a shift I made like I was going home when really, I was going straight to Pearl's apartment where she'd be waiting for me wearing nothing but a smile.

If it sounds like it was difficult to be together, it really wasn't. These were sepia tinted days where everything she did only served to fuel my fire for her.

But while things were going well with Pearl, things with Clarence were about to get murky.

Seemed like every drop off either the law or the Abels were lying in wait having got the rumble of what was going on. You couldn't leave your apartment without looking over your shoulder, scared spitless that you'd be filled with daylight by some goon packing a gun.

Clarence was sore as a bear. He'd thought that burning down that house would warn them off but now the Abels' had him behind the eight ball. Clarence was losing his crown, but he refused to see it.

Truth was, for the first time in his reign Clarence was scared. And when old men get scared, they get desperate. And when they get desperate, they become sloppy.

It was only when I stopped by to see George at the drugstore that I heard about the meeting at the Blenheim Hotel. Instead of it being opening time, George stood at the door, coat on, locking up.

'What's going on?' I said.

'Didn't Clarence call you about the meeting at the Blenheim?'

'Yeah,' I lied, I was just checking that *you'd* heard.'

The real reason I'd missed the call at my apartment was because I hadn't been at my apartment. While the phone was ringing out, I was lying next to Pearl on her bed at her apartment, but I couldn't let that slip to George in case it got back to Charlie.

'You wanna drive in together?' he gestured to his battered Ford.

I shook my head. 'I'll take my car. I've got places to go afterwards. I'll see you there.'

By the time I got to the Kelly Mansion, George had already gone in without me.

The first sign of something being hinky was the hired brunos in the entrance hall. All of them packing guns. They seemed so out of place under the crystal chandeliers and expensive artwork. There didn't appear to be any regular guests there that I could see either. Clarence had hired the place out.

One of the guys led me down the hallway to a waiting Clarence. This wasn't the calm, confident Clarence I knew. His face was pale and sweaty and judging by the dark circles under his eyes he'd barely slept a wink. I don't mind admitting that I was a little unnerved. He'd never seen him be anything less than calm before.

He smiled and pushed a wall that concealed a passageway.

'You first,' he said, and he placed his hand in the small of my back, steering me down there. The sound of my own footsteps echoed off the cold stone walls. I understood now why he had brought us all here. The hidden cellar of the hotel was his safe house.

To the right, illuminated by a lantern screwed into the bare bricks, I could see an open door. The lights were off, but I could hear George's hearty laughter drifting from the room.

'Just through here,' Clarence stood back, ever the gracious host, letting me walk in first.

I made some crack about him switching on the lights, but as I stepped over the threshold, I was socked in the guts with a punch so powerful, it knocked the breath out of me.

Gasping for air, I stumbled backwards, trying to get a hold on something to pull myself up but arms flailing in the dark. Pushed back by unseen hands, I fell backwards and into the seat of a chair already placed to catch me.

It was a stitch up.

The glow from the kitchen door illuminated the heavyweight ass-hole, Jesse.

I should have known the sucker punch came from him.

Clarence stood next to him in the half-light, shark eyes eyeballing me the whole time, as Elmer, who'd emerged from the darkness, quickly tied my hands behind my back. Where Jesse was gloating, Elmer was unreadable. Yesterday I had been Clarence's golden boy, now I wasn't sure what I was. I hoped it didn't mean I'd be leaving the mansion in a body bag.

Elmer lifted my shirt and snatched my gun from my holster. I was trying to catch my breath, preparing myself for another sock to the guts. See, I knew how this thing worked. I'd seen it enough times. Whatever it was they thought I knew, they would hurt me again and again and again, until I confessed it to them. A punch to the ribs was nothing compared to the torture I knew I was about to be dealt, and I was hardening myself ready for it.

'What the hell is this, Clarence?'

Clarence didn't answer the question.

'Where were you this morning?' he said.

'At home,' I said but my voice sounded like a stranger's.

'What are you lying for? The hell is wrong with you?' Clarence stepped forward only inches away from my face, eyes wide. 'You think I dunno that someone is feeding information to the Abels? The Pro-hies too? Elmer, pass me the gun.'

Elmer started to take out his own revolver.

'Not yours numbnuts! His...Milton's!'

Clarence snarled with fury and took his handkerchief from his top pocket, handing it to Elmer, so that he didn't leave any of his fingerprints on the grip.

My breathing became shallow now. Clarence wanted me dead. Maybe he was bluffing. Sometimes guys did this to put the frighteners up you. Made you blurt out confessions, mob secrets. Once you'd spilled your guts, they'd tell you it was a ruse all along. They never planned to kill you but there's no taking back the names you've said, and it would confirm what everyone believed all along: that you were a rat. And then they'd kill you anyways.

The only way to bide time was to tell Clarence where I'd really been when he made the call but even that I knew it was unlikely to go down well. His son Charlie was sore at losing Pearl. If he knew she'd left his son for me, he might be just as rage filled. And I'd promised Pearl I wouldn't spout a word.

Clarence raised the gun, the cold metal of the barrel against my temple. I closed my eyes tight. This was it. He was going to blow me down, right there in front of Jesse and Elmer and blame it on me, saying I committed suicide with my own gun.

The air buzzed around me, and my hands were trembling. I didn't want to die. Not there. Not like that, trussed up like a thanksgiving turkey, shaking in my boots. Who would look after Champ? He'd be waiting there for me looking out of the window and I'd never return.

And then there was the thought of my Ma believing I'd done it to myself. That would just break her heart.

To hell with it, I thought. What did keeping Pearl's secret matter if they were going to kill me anyway?

I spat the confession out. 'I was with Pearl.'

'What?' Clarence looked confused.

But Jesse understood right away and started to laugh. 'You and her together? How did you manage that?'

Still too spit scared to open my eyes, I ignored Jesse and tried to explain for Clarence's benefit more than Jesse's. I figured he'd be the one pulling the trigger. Or at least the one making the decision whether to or not.

'I didn't get the call because I was at Pearl's apartment. I stayed the night at hers.' I clarified just in case he still didn't get it. 'I stayed *with* her. I'm not a rat, Clarence, I swear I'm not.'

But the cold gun metal didn't move away from my temple.

'So, you thought you'd just lie to me instead about where you were?'

I had dug an even deeper grave. May as well have asked for a shovel and dug it myself.

'No, no. I didn't mean to lie. I just didn't want anyone to know about Pearl.'

I dared to open my eyes. I had to face Clarence, or he'd think I was a coward. Only, seeing his face red with rage, made me even more afraid of him. He jabbed the gun to my temple harder.

'Well, if you don't want me to fill you with daylight with this revolver here, you'll promise me right now that you ain't ever going lie to me again.'

I nodded, but that wasn't enough.

'Say it! Say it godamm it!'

'I swear that I won't ever...'

He jabbed the gun barrel again. Clarence looked so screwy that I couldn't get the rest of the words out.

'What are you waiting for? Do you want me to blow your fucking brains out?'

'No, no! Of course not. I swear I won't ever...'

Fear caught my tongue again.

'...lie to you ever again.' Clarence barked the words at me to parrot back.

'...lie to you ever again.'

When I got to the end of the sentence I held my breath, and closed my eyes again, waiting for the gunshot. For the searing pain and darkness. I wondered if I should repent for the bad things I'd done while I'd got the chance. From the recess of my brain, I remembered the look on Joe's face as he opened the door to see who had thrown the brick threw the window.

To my surprise the gunshot never came. The cold barrel of the gun moved away from my temple, and I sensed Clarence stepping away. Finally, I opened my eyes, to see Clarence wiping his fingerprints off my gun with his handkerchief.

'Well, Milton, I'm glad we understand one another. The last thing I wanted to have to do was kill somebody today.' His voice was calm as he tossed the gun into my lap. He gave a smirk and turned to Jesse and Elmer.

'Boys please untie him before he pisses his pants. Then the two of you go and fetch my son. For god's sakes don't mention anything about Milton here rutting with Pearl.'

Jesse and Elmer nodded and left.

When they were gone, he turned back to me.

'I understand why you lied, and I'm touched you would try to protect Pearl's reputation, but truth is I'm delighted someone's taken Pearl off Charlie's hands finally. I've been telling him for some time that a girl like her is no good, but it doesn't seem to matter what I say, he's still sweet on her. Now that doesn't mean I'm happy about you disrespecting my son, but this situation could actually turn out for the best.

So, here's what we're going to do now. I'm going to help you up and you and me are going to go downstairs. I'm going to make sure everyone is settled and has their drinks topped up and you're not going to spout a word about what just happened to anyone. You understand?'

I nodded and Clarence held out his hand to get me to my feet. My legs were still trembling as he put his arm around my shoulders in some attempt to reassure me, ignoring the fact that I was shaking all over. His soft friendly voice remained, like we'd just had any other man-to-man bull session.

'I'm sorry about all that Milton. It's just that I can't be too careful nowadays. It's a risk bringing people into my inner circle, you understand?' He finally switched on the light, and I could see that this was just the entrance to the room we were about to go in.

'There's still a rat among us, of that I'm certain, but here I'm in control. Take this room, for example. Only I have the key to it. Even the hotel staff aren't allowed in. Every day I sweep the room for bugs, under tables, behind paintings, in the light bulbs, everywhere. It's the only way I can get to sleep at night knowing I can talk openly about business here and know the people and the room itself is clean. You know what I mean?'

I nodded, still too balled up to speak. All the time I was aware my legs might collapse at any moment. And all this talk of rooms being bugged. Clarence really must have been losing it. He opened the door and walked right through while I trailed behind him, not sure if I wanted to puke or cry, or both. I daren't do either. Not until I was out of there.

The air was heavy with the scent of floor wax and table polish, making me feel even more nauseous. The rose filled crystal vases that lined the oak table, gleamed under the lamplight. There were no tablecloths, presumably because it would make it too easy for someone to hide something underneath. This way it was clear to see what everyone had laid out on the table.

Most people were so busy chatting that they didn't even look up when I entered the room but from his spot at the table, George nodded and raised his whiskey glass in my direction to call me over.

'Go on. Take a seat.'

Clarence gave his permission, and I walked over, legs still Jello, snatched George's whiskey out of his hand, and gulped it straight down; grateful for the way it burned in my chest because at least it meant I was still alive.

Chapter Twenty-Six

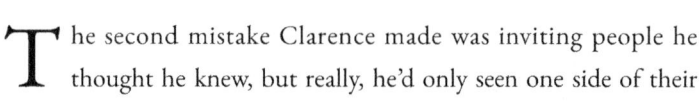

The second mistake Clarence made was inviting people he thought he knew, but really, he'd only seen one side of their faces. Lawmen, city officials; not a single one of them was on the level.

Take Clyde for instance. Sure, he'd been getting the jack from Clarence for years, but he was getting the jack from everyone – and just because he was getting paid, it didn't mean nothing in terms of loyalty. I'd seen how tight he was with the Abels that night me and George drove out to Princeton, and it was pretty clear to me that Clyde was getting paid by the Abels too.

Given that Clyde's day job meant it was the law paying the most of his money, he was the best placed to be a rat out of everyone. Why Clarence still trusted him, I never understood, but then Clarence wasn't exactly behaving or thinking like a rational human being at that time.

Other associates were notable by their absence, golden boy Charlie being one of them. Not that I missed him, given that I'd just admitted to his Pa that I was seeing his girl.

After downing George's whiskey, I sat down my heart still pumping, hands still shaking.

George leaned over. 'What's eating you?'

'I can't spill here,' I whispered. 'I'll tell you another time.'

Clarence stood up and cleared his throat to show he was about to hold court, and his congregation hushed their voices to listen.

'Thank you everyone for coming at such short notice. A lot of you will have heard about our recent disagreement with the Abels and the games they're playing. Well, I'm afraid they've played their final move. They may think they have us in check but they're entering into the endgame with only pawns to play. Clyde tells me they've put an embargo on selling or trading with us.'

Clarence took a sip of his water, hand steady.

'Anyone who trades with them will no longer trade with us, which puts Kings in a bit of a predicament. You see, in only a week's time, if we don't find someone else to supply us, we're going to be running a dry bar. And let's be honest, no one comes to Atlantic City for a dry bar – they're in plenty of supply all across America.'

It was meant as a joke, but nobody laughed. Clarence was trying to pass this off as a minor inconvenience when it was clear the Abels were the ones making the moves of a king, not Clarence.

Looks were exchanged across the table. This wasn't what anyone was expecting.

'I've managed to get a temporary supply from one of the bars we offer protection to, but I need to call more favors in. The other issue is the Abels themselves. No doubt they believe they have us on the ropes but just cause I'm old doesn't mean I'm weak and we need to show them that they can't get away with it. Even if it means all-out war.'

Across from me, Clyde cleared his throat to speak.

The air around us stiffened. Was he about to speak up against Clarence? Clyde stood up from his seat. Yes, yes, he was.

'Look Clarence, I've always offered you my support and turned a blind eye to a lot of things, but all-out war? You can't be serious. As an officer of the law, I can't be a part of this. It's against the oath I took...'

Clarence eyeballed Clyde.

'So's taking bribes the last time I heard.'

Clyde smirked.

'Clarence, I say this with the utmost respect and as a friend, but if it wasn't for me intervening every time you were raided, you'd have been thrown in jail a long time ago.'

I daren't move. Daren't breathe; the anticipation of imminent violence hanging in the air.

For anyone to have the audacity to speak out against Clarence and mock him in front of everyone, there had to be some payback. I wasn't the only one to feel the threat. All around me, fingers were twitchy, hands moved beneath the table, caressing the grips of hidden revolvers in preparation for the imminent firefight.

You could see by the look on Clarence's face that he hadn't expected this at all. And for the first time I witnessed something I never thought I'd see: Clarence backing down.

He let out sigh. 'Well, I suppose war is a strong word for it. It goes without saying Clyde that the last thing anyone wants is trouble in Atlantic City. Least of all me...' The old man looked exhausted.

As Clarence was talking Charlie burst in through the door, Martini glass in hand, with Elmer and Jesse coaxing and shepherding him in. And that was Clarence's third mistake: choosing his son to inherit the family business when it was clear he had no interest in it whatsoever.

Jesse led him to the empty chair next to Clarence.

'Sorry I'm late. I got caught up in business,' Charlie slurred.

Clarence's face was getting redder and redder. First his police protector had turned against him in front of everyone and now his own son couldn't even show him enough respect to turn up to a meeting sober and on time.

'I was just explaining,' Clarence said. 'How you're going to be helping to secure some new suppliers.'

An awkward silence fell across the table.

Charlie sucked the meat off the olive and spat the stone into the bottom of his glass.

'Do I have to? I thought you said you were going to send Milton to do it.'

My stomach dropped at the sound of my name.

Clarence flashed a cardboard smile and said, 'Sure son. That's a great idea.'

Now why would Clarence, a man who half an hour before had a gun to my temple because he thought me a rat, agree to send me on an errand?

Because all that talk about being happy, I was taking Pearl off his son's hands was a lie. Because no man wanted a dead body on his hands that he'd have to explain away or dispose of. Because Clarence still believed I was the rat and wanted me dead, and this was the opportunity to do just that.

A big shot never gets his own hands dirty. He always gets someone else to take someone out.

This is how it works:

A guy gets given an errand to do alone, or maybe he's just going out for breakfast same way he always does. He senses he's being tailed but every time he turns there's no one there so he tries to shake the feeling off. He's at the waffle house sitting in his favorite seat by the window when he feels a pain in the back of his head. Next thing he knows is him lying face down in maple syrup, a bullet in the back of his head.

Why else would they send me? Unless Clarence could trap the rat, he would always be hinky about me and the longer he didn't trust me, the more likely he was to take me out of the equation altogether to protect himself.

I came out of Clarence's meeting knowing I was a dead man walking.

As soon as I was out of there, I stopped to puke in a bush before getting straight in my car and driving away, leaving George standing on the sidewalk without chance to say another word.

28

CHAPTER TWENTY-SEVEN

❖ ⅲ———————ⅲ❖

I was convinced I was a dead man walking.

If my suspicion was correct, then that meant I couldn't go back to my own place. Clarence might have already sent someone to lie in wait for me. Pearl was out at rehearsal and given that Clarence had only just found out about me and her, it would be the safest place for me to be.

And, I decided, even if he did send someone after me, I would be the one lying in wait with a gun in my hand.

As I came up to the lights, two guys in trench coats paused on the sidewalk. I caught the eye of one of them as he reached inside his coat. Who knew what he could be reaching for? A 45. I slammed my foot on the gas, pushing through the lights just as they turned red waiting for the shot to shatter the rear window screen that thankfully never came.

The Chrysler behind me sped through the light too. And they were speeding up, their chrome bumper getting closer and closer.

In the rear view mirror the top of the driver's face was obscured but I could see his smile.

I reached for my revolver but in my panic to do so, it slid through my grasp and fell to the floor. When I looked in the mirror again the car was gone.

Still frantically searching for the gun, the car pulled up alongside me now.

I could see his face. The face of an old man, not too dissimilar from my Da. He sped past not even looking in my direction, turning right when he came to the next block.

Sweat dripped down my back, my forehead, my palms. My heart ready to burst. I had to get to safety before I gave myself a heart attack.

But even when I arrived at Pearl's things still felt hinky.

The first sign that something wasn't right were the red drapes billowing out of the open window, waving like a flag in the breeze. Pearl had closed the window before we left. I distinctly remembered her doing it.

I sunk down in my seat, just watching the window for a moment. As the drapes billowed and blew upwards, I caught a flash of a figure inside the apartment moving past the window. It wasn't long enough to see his face, but I saw his cropped hair.

Was Clarence really so evil that he would send someone to lie in wait and take out my innocent girlfriend, as well as me? I thought back to the wild look in his dark eyes when I was sat with my own revolver pointed at my temple and I knew the answer was unfortunately yes.

I reached for my gun and slowly got out of the car. I glanced up and down the street and when I was certain it was safe, moved quickly to the fire escape at the back of the building. Pearl was always complaining about how someone was always leaving the door wide open.

Peering round the door I was relieved to see the corridor empty, the broken light at the end of the hallway flickering on and off. The sound of jazz music drifted up from the floor below. Once I was certain the coast was clear I walked slowly, keeping close to the wall, loaded piece in my hand.

When I reached Pearl's apartment, the door was ajar, just enough so that I could peer through the gap.

Then I saw her, Pearl in a yellow dress, her hair newly cropped. Boy-like, like one of those flapper girls, with a cigarette in one hand, glass of gin in the other.

Unable to hold back the storm inside, I pushed the door open with such rage that it slammed against the wall, causing Pearl to jump back and spill her gin.

'Hey! What's the big idea?'

Pearl slammed her glass down on the table so the gin that remained leapt over the edge of the glass, making a tiny pool on the table.

'For god's sake, Pearl, I almost killed you! What are you doing at home? And what happened to your hair?'

Pearl came over all kisses and wrapped her arms around me to soothe me.

'You don't like my hair?'

'No, I don't.'

I slumped down on the couch, exhausted.

'Booker was sick. Rehearsal was cancelled, so I went and got my hair cut. I didn't realize it would make you so upset. Jeez Milt. What happened today? You're shaking.'

I spilled my guts about there being a rat. About Clarence's interrogation.

'I think he's going to kill me,' I said to her.

'You dunno that...'

She had that soft voice that I'm sure she thought was meant to be comforting but it just made me grind my teeth at her naivety. It wasn't her fault. She didn't understand the way mobs worked.

'Pearl, I hate to be the one to tell you this, but that's the sort of Clarence he is. He's not just a speakeasy owner. He's had people killed for less.'

'You sound like you have experience of that,' she gave an uncomfortable laugh.

I didn't answer.

'Well, what can we do?' She sat down next to me and took my hand.

There was only one way to stop Clarence. I was surprised when it was Pearl who suggested it.

'People disappear all the time in this town and the coppers, they don't do anything because they're all on the payroll. That's what you said, right?'

I knew what she was hinting at.

'Pearl...'

I tried to close down the conversation. I mean, of course I'd thought about what she was about to suggest but this was different to that night in the cave. That had been self-defense. It had been different to me setting that building alight. That was just a job. What she was suggesting was cold, calculated murder.

She gave my hand a squeeze.

'Well, if someone doesn't get rid of Clarence soon, those boys from New York will. And what will happen to Kings and the drugstore then? Charlie doesn't want any of it. He told me that as soon as Clarence died, he would sell everything to the highest bidder and get out of there. So, who's going to take over if he does that? Jesse?' She gave a snort at the thought.

'Pearl look...'

But she wouldn't stop. Just kept on flapping her jaws.

'Say someone did whack Clarence. Clyde wouldn't wanna get on the wrong side of them. You could walk right in there. You're a born leader. You don't wanna live with a leaky kitchen tap that drips all night long. That mansion of Clarence's could end up being ours.'

Ours? Neither of us usually thought further than the next week but here she was already building a future life in her head. I changed the subject.

'Do you really think I'm a born leader?'

Another hand squeeze.

'Sure, I do, but it's just a thought. I know you'd never do anything. You're too loyal for that.'

She said 'loyal' like it was a dirty word. Pearl dropped my hand and stood up. She walked over to the table and poured me and her a gin without another word about it.

It was like she'd dipped her toe in to see how warm my waters were, then backed out quickly when she realized it was stone cold.

But the seed of murder had been planted, and it didn't matter if she fed and watered it, or if she did nothing. It was already beginning to grow inside my head. Bigger and bigger, its leaves and buds blooming until there was no room for thoughts about anything else.

Chapter Twenty-Eight

❖▸▪────▪•▪────▪◂❖

I heard the car pulling up outside and I knew instinctively that it was for me. It hadn't taken them long to figure out I was at Pearl's. I gulped down the last of my coffee like it was my last.

'It's them, isn't it?' Pearl, who had sounded so calm before, had a slight tremor in her voice.

I nodded. What more was there to say. I felt bad for bringing them to her door, but she couldn't have been that naive if she'd been fooling around with Charlie. It was pretty clear the Kelly family weren't straight down the line. They ran a speakeasy, for goodness' sake.

'Stay there,' I gestured for her to sit still on the couch, for her own protection.

Taking my revolver out, I kept my back to the wall, getting close enough to the drapes to be able to take a sneaky peek out of the window without stepping into plain sight.

It was George's car, but that didn't mean I could assume that he was the one driving it. The car door opened. For the second time that day, the fear that these could be my last moments overwhelmed me.

'Pearl,' I said. 'Listen if anything happens to me make sure my Ma is okay won't you. My dog too.'

'Why are you talking like that...'

'Just promise me you'll look out for them.'

'Okay I promise.'

George stepped out of the car, and I relaxed a little. Not because I trusted him, but because I'd seen him piss his pants with weasel-face and I knew that should things turn ugly the dice would fall in my favor.

I watched him on the sidewalk, looking up at the apartment building, scanning across each window like he was figuring out which one we were in. He appeared to be alone.

'I'm going down there,' I said to Pearl.

'What? Are you crazy?' Pearl stood up and followed behind me as I went to the door to exit.

'It's safer for you this way. Don't worry about me. I can handle it.' I kissed her on the forehead and left.

I took the elevator down to the ground floor and found George waiting to take the elevator up. I immediately went for my gun.

'Whoa there!' George held up his hands in surrender. 'It's me, Milton. It's George.'

I left my revolver pointing at him, just in case.

'Who sent you?'

'Clarence. It's about that errand he wants us to do.'

'Us?' I laughed at his use of the word. George had no idea how it felt to have been through the sort of interrogation I'd just been through.

Yes, us.' Jeez, I don't know what's gotten into you Milt, but you need to get back on the level. Now can I please put my hands down?'

Perhaps I overreacted. Perhaps not. He had that same old earnest look about him, even with a revolver pointed at his face and it finally dawned on me that even if Clarence was planning to get me whacked at some point, today was not going to be that day.

I put the revolver away and George dropped his hands to his side.

'You need to get more sleep,' George grinned. 'Now get in the car. We're going for a drive.'

***

We'd only been driving for thirty minutes, and already little rivers of sweat were pouring down my spine. It was a damn hot day.

'Just how the hell did we end up doing Charlie's job for him?' George shook his head. 'Dunno bout you but I think the way he behaved at that meeting made Clarence look a sap.'

I'd never heard George speak out against Clarence before and I was surprised he was as sore as I was about this errand we'd been sent out on.

'Yeah, I gotta admit, the more I see of Charlie, the less I like him,' I said.

'I would just rather be doing anything but this right now, no offence Milton. I'd planned to take Lou to the beach today.'

I tried to make out that I was just gazing out of the window, but whilst I looked calm on the outside, inside my heart was thumping at the memory of the day before: the cold of metal against my temple. The click of the hammer being pulled back.

'You know, Clarence thought I was a rat. Shook me down trying to get a confession out of me.'

'Oh, I see now why you've been so on edge,' George kept his eye on the road, but his tone of voice told me he knew what 'getting a confession' meant.

'So, he thinks there's a rat? What gave him that idea?'

'Just that we've had a lot of busts lately. And the fact I didn't pick up the call yesterday morning on account of being with Pearl.'

'And how did he take that? I mean, you're playing a risky game there, Milt. Of all the broads to cheat with, choosing the one who is with the Boss' son...well, it's probably not the wisest move.'

'I know, I know.'

George changed the subject. 'Well, you know, I think Clarence is losing his grip anyway.'

'Really? You think he's too old now to be in this business?'

George shrugged. 'Clarence is getting old, true, but that's not what I meant. He still knows this business better than most. He knows how to work people and that's what Charlie don't understand. It's not all about money, it's about people and how you make them feel. And Charlie doesn't give a damn about how others feel. He's like a spoiled child. God knows why Clarence is insisting on handing over to him when he's gone. You'd do a better job than him and you ain't even blood.'

It was a joke but to me it wasn't. It couldn't be a co-incidence: George's words echoing Pearl's. If each word could have been a golden coin, then this was the jackpot pouring from his lips.

'Let's say by some miracle I did end up running Kings. How would you feel about that?

He didn't have to think for long. Theoretically, I'd be pleased for you, but we both already know that Charlie is going to inherit Kings and then run it all into the ground so ain't no point dreaming.' He laughed.

'You're right. Charlie's a coward for starters. Second, he ain't got the drive or the smarts to make it big...'

'And you think you do?' George was staring right at me now. I wished I'd kept my kisser shut.

'Well, I'd do a better job than Charlie does anyway but that's not difficult.'

'Here's us.'

Thank God the house we were looking for appeared just then. If nothing else, it taught me that George was loyal to Clarence which meant he wasn't the rat neither.

He slowed the car down and pulled in, just opposite the house. It didn't look much. Two up, two down. White paint flaking off the front porch. Barrel houses always looked like this. Richer than their neighbors they may have been, but moonshiners never showed off their wealth. Not the way big shots like Clarence did.

George turned the engine off.

'So, what now?'

'We wait a while. See if there's any movement.'

George saw this as an opportunity to sit back and chew, taking a paper bag of boiled sweets from his pocket. He offered one to me and I shook my head.

'Hey, he's dusting out.' George mumbled with his mouth full.

At the house opposite, a guy wearing slacks and shirt with a flat cap pulled the front door behind him and took the steps down the stoop two at a time.

George stuffed the sweets in his pocket.

'Clarence said to put the screws on this chump. Do anything to get him to do business with us.'

George opened the glovebox, but I pushed it shut, and I pulled out my revolver again.

'I'll take this one.'

George almost choked on his boiled sweet. 'Hey Milton, look I'm not being funny but you're not actually going to use that, are you? There's no need to get trigger happy here.'

For a mob guy, George was a little soft sometimes.

'Look, we want this done quickly right so you can get back home to Lou? As long as this guy says yes, I won't have to use it will I?'

CHAPTER TWENTY-NINE

✦ ┉━━━ •●• ━━━┉ ✦

The guy in the flat cap was Mickey Saunders and no doubt Mickey was expecting to have a swell day. His wife Maud was at home with the kids while he was on his way to the station. He was headed to New York, hoping to see Babe Ruth hit a few home runs.

Mickey was a simple guy, not used to the new-found wealth making moonshine had bought him. To me, he just looked like every other chump who was planning to drink away his money with his beer buddies over the weekend.

The train was at ten thirty. Mickey glanced at his watch. He figured he'd have time to grab a cup of joe and a stack of pancakes for breakfast. It was as he came to the crosswalk that he finally noticed me and George, walking steadily, ten paces behind him.

He walked a little more quickly, every now and then glancing behind to check we were still there, which of course we were. We were in no rush. We would soon catch up with him.

At the crosswalk, Mickey sidled up to a pregnant broad in a floral cloche hat. A move that smelled of desperation. Although George and me hadn't done anything except follow, Mickey's instincts told him trouble was coming his way. By the time we reached him, all his Saturday morning pep had drained clear out of him.

George slipped in on the left, between Mickey and the pregnant woman, whilst I stood next on the right and showed him a flash of the revolver I had in my pocket. When I spoke, I made sure that I did it softly and without any sound of threat in my voice. I didn't want to scare the broad next to him.

'Morning Mickey,' I said. 'You off somewhere?'

There was a shake in his voice. 'Look, I dunno you guys and I don't want any trouble...'

'Well, you're in luck because we're not looking to make any...'

'Steady there, Mickey,' George stepped in to pat him on the back. 'We're all friends here, ain't that right Milton?'

I nodded, sore that George had used my real name, not that there was much I could do about that now.

I cut back in. 'So, you didn't answer my question. Where are we going Mickey?'

The poor guy was so scared spitless he could barely get the words out. This would be easy as pie.

'B...b...breakfast, 'he stammered. 'A ball game.'

'Well, we could do with breakfast, eh, George?' I looked over at George, who nodded. 'Great, where are we dining Mickey?'

Mickey let out an exasperated sigh. He was going to have to deal with us whether he liked it or not.

'I...I was going to go to Stacey's Waffle House.'

'Good choice,' George said.

Truth be told, I didn't want to have to do anything bad to this guy. He just needed to agree to help us out and not get smart and everything would turn out just fine for him.

Stacey's was the sort of diner, my Da would have taken us to. The kind where regulars nodded to one another and the waitresses remembered your favorite order. That's fine if you're a regular patron but we wanted to just get on with the job and get out of there without anyone paying us much attention. I found a quiet booth at the back.

Mickey ordered a pot of coffee whilst George, unsurprisingly, ordered the biggest item on the menu; eager to fill up with waffles and chicken on Mickey's hospitality.

I waited until the coffee and food arrived before I got down to business.

'Listen Mickey, we wanted to talk to you about your friend William Abel.'

'Oh, the Abels are not my friends...'

'You hear this, George? We got ourselves a smart guy here in Mickey. Well done, Mickey, that's the right answer.'

Mickey poured himself a cup of coffee, his hand trembling slightly.

'Look, I wouldn't know anything about anything. I just make the shine I get told to make, I get paid and that's all there is to it.'

'Yeah, and we heard you make good stuff, and you should know that our Boss, Mr. Kelly, is a few hundred bottles of whiskey short, given that William Abel and his brother Thomas have stopped supplying him. Now I don't what your financial situation is Mickey, but Mr. Kelly is willing to pay over the odds for the shine you produce as long as you promise to just keep on selling it to us exclusively.'

Mickey was silent for a moment. I watched the dull look on his face like he struggled to think, never mind think anything over.

'I dunno. I mean, the Abel brothers are going to be pretty pissed about this. I'm going to need a lot of money and some sort of protection...'

'Which you'll have. For you and Mrs. Saunders and all your little ones. So, what do you say? Do we have a deal?'

I held out my hand and he let it hover there for a moment. I knew he'd shake on it, because there was no other choice.

He put his sweaty palm in mine, and the deal was done.

I swigged the last of my coffee and stood up.

'Anyway, we'd better get going, and so had you, or you'll miss the ball game. We'll see you on Sunday for the pickup.'

***

George waited until we were a little way down the road before he spoke.

'You're a real piece of work, you know that? Did you see that poor chump's hand shaking as he poured your coffee? And to think how timid you were when you first came to Clarence. I swear he thought you were going to kill him.' He laughed.

I changed the subject. 'You know what'll kill you? All those waffles and fried chicken. I swear I've never known anyone eat as much as you do and not put on weight.'

George patted his stomach. 'I'll tell you my secret. Every single day, around dusk, I go out in the front yard and pitch a few balls with Lou. Keeps the pounds off.'

Something moved in the bushes. I moved for my revolver before I even registered what I was doing. I aimed it past George and towards the rustling sound, fingers wound so tight round the trigger, my knuckles were white.

George ducked down beside the car, his own piece out, following my lead. Both of us froze, watching the leaves on the bush trembling in the breeze.

My head hurt; my brain a balloon swelling up with air, ready to burst. Fear crept over me again, the way it had when Clarence had me tied to that chair, sweat dripping down my forehead.

Realizing it was a false alarm, George stood up and hissed at me.

'Jeez Milton. What's wrong with you? Put the damn gun away.'

'I'm sorry George, I dunno what happened.' I glanced around in case there were any witnesses but thankfully we were alone. I put the gun away.

George walked ahead a few paces.

'What is going on with you? First you were acting twitchy at Clarence's, you've started drinking whiskey when you used to be dry and now this.'

'George, look, I'm sorry. It won't happen again, I promise.'

'You're damn right, it won't. Damn nearly took my head off,' he said. 'You're going to give me that gun at least till we get home.'

He held his hand out for me to give it to him, the way a parent takes away a sharp stick.

'When we get to the car, you're going to sit there in the passenger seat and tell me all about what happened with Clarence.'

'Sure George.'

How could I explain the terror the interrogation had planted in me? I couldn't explain the conversation with Pearl that played like a stuck record over and over, nor the fear that told me that if I didn't do something about Clarence, that he might end up doing something terrible to me.

Chapter Thirty

❖⊱————••◦••————⊰❖

O f course, I knew I was paranoid but so was Clarence and that made him even more unpredictable and dangerous.

I'll give you just one example off the cuff. Clarence was so off his nut that one day I walked up to Kings to start my day, and Jesse stopped me at the door and ushered me away.

'Look kid,' he said. 'Best thing you can do today is get right back in your car and drive home. The mood Clarence is in; you'll only have to look at him the wrong way and he'll me ordering me to take you out and I can't have that weighing on my conscience.'

And you have to remember that Jesse, for the most part, hated my guts. For him to look out for me meant things were getting desperate. I was becoming more and more like a dog backed into a corner. If I didn't bite soon, Clarence would bite first and savage me.

The more I thought about it, the more it seemed like the right thing to do. Like Pearl said, someone would whack Clarence sooner or later, so it was probably kinder if it was me.

Once I'd made my mind up to go through with it, it was like a huge weight was lifted off me.

The plan was simple. I knew that every morning, come rain or shine, Clarence made himself a coffee and went for a walk along his private beach just as the sun was coming up. And when he did, I would be there, hiding behind the sand dunes, waiting to take him out.

It would only take one shot, and it would all be over. Almost painless.

I'd drag the body into the sea and when he did wash up on the shore, everyone would assume the Abel brothers were behind the hit. Clyde would do a half-hearted investigation but as he got the jack from every gangster in town, wouldn't want to arrest anybody. And when the case was closed due to not having enough evidence to convict anyone, I could get on with my life again. I'd just have to be patient and wait it out.

I didn't tell a soul about the plan. Not Pearl. Not George. No one.

Of course, as always happens when you're about to do something big, quit your job or leave your lover, the universe hears about it and decides to test you. And only the day before I'd planned to do it, Clarence called me up to his office at Kings.

I hadn't prayed for months. Not since I left Ma's but as I stood outside the door expecting this to be the last time, I spilled my guts with what I thought would be my last breath, hoping for forgiveness if Clarence did take me out.

When I stepped inside, Elmer patted me down to check for weapons and whispered in my ear.

'It's okay. He's in a good mood.'

Like everything Clarence owned, his office was the bees. Heavy drapes, leather chairs and mahogany furniture. A pool table in the corner of the room. When I went in, he stood facing the window, sipping coffee and looking down on the boardwalk below and the tourists rushing like termites back and forth. He put his coffee cup down and turned to me, a smile on his face.

'Come in, come in, Milton. Sit down.'

It was difficult to believe this was the same man who had held a gun to my temple. I did as I was told and watched nervously as he rummaged around in his pocket. When he pulled his hand back out, he opened his palm, revealing a gold sovereign ring and placed it on the table in front of me.

Clarence's sovereigns were only given to those closest to him. Charlie and George had one. Elmer and Jesse too. It was a sign that you were trusted. That you were as good as blood. If he had offered it to me even a month before, I'd have snatched it up. But knowing what I was planning to do to him, right then, it was the very last thing I wanted.

'Thanks Clarence, but I can't accept it.' I pushed the ring back across the table towards him, but he slammed his hand down on top of mine to stop it from moving.

'Come now Milton, don't be modest. You've earned it. You must take it, or I'll be offended.' He pushed it back towards me. 'We think we caught the rat, you know.'

'We did?'

'Clyde is talking to him as we speak. Take it.' He forced the ring into my hand.

I put it on but every time I looked down and saw it wrapped around my finger it may as well have been a goddam albatross.

Back home, I showed the ring to Pearl. I've never seen her so angry.

'You've got to be kidding me!' she said. 'Have you forgotten what he did to you? He almost killed you.'

'Yeah, but he was just scared. We all were. Things are better now. We've got shine coming in and Clarence is back to his old self.'

'Yeah, until the next time. People don't change Milton. Bad people even less so.'

I heard echoes of my Da in her words. He knew that once demons got his claws in him, he could never shake them off his shoulders. If

I'd have taken him out the way I did my horse, it would have saved me and Ma a lot of trouble.

That was enough to set me straight again. I had to remind myself that Clarence deserved to die.

Not just for what he did to me. For what he did to anyone who crossed him.

I thought of the shopkeepers on the boardwalk struggling to make ends meet because they had to pay their dues. I thought of the families struggling to pay their debts to him, the interest spiraling out of their control. Their children going hungry because they could no longer afford to feed them.

Me killing Clarence would be a blessing, and I, the avenging angel.

Chapter Thirty-One

❧ ⊷————⊷————⊶ ❧

The morning Clarence got shot it should have been raining. That's what they'd said on the wireless, but as I stood out in the yard while Champ did his business, my brain was having a boxing match with itself.

Was this a bad omen? Was I doing the right thing? What if I got caught? It didn't matter. Things couldn't continue the way they had been. Killing Clarence would kill the worry in my mind.

So, I left Champ at home and drove to a couple of blocks away from Clarence's place. His beach may have been signposted 'private' but that didn't mean there wasn't access to it. Just that if you got caught there, you'd better be packing a gun, which luckily, I was.

As it got closer to the time, I knew Clarence would make an appearance my heartbeat in time with the moving of the hands of my watch. As my heart began to out beat it, that was when I saw him strolling down to the edge of the sand, coffee in hand, looking out at the sea like he owned that too.

I watched him for a couple of moments, but guys catch change on the breeze the way dogs catch a smell. He turned in my direction and stared hard.

'Who's there?'

My heart sank into the pit of my stomach. I curled my fingers tighter around the gun handle.

He took a couple of steps forward, straining to see. 'Milton, is that you?'

Shit! No way of backing out.

I raised the gun, trembling, that damn sovereign on my finger glinting in the sun. Too scared to watch the next part, I closed my eyes tight and pulled the trigger.

The gunshot exploded, my ears ringing above the silence. I opened my eyes to see Clarence standing there, very much alive, coffee cup in pieces at his feet; a brown stain spreading across his chest where his blood should have been.

Now my heart really was thumping. How the hell could I have missed him from that short distance?

'What the fuck! You little shit! Where the hell are you?'

Clarence reached for his gun, and I knew it was either him or me and I didn't want it to be me, so I raised the gun once more and shot once. Twice. Three times. Until he stumbled backwards and fall down onto the sand.

A quiet hush fell like snow, dampening any other sound. There was no movement except the gentle ebb and flow of waves against the shore. I waited to be sure, but it was clear that Clarence wasn't getting up again.

When I was absolutely certain he was dead, I walked over to take a look and saw the blood flooding out of him, staining the sand underneath him dark crimson.

I rolled him over onto his back.

'Oh, Jesus Christ!'

The sight of him! I was reminded of one of Da's war stories about a soldier who had half his face blasted away. I thought I might puke but

I held it together long enough to grab Clarence's ankles and drag him through the sand down to the sea. I hadn't planned on the snail trail of crimson that would signpost the way to his body.

The waves weren't big enough to carry him out to sea neither but at least it might help wash away the blood. I hated Charlie, but the thought of his son finding him like that unnerved me.

When it was over, I walked back to the car with everything hazy, unreal; dreamlike. There was no relief. Not yet. The enormity of what I'd just done hadn't really sunk in.

When I got to the car, I sunk down into the driver's seat and wiped the sweat from my brow with my handkerchief. I closed my eyes and saw the image of Clarence lying on the sand with half a face.

I opened the door and puked in the gutter.

33

CHAPTER THIRTY-TWO

P eople think the hardest part about taking someone out is the physical killing itself but that's simply not true.

When you're involved in something intense like that your adrenaline is the one calling all the shots. There's no time to think or feel anything. You're so detached from rational thought that sometimes it feels like you're floating above your own body watching someone else do it.

In my experience, the worst part isn't the killing. It's the waiting. Waiting for someone to find the body. Waiting for them to announce who that body is. Waiting for the law to come knocking at your door.

Waiting. Waiting. Waiting.

After what happened to Clarence the waiting immediately began. I went home, took a shower, had a sleep. Played fetch with Champ. Ate a fried egg sandwich. I smoked cigarette after cigarette, waiting for the phone to ring.

When there hadn't been a call by eleven o clock my mouth was as dry as sand. Surely, someone should have found him by then. Charlie? His wife? The help even? The fear came over me that maybe the shot hadn't taken him out after all, and he was still living and breathing but I had seen the state of him after three shots to the face. It was impossible. There was no way he was getting up after that.

I was pouring myself orange juice when the phone finally rang with the news.

The voice on the other end was shaking.

'Milton. It's George. Have you heard the news yet?'

This was it. They'd found him. I could have punched the air; I was so stoked but I still needed to play the chump so no one would suspect anything.

'What news are you talking about?'

'It's about Clarence. I'm so sorry to be the one to tell you Milt, but he's dead.'

I had to pretend to be surprised.

'Dead? What do you mean dead? How?'

'He's been shot.'

Dramatic pause for effect. I counted to three to give him enough time to think that I'm mulling it over in my mind.

'Okay, are you at Kings?'

'Yeah.'

'I'll be right over.'

I patted Champ on the head. 'Well buddy, can you believe they told George before they told me?'

I'd expected the news to come from Charlie, but I suppose it didn't really matter who delivered the news. The important thing was that Clarence had been found. Now all I had to do was get through the part where everyone else was upset.

Then it would all be plain sailing.

Or so I thought.

CHAPTER THIRTY-THREE

I hadn't accounted for the reporters swarming round the place, poisonous wasps that they are.

As I stepped out of the car I spotted Jesse, fist balled, itching to sock someone. Next to him George tried his best to shoo them away, reports stepping right up to him, bulbs flashing in his face.

Of course it was going to be front page news, Clarence being the big shot that he was. I guess it was then that I realized that this wasn't something that was going to be cleared away quickly, like some broken vase that had been carelessly dropped. In killing Clarence I had smashed the whole legacy of the Kelly family into pieces.

And whilst I'm sure some bluenoses would be glad he had gone, (my own Ma for one) a lot of people still thought of him as having done some good for Atlantic City.

As I stood watching the crowd of reporters hustling for a scoop, guilt crawled into my collar and down my spine.

I needed Pearl right then. To make me feel better.

Angling my hat down, I put on my sunglasses and went round the back entrance. Of course, there was some moon-faced photographer waiting there and I'm not saying I manhandled him, but I did put the screws on a little to persuade him to leave.

It was Elmer who opened the door and let me in, his cheeks tear-stained, eyes puffy. If I hadn't felt bad before, I certainly did now, seeing him so upset when my own cheeks were bone dry.

'You heard then?' he said, his voice as solemn as I'd ever heard it.

'Yeah. I heard. How's Charlie bearing up?'

'As good as can be expected. It's got to have been the Abels.'

This was good. Everything was working out in my favor. If I could just keep the act up until the storm passed, everything would be jake.

'Had to be them.' I said, trying to match Elmer's tone. 'Does Pearl know yet?'

He nodded. 'She's really upset. Shut herself away in her dressing room but I wouldn't go in there if I were you.'

I headed straight to Pearls' dressing room anyway. The door was ajar slightly. I didn't bother to peer in or knock before walking in.

When I did, two figures pulled apart like they were spring loaded. It was a sobbing Charlie that she had been holding.

Some other time I guess I would have flown into a jealous rage, but I had no kick with him. Not when his father had just died. I was so stunned to see him there at all. I was more annoyed with Pearl who looked down at the floor, not acknowledging me, or daring to meet my gaze.

Charlie looked confused.

'Milton, what are you doing here?'

He still didn't know about me and Pearl.

'I just wanted to see if there's anything I can do,' I said, unmoved. 'I'm so sorry to hear about what happened to Clarence.'

'Thanks Milton. You know Dad always said you could be relied on. I'm just waiting for Clyde to get here and take statements.'

If it was any other flatfoot I might have been shaken but Clyde would have this case dismissed and closed in no time. It didn't serve his interests to have anyone look too closely at Clarence's business affairs.

'That's good news. I'm sure he'll have one or two theories about who did this,' I said. To my surprise, Charlie shrugged this off.

'I don't care about that. Dad upset a lot of people. Did a lot of bad things. He had it coming to him.'

Well, this was a side to Charlie I'd never seen. He carried on.

'If I'm going to be taking over, I want everything to be above board from now on.'

All of the heat was draining out of me. Pearl still gazed at the floor like a pup who'd done wrong. I knew why.

She had said Charlie wanted nothing to do with any of it. That we could just walk right into Kings and take it from under his feet as easy as a magician pulling away a tablecloth. And I'd believed her – what a chump!

I gritted my teeth. 'I dunno about that Charlie,' I said. 'The Abels are ruthless. They're not going to let up just because your Dad has gone. Honestly, the best thing you could do is take a vacation right now. For your own safety.'

Charlie's gaze hardened into a stare.

'I'm not going anywhere.'

I would have to play dirty if I was going to get rid of Charlie without killing him. I still had an ace card hidden under the table.

'Well maybe talk to Clyde about it when he gets here.'

I walked right up to Pearl and planted a huge kiss on her forehead.

'I'll see you back at your apartment.'

I could see the horror on his face as the truth about me and Pearl began to register. Maybe you think I was cruel, but if Charlie thought he could worm his way back into Pearl's affections after rejecting her, just because he was hurting then he needed to know that wasn't about to happen.

Everything that happened afterwards happened so quickly: the funeral, Clyde's closing of the case due to the Abel brothers' alibi, Charlie finally giving into his grief and going on vacation just as I'd suggested.

Of course, Charlie was sore with Clyde. Everyone heard their parting conversation. Their voices so loud that it didn't make a difference that they were behind closed doors, they may well have been standing out in the hallway with a megaphone.

Charlie was pacing the room.

'What do you mean, there's nothing you can do? My father's been murdered, we all know who did it and you still can't arrest them? That's ridiculous! You're meant to be a copper, or have you been so busy waltzing around town accepting bribes that you've forgotten that's the reason you're here?'

Clyde tried to reason with him.

'Look Charlie, I know you're upset. We all are. It's why I think it would do you good to take a couple of weeks away. Go to Long Beach. Or Princeton. You have friends in Princeton, right?'

'And what about this place? I can't just up and leave Kings to run itself.'

Clyde kept his voice calm. 'These guys have been running the place for your Dad for a long time. Ask one of them to caretake.'

Charlie exploded. 'Jesus Clyde! You've seen Elmer and Jesse. They can barely tie their own shoelaces. I'm not going to let them caretake the place.'

'George then.'

'No, we need him to run the drugstore.'

'What about Milton?'

Silence.

I wished I could have seen his expression. I understood anger. Hatred even. But silence was impossible to read.

'Look Charlie, you can't hold a grudge over that girl. Milton's a good guy. He loved your Dad. And Clarence trusted him. A couple of weeks' vacation would do you good. Give you time to grieve.'

I had to hand it to Clyde; he hit on all eight to persuade him. Of course, it was all out of self-interest. He couldn't have Charlie running things above board. If he did, Clyde would be out of work.

Charlie cracked.

'Okay, maybe you're right.'

Charlie promised he'd be back in two weeks.

But two weeks passed, and he called to say he was enjoying the peace and quiet in Princeton and was staying. He'd spoken to his accountant and the bank and had my name put on the accounts so I could run the place however I wanted until he decided to return.

It was such a shame that poor grief-stricken Charlie never did come back.

Chapter Thirty-Four

❖ ▸────◦◦────◂ ❖

Sometimes I saw Clarence in my dreams. In them he was a real hot sketch, joking and slapping me on the back the way he always used to. It was his bloodied face that had me waking up with soaked sheets night after night.

Pearl, on the other hand, popped sleeping pills like candy and slept soundly as a princess, unaware of the night terrors I was experiencing.

I hadn't realized until I took over just how many people Clarence had in his pocket in order to keep things running smoothly. There were payouts to every big shot in town. No wonder Charlie had had second thoughts – it was impossible to run Kings above board when Clarence had been paying out the jack for so long. He'd learned the hard way with the Abels what happens when you suddenly stop giving people what they think they're due.

Even though Clyde deemed the case closed and everyone else was getting on with life as normal, I couldn't shake this feeling of doom that hung cloudlike over my head. Every time there was an unannounced parcel delivery at Kings, I would sweat. Visions of the delivery guy packing a gun and a message from the Abels, explaining the beef wasn't over. A guy I didn't recognize eating dinner was a Dry Agent planting a bug beneath the table, hoping to make an example of the lawbreakers in Atlantic City. Every time Champ barked at a moving shadow, I'd draw my revolver convinced it was the ghost of Clarence or even Charlie, back to take his rightful place.

I swear, in those first few weeks, I thought I was going screwy, the buzzing in my head getting louder and louder with each passing day.

But just as grieving becomes easier as time passes, so did my guilt over Clarence's little accident. By the time Summer came, I'd almost forgotten I was ever a part of it.

But I had other problems with Pearl.

'I keep on thinking he's watching us,' she said, pulling the covers up over her naked body as we lay in bed.

'Who's watching us...?'

'Clarence. Watching us take over Kings. Sleeping in his bed. Living in his house. I think I preferred living in my apartment with the flickering light and leaky tap.'

It took every ounce of my self-control not to point out that the whole thing had been her idea in the first place. That if she hadn't set me off on the idea, Clarence would still be sleeping in his own bed. She had everything she could have wanted, furs, a mansion, money, a dog in Champ, a stage she could headline every single night if she wanted. I had sacrificed everything for her, and I told her so.

'I know,' she said. 'I'm sorry Milton. I shouldn't complain.' She looked like she might cry.

I didn't mean to hurt her. It was just that sometimes I had to extinguish the fire in her so she could see through the smoke. Perhaps there was one more thing I could give her.

Pearl was in her dressing room, putting on her makeup, getting ready to go out on stage when I sneaked in to see her. I had sent her the most beautiful bouquet of Russian cut roses that had cost me a small fortune. There were so many she'd had to send for more vases to put them in.

I tapped on the door and walked in.

'How do you like the roses?'

'They're beautiful,' she said but her voice was flat.

I put my arms on her shoulders and looked at her reflection in the mirror. She looked tired.

'Pearl, I think we should get married.'

Now you'd expect someone you'd been through so much with to be happy; grateful even, to have someone want to marry them, but instead she eyeballed me in the mirror, disgusted as if I'd sent her a bouquet I'd stolen straight from Clarence's headstone.

'Are you serious, Milton? Is that your proposal? I'm sat in a damp dressing room, five minutes before a show.'

She wanted more. I understood.

'I'll give you a proper proposal if you want. A ring. A goddamned parade in your honor if that's what it'll take to make you say yes.'

She got up from her chair and tried to push past me, but I reached out and grabbed her arm to stop her.

'Look Pearl, I know these past few weeks have been hard, but you and me, we're meant to be together. We're made of the same clay and stars. Bound together. Nothings ever going to break that apart so you may as well just say yes.'

She softened a little at the part about clay and stars and I pulled her in to kiss me. 'C'mon Pearl, just say yes.'

She had a wry smile on her lips. 'You don't give up, do you?'

I smiled back at her. 'Nope. Not if I really want something.'

'I'm sorry Milton. I just can't.'

I don't why I wanted her to say yes so badly. I guess in the beginning I thought she was perfect. And sometimes you'll do anything to keep someone by your side.

I sent her a new bouquet every day. Sometimes roses. Sometimes gladioli. Kept her guessing. Still, she said no.

Then one night, just as she finished performing and was taking her bow, I came out from behind the curtains and popped the question there and then right under the spotlights with a ring set with the biggest diamond I could find.

Of course, she said yes. She couldn't disappoint the punters.

We served platters of the finest foods on the house: deviled eggs, salad supreme, freshly caught oysters, pineapple upside down cake and bottles of fizz.

Even though I'd given her what I thought she wanted, there was still something wrong. She seemed on edge all the time. Couldn't sleep without those damn sleeping pills.

I mean, she was never much of a housekeeper, I knew that when I met her, but I'd get home from work and the place was always overflowing with lipstick marked glasses and shoes cluttering up the floor where she'd just kicked them off when she came home. Still, I didn't want to make too much of a fuss. It weren't no kick.

We'd been through a lot together those past couple of months, what difference did a few dirty glasses matter? I knew she'd become more excited once she started looking at wedding dresses.

Besides, now the tourist season really had kicked in, I barely had the time to worry about Pearl. Business was booming and word had quickly got round that whilst Clarence was dead, Kings had very much risen from the grave. Since taking over I'd been hitting on all eight.

But you can't blow gum and not expect it to pop. And my sweet bubble was about to burst.

Chapter Thirty-Five

❖ ▪──────▪▪▪──────▪▪ ❖

The first time I got shot was the one and only time I'd gone to a pickup at Mickey's place. I didn't usually do my own run, but we were one guy down and with the summer season in full swing, I couldn't risk us running low on liquor. Besides, it was good for morale for the Boss to be seen to get his hands dirty occasionally.

I'd vowed to give both Jesse and Elmer the push when I took over, but I quickly realized how useful they could be.

Jesse was a bimbo sure, but he was happy to follow orders no matter who gave them. I'm pretty sure I could have asked him to wipe my ass, and he would have if there was a paycheck at the end of it. All those times Jesse had mocked me or that time he socked me in the guts, it was all because Clarence had told him to. He was playing the role of goon and now he was playing that role for me. He knew that I controlled him and that made things a hell of a lot easier.

Elmer was different. The quieter of the two, he had always been more than just hired muscle. Sure, he collected dues from local businesses on the boardwalk, but he also answered phone calls, arranged meetings in fancy hotels and made me the best cup of joe in all of Atlantic City.

Elmer was responsible for organizing the fortnightly pick-up from Mickey's, but the routine was always the same. Early Sunday morning, when the sort of folk who might report anything were too busy repenting for their flimsy sins at church, Elmer and the boys would meet at the boardwalk and drive over to Mickey's place. Now it was risky doing this in the daylight hours, but the way Elmer saw it, the prohis expected running to happen late at night under the cover of darkness. On a Sunday morning, they would be just as likely to be attending church as Mickey's neighbors were. Everything about Mickey made him look above board. His pious wife and their two kids skipping to Sunday school. The white picket fence round the yard and neatly trimmed lawn. Mickey himself, clean shaven and an all-round 'nice guy.'

We stopped at the kid's treehouse first and Elmer, who was the lightest, hoisted himself up and took the bottles hidden under the floorboards. While Elmer was busy doing that, I ordered Jesse to go and lift up the seat of the wooden bench against the wall, revealing another row of bottles, all wrapped in brown paper and straw to stop them from rattling against each other.

While the two of them filled apple crates with shine, I followed behind Mickey down to the shed. Now it might seem goofy to store shine somewhere so obvious, but Mickey was a whole lot smarter than he looked. If you went inside the place you could search for a week under floorboards and inside clay pots and not find a single thing that wasn't legit. But outside, around the base of the shed, there was a series of panels that could be lifted off. Behind them, tucked into a cavity in the wall, were the rest of the bottles lined up like soldiers on drill. I started filling up the boxes the way we always did, waiting for Elmer and Jesse to join me.

Mickey and I had been standing there for several minutes chatting about baseball when I stopped what I was doing. I couldn't put my finger on what was off exactly, but it was like the air felt different.

'Mickey, where the heck are Jesse and Elmer? It can't take this long to fetch those bottles.'

We stared at one another, fear rising like the tide as it dawned on us that something was wrong. Both of us reached for our guns a little too late as the dull popping of a silenced bullet whizzed past me.

My ear lobe buzzed and stung like a wasp bite. Instinctively reaching for it, I pulled my hand away and saw the blood.

Behind me a terracotta pot smashed, and Mickey crumpled into a groaning heap on the floor, blood spurting out his neck where the bullet embedded in his neck.

I dropped to my knees, crawling across the floor like a baby, heart pounding, praying they couldn't see me. There was a loose floorboard around here somewhere housing a tommy gun. If I could just get to it before they got to me, I could fight back and be guaranteed to win. There it was: the wonky floorboard that wasn't quite flush against the others. I could see it up ahead.

There were footsteps and hushed voices outside the doorway.

'You sure it was Milton?'

'I swear it was him. He's in here.'

I had to get to that tommy gun. I crawled as quickly as I could but one of them spotted me as they entered the shed.

'There he is!'

I didn't know this guy, but it didn't take a genius to figure out the Abels had sent him. He grinned as he lifted the gun and pulled the trigger. I rolled to the side and the bullet hit right through the sack behind me, soil spilling out all over the floor. I was up and, on my feet, before he had a chance to reload leaping over the seed boxes but just as my feet landed, a searing pain took over the back of my calf, so painful the whole world moved in slow motion around me. Powerless to stop the pain, or light-headedness that came over me my legs buckled, and I dropped to the floor.

I reached out and lifted the floorboard, the gun only inches away from my fingers. Footsteps walked towards me. He was in no hurry. He knew he had me on the ropes now.

He raised his boot and placed the weight of his entire body down on my fingers. He ground down his boot like he was extinguishing a cigarette, each finger snapping like a twig.

'This is for what you did to our boys.'

As my body grew limp, drifting in and out of consciousness, the guy lifted up the floorboard and threw it to one side.

'Hey, Jonny, look what I got myself. A new tommy gun.' He showed it to his associate before aiming it at my head. I was a goner now. I was certain of it.

'Just get it over with,' I said.

He grinned.

'No!' Jonny called to him. 'You can't just kill him without the boss' say so.' Jonny dashed over to stop him and grabbed hold of the gun. He knew that there were rules to this thing.

'Aww c'mon Jonny. It's a gift him being here.' He was whining like a kid who'd had his toy confiscated.

Jonny shook his head. 'But that's the point. He wasn't meant to be here. Thomas said to just shake things up with Mickey. This isn't just some Bruno we got here. This is Milton Costello. You can't just kill him without the Boss's say so. Unless you want to get whacked yourself.'

'So, what do we do?'

'We do what we said we'd do. We take the stuff and leave.'

I felt a boot to the ribs and passed out. When I came to, they had cleared the place out. Took everything Mickey had.

I had to find Jesse and Elmer. Get us out of that place before they sent someone to come back for me.

Somehow, I dragged myself outside, leg bleeding all over the place. Elmer lay unconscious on the path, his face a bloody pulp. Next to him, Jesse lay limp, knee smashed in with a shovel, blood spilling out of his skull like the yolk of a cracked egg.

Clarence had been right all along.

This was a war.

CHAPTER THIRTY-SIX

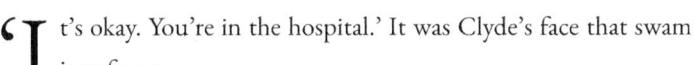

'It's okay. You're in the hospital.' It was Clyde's face that swam into focus.

I raised my hand to shield myself from the scalding light shining in between the blinds and didn't recognize my bloated fingers taped together. I tried the other hand but in that one the tap of the drip grew out of my veins. I shot up, almost pulling the trolley and fluid bag clean over.

'Hey, hey, calm down Milton.'

My heart slowed, the colors around me morphing from nameless shapes into hospital furniture. A bed. A piss pot. A chair.

'You want me to call the nurse?' Clyde asked.

'No. Just help me to sit up.'

Clyde plumped the pillows. Helped me to sit up whilst I tried to remember what had happened. The memories were fuzzy, except for the one of Jesse lying on the floor with his head cracked open.

'Where's Jesse? Is he okay?'

Clyde sighed. 'I'm not gonna lie Milton. It don't look too good. They say the impact on his skull might be too much for his brain. That he could have brain damage for the rest of his life.'

Another flash of memory: gunshots, blood.

'What about Mickey? Elmer?'

'Elmer's in the room down the hallway. He'll be okay. Mickey's dead.'

The first death on my watch. He wasn't even part of the mob. Not really.

'The Abels can't get away with this. You have to do something Clyde. They can't just go around snuffing us out like candle flames.'

Clyde nodded. 'I'm sorry Milt. My hands are tied on this one.'

'What's that supposed to mean? How much are they paying you? I'll double it.'

'It's not that. Mickey's wife called the law. She had to. She came home from church with her kids to find her husband murdered in their back garden. As far as the authorities are concerned this was an unprovoked attack on an ordinary man. Mickey was careful. He had no criminal record and as far as bootlegging is concerned, well the Abel boys did a clean sneak. Took everything so there's no evidence that there was ever any wrongdoing. His wife never knew anything about his little sideline. And now there's this.'

He threw that day's paper onto my lap and there on the front page was a photo of Mickey and his friend posing with his hero Babe Ruth after the ball game they went to. The headline read 'FAMILY MAN MASSACRED IN HIS OWN HOME.'

I handed the paper back to him. 'So, what you're saying is that you can't help sway the investigation on this one?'

'Milton, I'm not on the case, full stop. They called in law from out of town. Some broad called Simpson. Some guy called Brooke. Both of them as straight lined as a ruler. Anyways, I think someone's been talking with the commissioner about me. They said I'm not to touch anything to do with it. Got me patrolling the boardwalk for god's sake.'

I threw my blanket off and moved to the edge of the bed, despite the shooting pain in the back of my calf.

'Well, the least you can do is help me scram outta here.'

***

W hen I limped into Kelly & Son's, George stared like a ghost had walked in. Some guy was spouting to him about his father's hemorrhoids and George was doing his best to stay focused, but I could see how haunted he was by me being there.

'Why don't you go out back,' he nodded across to me and pointed to the back room. 'I'll be through to see you in just a moment.'

I sat on George's seat and watched him through the glass. Finally, the guy bought the remedy George recommended and left. George locked the door and pulled the blinds down.

'Jesus Milton! Just look at you. You'll scare all the customers away looking like that. I can't believe the hospital discharged you.'

'Discharged myself.' I kept to the point. It still hurt to breathe where I'd had my ribs kicked when I was down. Everything hurt.

'I just need painkillers. Anything. I don't care what it is.'

'Yeah, of course.'

George gathered various pots of powder, yapping at me as he weighed them out.

'You know, the law came round asking questions. Not Clyde neither.'

My ears prickled at this. 'Yeah, he said he's off the case. You know who it was?'

'Said his name was Brooke. Not too bright. Searched everywhere but totally missed the trapdoor to the cave, thankfully.'

He mixed the powders, not daring to look me in the eye.

'He asked about you and Clarence too.'

'What about me and Clarence?'

'Asked If there'd been any tension between the two of you. If I thought, you were capable of hurting him.'

I didn't know if it was just the hospital painkillers wearing off or what, but I felt sick to my stomach.

'And what did you say?'

'I said, I didn't think so.'

'You didn't think so? George, you're kidding me, right? Didn't think so! You know how that looks? You've set the bloodhounds on me.'

It hurt to raise my voice. George just carried on making the pills, not looking up.

'What was I supposed to say Milt? Do you even know how it looks to everyone? First Clarence dies, then Charlie leaves and never comes back. You move into Clarence's mansion. Drive his cars. If you want me to spell it out it's like you almost planned it all to happen.'

Rage bubbled up from the pit of my stomach.

'Don't you remember how I saved your life that time down in the cave? Doesn't that mean anything to you? I came here for your help. Jesse might never be the same again and Mickey is dead and here you are accusing me of...well, what are you accusing me of?'

George stopped what he was doing. Clearly, he hadn't heard the news.

'What do you mean, Jesse might not be the same?'

'He got jumped. Real bad. Could be brain damaged.'

'I didn't know.'

'Yeah, well now you do. And we can't let the Abels get away with it. We need to do something.'

George put the pills in a glass bottle and handed them to me.

'And you want my help getting revenge on them? Is that it?'

'You don't need to put it quite so bluntly, but yes. I was hoping you'd help.'

He was quiet a moment like he was thinking it over but instead he was just selecting his words carefully to avoid pissing me off any further.

'Milton, can I speak freely? Not as your associate, but as your friend?'

I shrugged. Looked like he was going to anyway, no matter what I said.

'Yeah, of course.'

'Go home. Check in on Pearl. Get some rest. If you don't stop now, this feud will never end, and you'll be so deep in blood and dirt that there's no way out of it. Go back to your mansion and sleep on it before starting a war you can't ever finish.'

I took the bottle of pills from him. He was right, of course but I was already in this up to my neck. Now I was stuck and there was no climbing out of the quicksand once you were in deep.

'Thanks for the pills and the advice. Say, do you remember that girl from Zelda's on the pier that one time?'

George nodded. 'Of course.'

'Is this what you think she meant about you being greater than me? That by backing off, you're gaining the moral high ground?'

His face reddened. I was turning him like a key.

I continued baiting him. 'Cause it must feel good sitting on high watching the rest of us wading through shit while you sit here making your pills and potions, never getting your hands dirty.'

He leapt forward like a cobra and gripped my collar. He raised his fist, ready to sock me one.

I didn't fight back.

'You feel good attacking a sick man?'

He let go. Pushed me back. But I saw the look of shame on his face. I always said we drank from the same bottle, but this little outburst of his proved me wrong. He'd let his temper get the better of him. Like a chump.

I was sick of his yapping. Before he had chance to apologize, I was already out the door.

He was right about Pearl, of course. And I would go home to her, but not yet. I just wasn't in the mood for a grilling.

But George had reminded me of the girl on the pier. Outside, the sun was high. The tourists were out.

And the door of Zelda's was wide open.

CHAPTER THIRTY-SEVEN

❖▪━━━━▪▪▪━━━▪▪❖

It had been a while since I'd thought of the girl from Zelda's. Her red curls. Her eyes that shined metallic in the sunlight.

I hadn't even asked her name. I didn't want to know. I wanted to think of her, ethereal, perfect. Knowing her name would have taken that away from me. Made her like any other broad.

We had promised to go to Zelda's if any of what she had said came true. Her predictions for me certainly had. I had a promotion. I was running Kings. I walked right up to the door and went inside.

A bell tinkled as I entered. There was too much for the senses to take: the smell of patchouli, posters on the walls showing the map of the human hand, paneled walls painted bottle green, jazz playing quietly on the wireless. The color and incense smoke felt oppressive; walls and ceiling pressing down heavy on me. Pressure built inside my head the way it does before a rainstorm.

The girl from the boardwalk got up from her seat behind the front desk, trying unsuccessfully to hide her grimace at the sight of my cut face and goog around my eye.

'It's you,' she said. 'You're hurt.'

She walked to me and touched my cheek. I resisted the urge to flinch back. I wanted her to stop and yet at the same time, I didn't.

'I'm fine,' I said, and she dropped her hand. The brief moment of intimacy had thankfully passed.

'I want to see Zelda,' I said.

She lowered her voice and leaned across so no one else would hear.

'It's not worth it.'

'What?' Was she admitting it was all baloney? It couldn't have been. What she'd said had come true.

'I'm sorry. I wasn't very clear. What I mean is, nothing has changed for you yet. Sure, you've been promoted and you're the head of the business now, am I right?'

I nodded. She remembered.

'Well, that's great but I can sense there is still something, or some-one in the way. And until they're out of the picture, well, there's nothing else to tell. I'll book you in with Zelda, if that's what you want but I can tell you now, she's going to tell you exactly the same thing.'

The bell at the door behind me tinkled and a drunken couple stumbled inside. They were laughing and acting sozzled. I stayed put. I hadn't wanted to leave. There was something about her that made me want to stay.

She scribbled something down on a piece of paper and handed it to me. It was an appointment for a week's time.

'If I'm wrong, we can cancel it,' she said.

I took it from her outstretched hand and stuffed it into my wallet. I felt like I was cheating on Pearl somehow, even though I hadn't done anything wrong.

'I'll see you then,' I said, and I turned my back on her and left.

Outside the sun was almost blinding and I was glad of the seaside air. I knew exactly who she meant when she talked about someone blocking my way. She meant George. Had to. Who else had told me to stop the feud with the Abels? I no longer trusted George the way I had once. He was getting to be more and more of a mug every day.

***

I'd expected Pearl to be pleased to see me but as I struggled to walk down that driveway, she came rushing out of the open door, her face red, with Champ bounding after her.

'What are you doing here? Who discharged you? You look awful.'

'Thanks. You missed me I see.' I gave Champ a stroke and he jumped up to lick my face.

'Down boy!' Pearl said and he obeyed her straight away. I could see her glancing back at the house.

Maybe it was my own thoughts of cheating that caused my demon to rise.

'What is it? Who's in there with you?' I had visions of Charlie sitting in my chair with his feet up.

Pearl soothed me. 'It's some flatfoots. Two of them. They both wanted to talk to you about what happened. I told him you were too ill for questioning. That you were in the hospital. And now you're here. Oh god, they're going to think I was lying.'

'Its fine,' I said to Pearl. 'I'll just go and talk to them.'

Maybe it was cocky of me, but I was eager to meet them both. First, they questioned George. And now my fiancé. And in my own home too while I was out at the hospital. Of course, I was curious.

Pearl helped me up the driveway and up the steps into our house where Simpson and Brooke were waiting. Brooke had the cheek to be sat at the head of the kitchen table, sipping on a cup of my coffee. When I walked in, they stood up, eyeballing one another.

He must have been shorter than Pearl, about 5ft 5. His blond hair was waxed into position, not a hair out of place. His skin lightly tanned from his holidays in the Hamptons. He wore his shiny officer's badge like a good boy scout. He went to shake my hand and saw my broken fingers taped together.

'Looks like you've been in a bit of a scrape, Mr. Costello.'

'Yeah, I'm sure my fiancé here has filled you in on the details.'

The woman, Officer Simpson spoke. She looked like the sort of girl who attended the anti-saloon league because she'd been tempted too often herself. The sort who said hail mary's every night and wanted to save every person she met.

'Those guys on the pier sure beat you up, real good,' she said. 'We'll leave you two to talk.'

Pearl led her into the garden and the two women sat down on loungers placed directly in front of the glass doors. I didn't know if she did that to keep an eye on me or so I could keep an eye on them.

'My name's Brooke,' the guy officer said, pulling his buzzer from his wallet.

'Don't you guys have first names?' I smirked.

'With my friends, yes I do.'

Sharp. And he was making it very clear that he was straight down the line. He wasn't about to be easily bribed like Clyde was. I took my seat and the table and poured myself a coffee.

'I would offer you one, but I see you already helped yourself.'

'Yes, Pearl has made us feel right at home. This is some place you got here.'

'Thank you.'

'Only, I find it fascinating how you came to live here when little more than a year ago you were still living with your mother.'

The Boy Scout had done his homework.

'I'm just caretaking till Charlie Kelly comes home. That's Clarence Kelly's son, if you want to write it down in your little book or whatever it is that you do.'

He didn't flinch.

'I know who Charlie Kelly is. Such a sad tale; his father murdered right out back on his private beach. But I mean, what good fortune for you. You get to move in here. Take over Kings. The Kelly drugstore. Have you any idea when Charlie's planning on returning?'

I shook my head. 'Nope. Seems he's having a spiffy time, wherever he is.'

'Because there are rumours...'

This guy was getting on my nerves. I couldn't be bothered with all this cat and mouse baloney.

'Look Officer Brooke, if you're trying to accuse me of something just come right out and say it.'

But he was still playing the game. 'I'm not accusing you of anything. What could I possibly be accusing you of?'

'You tell me what you're thinking, and then I can tell you you're wrong so you can leave. Save us both a lot of time.'

He paused for a moment. Then words spouted out of him like exorcism.

'Okay, here's what I think. I think you had something to do with Clarence Kelly's murder and his son's disappearance. I think you're lying about the attack on yourself and your associates, and I think you're into bootlegging so deep you may as well be living in a swamp. That's what I'm thinking.'

I sat back on my chair and took a slow sip of my coffee and smiled.

'Guess what, you're wrong. And I know you don't have a shred of evidence for any of it.'

He nodded in agreement.

'You're right, I don't. But one day I will. All it will take is one wrong move and it'll be judgement day for you.'

He stood up and pushed his cup away. 'Good coffee. I'll be back for another.'

'Yeah, when you have something on me, I scoffed. 'I'll let you see yourself out.'

He walked over to the patio and whistled to his partner.

'Nancy. We're leaving.'

The two of them walked out. I didn't even bother to check they weren't sneaking about the place on the way to the door. I knew they wouldn't find anything even if they did.

My head ached and I longed for sleep. The last thing I needed to care about was the law getting on my case.

But things were going to get worse. Much worse.

Chapter Thirty-Eight

❖•———••———••❖

Now, I had real beef. I had a club that hadn't opened up for a week. My employees were either dead or in the hospital. The Labor Day Pageant was looming over me and unless I could find a new supplier in the next few days, it would be a dry one.

Already the town's mayor had called to ask if we should cancel it for this year 'given the circumstances.' And to top it all off, I had just joined Officer Brooke's hit list as well as, presumably, still being on Thomas and William Abel's one.

Pearl was acting strangely too. Tiptoeing about, looking wide eyed, the slightest noise making her jumpy.

'Look Pearl, honey,' I said. 'You have nothing to worry about, I promise. No one is coming for you. If it's anyone they'll be looking for, it's me.'

But nothing I said seemed to help. When I tried to hold her, it was like holding a wooden plank, her shoulders stiff.

There was something changed in her. Had been since me and Champ had moved into the mansion with her. It was in her shaky hands and in her low soft voice she used when she spoke on the phone.

Suddenly, Eveline, the red-haired girl Jesse had been seeing on the side, was calling her up every day. They'd never been close as far as I was aware.

I tried to raise the question with her, but she got all defensive.

'It's all in your head,' she'd say. 'There's nothing wrong.'

I knew her too well to know when she was lying. And I was certain she was lying now. I just couldn't prove it. All I could do was carry on as usual while I waited for her to slip up.

One morning, a few days after I'd got out of the hospital I sat at the breakfast table drinking my coffee and reading the paper while Pearl fixed some eggs, when on page four was a story about the famous bootlegger and lawyer George Remus. Apparently, his wife was filing for divorce and by all accounts he was pretty furious about it. As I read through the story it mentioned how he owned several pharmacies all across America.

It hit me like a freight train. Why were we risking our lives on the run when we already had someone who could get us as much shine as we liked? George O Malley had a license to legally order as much medicinal alcohol as he liked. I dunno why Clarence hadn't thought of doing it before? It was probably to keep associates sweet but now that those associates had become rivals, we had no obligations to anyone but ourselves.

The pageant could go ahead again and the best thing about it was that Officers Brooke and Simpson wouldn't be able to do a damn thing because the alcohol would be signed off as legal. We could even sell cocktails at the pageant and call them health drinks. That would really make them sore.

I stood up from my chair so quickly I almost lost my balance, and Pearl almost dropped the plate she was piling the eggs up on.

'I need to go,' I said to her.

'What about breakfast?'

'I can't just sit here all day. Be a doll, call the press and the town mayor and tell them the pageant is still going ahead as planned. Tell them that I'm well on the road to recovery and that Kings is back.'

'Are you sure? I mean, Milton, you're still not well. You can barely stand.'

'Then I'll get myself a cane.' I gave her a long hard kiss on the mouth that she tried to wriggle out of.

'It's a shame that you hate the pageant so much. You could sing there if you wanted. I'd get you an entire float for you and your band.'

'Really? You mean that?' She smiled for the first time in months.

'Serious as a heart attack. Now make sure you call the mayor. I've got a couple of people I need to see.'

***

First, I stopped off at the hospital to see Jesse and Elmer. Jesse was sitting up in bed, which was better than I'd expected, but the attack we had endured had left him with his head sewn up; a crude scar from the center of his scalp down to his right eyebrow where they'd put in a metal plate.

'Jesus Jesse, you look in a bad way.'

I couldn't hide my horror, but Jesse's anger was close to bubbling over.

'I swear when I'm ready and able we'll go back there. Take them all out.'

His reaction wasn't what I had expected. The boy was a firecracker, lit and ready to fire off at any moment. At any other time, this would be an asset but now the law's eyes were on me, uncontrolled anger like Jesse's was a liability.

'Look Jesse, I understand your anger. I really do, but we have to think smart here,' I told him. 'One foot out of line right now and we'll all be dogmeat. And you need to get well again first before you go starting a firefight.'

'Doctors say I could suffer with headaches long after this has healed,' he said. 'And my leg might not ever be the same.' He pulled back the sheets to show the stitches around his kneecap.

I tried to mollify him with my words.

'I'm sure you'll heal in time. And then, we'll show them. No one can take us down. No one.'

I patted him on the back and promised him a raise when he came back to work.

Down the hallway, Elmer lay in his bed, ribs bruised, face swollen and the color of eggplant. The painkillers made him too drowsy to talk but the nurse told me he'd be okay. That if he was lucky, he would be out in a couple of days.

***

George was the last stop I made that day. By now the sun was low, the sunset casting a blood red glow across the boardwalk. He was winding down for the end of the day when I dropped in. He looked surprised to see me. Perhaps, after the ing bing I'd caused last time, he wasn't expecting me to be so chummy but quarrels between friends are soon forgotten.

My enthusiasm was palpable after speaking with Elmer, but it was about to be tempered by George. He listened to my plans to order in the liquor through the drugstore but to my surprise, George was sore about it.

'I dunno Milton, are you sure this is legal? I mean, if something goes wrong, it's my name on that license, not yours.'

'Of course, I understand,' I reassured him. 'But Remus went to jail for double crossing Jack Daniel and stealing from him, not for having medicinal alcohol. I've told you, it's all above board. It'll be easy. And once I make this pageant a success everyone will want to associate with us again. I swear, the law can't touch us on this.'

'What about Jesse and Elmer?'

'What about them?'

'Should we really be holding a pageant when the two of them are wound up in the hospital?'

'I've just visited them. Promised to pay their medical bills. Jesus, George, talk about a wet blanket. What's gotten into you lately? Why are you so critical of everything all of a sudden?'

George shook his head. 'I'm not. It's just...'he sighed. There was something he wanted to say but he wasn't letting himself say it.

'What George? C'mon, we've been friends for a long time. Just spit it out.'

He took a long deep breath. For a moment I thought I saw him eyeing up the rifle taped under the counter, like he was afraid I was going to go screwy or something.

'I've been thinking about it a lot lately Milton, and I don't think I can do this anymore.'

I'm pretty sure I laughed at first. 'What do you mean? Can't do what?'

He sat himself down on the stool next to the soda fountain.

'All of it. The drugstore. The booze. Everything. Mickey had a wife and kids. What if they had been there at the time, would the Abels have gunned them down too? It never used to be so risky in the early days but now I get scared to leave Lou with his grandma in case that's the last time I see him.'

I sat down next to him.

'This is just because we've had a setback. Everyone feels like this from time to time. Don't you think sometimes I just want to quit? Do the same? I'll be the first to admit these past few months haven't been great but just hold out a bit longer George. You'll see, everything will be just as it used to be. Kings will be back on top again. *We'll* be back on top. This pageant is going to be something special.'

George shook his head.

'I want out of this life Milton. I've made up my mind. I'll do this one last thing for you but after that, I'm done. You'll need to get a new pharmacist.'

I nodded.

'Of course, whatever you want to do.'

But I didn't believe he meant it. Not really. Perhaps if I had taken him more seriously, it wouldn't have been the last conversation we ever had.

Of course, you know what happens next. It was reported all over the papers. The next day George took Lou to his Ma's around nine. Mrs. O Malley often looked after her grandson while George worked. She told George he looked tired. He said he'd not been sleeping. He kissed Lou on the forehead and told him he'd pick him up later.

He got in his car and drove away to Kelly & Sons, only he never arrived.

His car disappeared without a trace.

And so did George.

40

PART TWO: PEARL'S LETTERS

41

SEPTEMBER 2ND, 1927

❖⊪———⊪⊪—⊪❖

Dear Grandma,

I've thought about writing this letter many times since leaving you in New York all those months ago but admitting the truth to anyone about what has really been going on is hard.

I underestimated what Milton is capable of, and whilst I keep on pretending that everything is the bee's knees, the truth is, being with Milton is not the bees at all. Far from it.

Last night I witnessed something so terrifying that no amount of sleeping powders will ever be able dull the images branded into my brain.

I guess I'm telling you because I have no one else to turn to and I want to make sure there's a record of what is happening before I'm forced to leave town.

Or worse, I wind up dead.

Before I spill the juice on what I saw, there's a couple of things you need to understand about Milton.

The first is that he can be incredibly charming. When Clarence Kelly was killed and Charlie left, everyone thought the Kelly legacy would fall apart. Clarence was such an important figure around here keeping the town afloat when every other tourist town dried up during prohibition.

Then, in walked Milton who charmed the papers, the commissioner, every mother and child he met.

If you read the papers, you'd believe he's a folk hero; a gentleman bootlegger who raised the town up from the dead. He wears fine suits and has friends in high places. Respectable and respected, Milton is the poor rural boy who made good in the big city.

The second thing is that this 'Milton' you see in the papers doesn't exist. Most girls think I'm the luckiest in the world to be engaged to him, but the Milton the public see and the Milton he is behind closed doors are two very different people. If I'd have known how dangerous he was, I would never have played so closely with fire.

Now don't get me wrong. I've met enough trouble boys in my time to guess Milton weren't an angel, but the Milton I know, spouts lies as often as the rest of us tell the truth. And just lately it's difficult to know for certain which is which. He has me confused so often that if he told me up was down, I wouldn't just doubt which one was which. I would question whether either existed at all.

It wasn't always like this of course. It never is in the beginning. In the beginning it was all red roses and petting parties.

I used to believe it was love. It was the sort of love that made you weak kneed and flipped your stomach like a pancake. I still have those feelings whenever I see Milton enter a room, but now it's not love that's causing that sensation. It's fear. Perhaps that's what it always has been.

You used to say the body knows when something isn't right, even if your brain hasn't got the telegram yet. And I think my body has been telling me to run for some time.

I have seen and heard terrible things here at the Kelly Mansion, but Milton tells me they didn't happen or that I've misremembered them. This is why I wanted to write it all down for you. To get my thoughts straight. You were the only one I trusted to shine a light on truth and as you're not with me here, this is the closest I can get to asking your advice.

First, let me explain how it all really began and then I'll tell you about what I saw.

***

*M*ilton loves to tell his own version of the story in the press of how we met. How he saw me in my blue sequin dress rehearsing at Kings and how I literally dazzled him under the spotlights. How he knew he had to have me, which I guess is meant to sound romantic.

But one month later, I hated the sight of that sequin dress.

Milton didn't say I couldn't wear it. Not exactly. Just that it showed a lot of my shoulders. Sometimes, he'd tell me that it looked cheap, and I deserved better. Other times, that no one would take me seriously as a performer if I dressed like a whore.

When I got upset at his words, he told me he would take me shopping and buy me a new dress but the only dresses he ever wanted to buy were buttoned up to the neck in black. I would wear them because he insisted but in the dressing room I would stare at this stranger in the mirror all dressed up like she was going to her own funeral.

I should have known then to give up and walk away but things aren't always that easy. Things are not always as black and white as people think they should be.

As the person I once was, faded like an old photograph, Milton too morphed into shades of grey. It wasn't bad all the time. Sometimes things were wonderful. Sometimes he was bursting with compliments and when he did say something kind, he made me feel like there was a spotlight all of my own upon me.

In those moments of kindness I would wonder if I'd misjudged him before. Misheard him. Misinterpreted the words he'd said to add my own meaning to them. The sweetness of his words made me forget the bitterness of his complaints.

He's had a difficult life, I'd tell myself. A strict father. A mother who dotes on him but who would never stand up to her brute of a husband. I used to tell myself that it wasn't Milton's fault he was the way he was and the worst thing I could do was to abandon him.

I just had to be patient. Be his verbal punching bag just a little while until he softened. Stay no matter what, until he trusted me not to leave.

By the time I got to know his anger, it was too late for anyone to intervene. I'd already started seeing less of Eveline and the girls. They were a bad influence and Milton preferred me to stay at home, or did I want to go back to my crummy flat doing whatever the landlord wanted to pay the rent?

If his accusations were true (which they were not) is it any better than living with Milton, hiding my bruises under a layer of powder? It's gotten to a point where my hands tremble whenever I pour his coffee in case it's deemed too bitter or too hot, or too anything that might send him into a rage?

Sometimes even the silence that follows is just as distressing. The deliberate refusal to speak to me, theatrically slamming the front door behind him and disappearing for hours makes my whole body ache. When he does come back, I end up apologizing for the things I haven't even done, just to keep the peace.

And then we start all over again to repeat the same pattern, an endless cycle of happiness and misery, going round and round like a twisted wheel of fortune.

In the end it's just become easier to stay in and never complain, than have an argument. My friends have quickly faded into the background like piano music in a bar, still there, but unobtrusive, not wanting to disrupt the mood.

So now I'm left with no one else to tell except you.

I know you will say I should just leave him. Well, I've tried. Several times.

Every time I build myself up to walk out, it's like he senses it. He'll come home arms full of roses and for a couple of weeks everything is like it used to be. And temporarily, I forget who the real Milton is. But of course, the real Milton hasn't gone. He always rears his ugly head again sooner or later.

And now, things only seem to be getting worse. When Clarence Kelly's body washed up on the beach, Milton closed down my contacts even further. I was no longer allowed go out without him knowing my exact location.

Thing is, it made perfect sense at the time. After all Milton had become a target for the Abel brothers. And me too by association. He just wanted to keep me safe.

For a while, I believed him. I believed everything he said.

Sometimes I still feel a little sliver of hope that things will be like they once were. That he'll realize what he's doing to me. That he doesn't need to control me anymore because I've bound myself. No matter how much I want to escape, I just can't bring myself to go anywhere else because the stepping away hurts more than the staying stuck.

Sleeping powders allow me to melt into oblivion night after night, the pain and fear of living with a man who terrifies me, temporarily eased. But the problem with sleeping powders is that the more you take, the more you need. And as fate would have it, last night I think I've finally reached my limit for both sleeping powder and Milton's behavior.

I'm not sure I'll ever be able to sleep soundly again.

***

I was lying semi awake, waiting for my powders to soothe me to sleep when I heard Milton's key turn in the front door. It must have been two in the morning as I lay there on cold satin sheets, eyes closed, pretending I couldn't hear his heavy footsteps coming into the room, his shadow blending into the darkness.

'Pearl, you awake?'

I dared not move, for fear he might see it as an invitation to do whatever he was in the mood for, so I lay like a corpse on the slab pretending I was asleep.

He moved in closer, so close I could feel his breath on my cheek as he stood over me. And there was this smell! The horrifying scent of the slaughterhouse and tarnished metal.

Milton leaned over to flick on the switch of the bedside lamp, and even though I was scared spitless of what I might see, I dared to open my eyes a crack but I wished I hadn't when I saw the scene: the blood-spattered shirt. His steady red hands wiping the blood onto a handkerchief.

I clamped my eyelids shut again, struggling not to scream. I dare not open them again, but I heard every movement he made.

Heavy steps walking to the bathroom.

A groan of the hot water pipes as they too woke up.

Afraid, but feeling compelled to look once more, I ignored the thudding heart in my chest and rising panic and opened my eyes just enough to see new flashes of horror: the white bar of soap, now a new shade of pink. A white towel so soiled it would need to be thrown away.

As the red water gurgled away, Milton stood on the toilet seat, slowly raising the lid of the cistern. He dropped something in. Looked like a revolver. He carefully placed the lid back on as if shutting the lid on a coffin then put on his pajamas and slipped in between the sheets like normal.

Within ten minutes he was snoring like a newborn, unbothered by the bloodbath that had occurred. Yet I lay there wild eyed, staring up at the dark wondering whose blood he'd been washing from his hands.

I still don't know yet, but I swear I'll find out. I just pray I do it soon. I'm afraid if he realizes what I witnessed, it won't be long until my blood mingles with theirs.

Sleeping powders make everything misty and dreamlike. You're not quite awake, not quite asleep, and now the events of last night seem even further away than they were before. Everything is hazy. And a night of drifting in and out of drug-induced sleep hasn't helped. Despite this doubt there's a sensation in my stomach; an ache, a pang of fear that tells me to trust in what I saw.

Love always

Pearl

42

SEPTEMBER 3RD, 1927

I couldn't stop my hands from trembling as I lit my cigarette at the breakfast table this morning. I'm sure Champ could sense something in the air, laying his head in my lap and looking up at me as if to ask what was wrong. Watching Milton stuffing his face with ham and eggs, yolk leaking out of the corners of his mouth, made me sick to my stomach.

Of course, Milton didn't notice a thing and for once I was thankful. You always used to say, a good night's sleep solves most of a girl's problems and time spent with friends helps solve the rest.' I hadn't been able to do either of those things.

'Got any plans for today?' he said, not even bothering to look up.

How he was able to sit and eat with the same hands that dripped with blood only hours before, was beyond my comprehension. I exhaled a huge plume of smoke and spoke with caution.

'I said I'd go and see Eveline today.'

He's loosened the shackles recently when it comes to Eveline and for good reason. Jesse is still in the hospital after the ambush at the pickup the guys did at Mickey's place. Milton assumed he'd be right as rain in no time but that hasn't been the case. Going to see her is the one outing I don't have to beg for permission at the moment. Milton doesn't want to have to face going to see Jesse's broken body, knowing it is his fault that he is there. This way, he can feign concern by asking me to pass on his best wishes without having to look Jesse or anyone else in the eye.

And as for Eveline, well, she hasn't been quite the same since it happened. Jesse's wife, already furious at him being so close to death, is even more heartbroken to find out he's had a mistress for most of their married life and that everyone but her has known about it.

At first, Eveline stayed away from the hospital out of respect, but after a while she realized he wasn't coming out any time soon. She's so scared he might die that she's been visiting almost every day when she knows his wife won't be there.

'That Eveline's a real firecracker.'

Milton grinned at me, looking for a flicker of jealousy in my eyes or a change in the way I held my body. I'm not giving him any fuel to burn me with anymore, so I just got up from the table and tried to walk away to the sink.

'Hey, what's eating you?' He stood in my path. 'I was only joking about Eveline.'

I couldn't hold it in any longer. I had to say something.

'I saw you last night.'

'Saw me where?'

'In the bathroom. You were covered in blood.'

He gave a hollow laugh. 'You were asleep. Must have been a nightmare or something.'

'I know what I saw,' I said.

But even as the words left my mouth, I began to doubt them.

He stepped in close, squeezing my right buttock so hard it hurt.

'Honey, are you sure you're feeling okay? Maybe I should ask George to up the dose on those powders.'

His stare bored into me. I held his gaze for as long as I could, not wanting to flinch away and show weakness but his grip on me tightened. I knew the only way to get out of this without being bruised was to look away, so I did.

He let me go and walked away chuckling to himself, all the way out the door and down the steps. I stood at the door in my nightgown, watching him drive away in his expensive suit, asking myself how I could have ever found him attractive and what he'd done with his bloodied shirt.

Once I was certain he was gone I ran up the stairs, two at a time, heart pumping, to the bathroom. I stood outside for a moment to compose myself before pushing the door open. I remembered the scene: the blood. So much blood.

I pushed open the door and found pristine white walls. No trace of the horrors of the night before. It was easy to clean blood off the tiles, but what about the gun? I remembered him climbing up to drop it into the cistern. All the evidence I needed was in there.

I kicked off my mules, stood up on the seat in my bare feet and lifted up the lid. If I stood on tiptoes, I was just tall enough to peek inside.

The gun had disappeared.

But this time, I know what I saw. It doesn't matter what he tells me I know in my guts that he's lying.

It's like something has shifted in me. Awoken. There's a realization of who Milton really is.

I'm scared to leave, but I know the time has come for me to get out for good. I just need a plan to get out of here.

Love always

Pearl

43

SEPTEMBER 4TH, 1927

❧ ▸━━━•••━━━◂ ❧

Dear Grandma,

Today I am at a loss as to what to do. The one person I thought I could open up to and who might understand, doesn't and now I'm not sure if I'll ever escape.

I went to see Eveline. I'm not sure she's ever really been a friend, but she's been a moll for so long that I thought if there's anyone who understands what it's like, it's her, so after Milton left for Kings, I went to go and see her.

I'd never seen Eveline without rouge or lipstick before, but she opened the door barefaced, still in her robe. She was beautiful without it on, but she looked so different. Young, plain. Not like the made-up Eveline I know from seeing her at parties draped on Jesse's arm. I don't usually drop round unannounced, and I could see the surprise on her face.

'Pearl. What are you doing here?'

She stood with the door so tightly pulled towards her body that I could tell she didn't want anyone else in the house to see me there. I knew it was a mistake, but it was too late by then.

'I'm sorry Eveline,' I said, I just didn't have anywhere else to go. Look, I'll leave you if it's an imposition.'

She shook her head. 'Jesus Christ, look at your face. Did Milton do this to you?'

I felt embarrassed. In my rush to get out of the house I'd forgotten to put sunglasses on to cover up the latest mark he'd left behind.

'Oh, that bruise. It's a few days old now. I'm fine.'

'Well, you don't look fine honey. Your hands are trembling. Look, give me ten minutes, okay. I'll tell Ma I'm just popping out to get milk.'

As she closed the door, leaving me waiting on the step, I heard two children arguing over the last glass of orange juice in the kitchen and it suddenly struck me that I don't really know Eveline all that well. What was I expecting from her turning up at her door like that? Advice? Pity?

I hate to admit it, but I have chosen this life after all. Chosen to be with Milton for reasons that made sense at the time.

And compared to the issues she's facing when Jesse finally leaves hospital, my problems look small.

Ten minutes later she came walking out of her house, looking like the Eveline I know: full make-up, comb in her hair, a pair of sunglasses in hand. She handed the glasses to me.

'Here. Put these on. Now do you want to tell me what is going on?'

Now that I was there, and I was about to say it out loud I wasn't certain I believed it myself. Still, I couldn't keep this to myself any longer and there was no other person to tell.

'I know this is going to sound crazy,' I said to her, 'but I think Milton might have killed someone last night.'

Eveline gave a snort and started to laugh.

I stared at her.

'It's not funny Eveline. I'm being serious.'

'I'm sorry for laughing Pearl but what did you think he did for a living? That he was a preacher?' She lit a cigarette.

I guess she had a point. I thought of the boy that walked into Kings in his cheap wool suit and who used to sit off stage to watch me sing. The boy who sent me so many roses I could barely fit them on the table in my dressing room. The boy who looked after his mother and who told me, rescued Champ from a fire.

'The Milton I first met would never have done something like what I saw last night,' I told her. 'He was covered in blood, Eveline. I mean covered head to foot. I've never seen anything like it in my life. And believe me, I've seen some things.'

Eveline paused like she was choosing her words carefully.

'I don't mean to sound heartless Pearl, but I bet he never hit you none back then neither. None of the violent ones show their true colors at first.

Men like Milton and Jesse do bad things sometimes. We all know this, and we keep our noses out of their business. Their work isn't anything to do with us. Look, you need to decide what you want.

If you want to stay you need to accept that he is going to be doing things you don't agree with. Or if you want to leave, then quit whining and do it. But remember, knowing what you know about him now, Milton will see you as a liability. If you leave him, you won't be able to tell a soul where you're going. And you'll never be able to come back. Not just to Milton, but back to this town. You understand what I'm saying?'

She laid the ultimatum out like a spread of cards.

How am I going to play my hand? I still haven't decided.

In the end she broke the silence with her own opinion.

'Do you know what I think is the best thing for you to do?'

I was grateful for any bone of wisdom she was going to throw at me.

'What? What should I do?'

She took a drag of her cigarette.

'Absolutely nothing. You let him sort out whatever mess he's got himself into and keep your head low and your mouth shut. If you're going to *be his wife, you'd better get used to it. And for goodness' sake, don't tell anyone else about this.'*

I got to say Grandma, it wasn't the advice I was hoping for. I'd wanted her to tell me to leave and that she'd help me.

When mom was still with us back in New York I remember seeing you and her friends gathering round her with gin and sympathy, every single time she tried to leave. You never judged her when she couldn't go through with it. Or if she left and came back two days later. You understood how difficult it was, but I could see I wasn't going to get any of that from Eveline, so I changed the subject.

'Say, are you going to visit Jesse today? Cause I wondered if I could come with you.'

Eveline raised an eyebrow. 'Haven't you heard? Jesse got out yesterday.'

I should be happy for them both, but the truth is I feel sick. When Milton finds out Jesse is okay, there will be no more visits to see Eveline. My one way to get out of the house will be taken away from me and I'll have no chance of escape.

Eveline paused outside the grocers and took one last drag of her cigarette before tossing it to the ground.

'Jesse's doing okay if that's what you were wondering.'

She must have sensed my mind was elsewhere.

'Doctor says he'll always walk with a limp now on account of how badly they smashed the knee bone, but it could have been worse. Much worse. You sure, you're okay?'

I told her I was and forced a smile. The sort of pained smile you give when you fail an audition, or you overhear your date telling a buddy that you're easy. But I am anything but okay. I have never felt so alone and so trapped as I do right now.

Talking to Eveline puts her in a difficult position now too. And me even more so.

Now that Eveline knows what I've seen, there's every chance she will tell Jesse, and I don't think I can trust him to keep it to himself.

It's one thing Milton knowing I saw him do what he did, but quite another me telling other people. It's only a matter of time for the news to get back to him.

I already know he's capable of hurting me.

Who's to say he wouldn't kill me?

Love always

Pearl

44

September 5th, 1927

❖ ⊶———⊷———⊶ ❖

Dear Grandma,

I've made up my mind. I'm going to leave.

I know I've said I would leave Milton before, but this time I really mean it. This time is different to all the times before. If Milton has killed a man which I know he has then there is no other option.

Of course, I'm scared.

I have to keep telling myself all of the reasons why I'm doing this over and over again every time I doubt myself. I stand there talking to myself in the mirror. And every time I repeat the long list of reasons, I see a glimpse of the shining woman I once knew, getting brighter.

Tonight, we are going to the Marlborough Hotel and that is when I plan to do it. I will make sure I pack my bag today with what I need, and I'll feign a migraine at dinner so I can leave and go back to the room.

Milton will want to stay with his buddies and will trust me to go up to the room to sleep it off. That is when I will take my things and sneak out of the hotel while he's too drunk to know.

I don't know where I am heading but anywhere will be better than staying here.

Love always

Pearl

45

SEPTEMBER 6TH, 1927

❧ ⊶————•••————⊷ ❧

Dear Grandma,

I couldn't wait another day to tell you what happened. Well, the Marlborough Hotel is just as spiffing as you would expect it to be. Walking up those steps to the entrance and having the doorman open the door for me and carry my bag to the room, it felt like a dream come true.

When I first came to Atlantic City I used to gaze up at the Marlborough hotel, layered up in white like a wedding cake and imagine what it must be like to have enough money to be able to stay there and eat the finest steak in town and drink champagne. Now finally I had made it there, but instead of it being the joyous occasion it should have been, I sat opposite Milton, the meat on my plate too bloody, the walls too bright. My nerves were on edge, knowing that in an hour's time I would be walking out that same door, never to return.

Everyone important in Atlantic City was there. A bunch of men all talking over one another to get their voices heard.

Everything about Milton made my skin crawl. The way he laughed too loudly. The way he slapped his gums when he ate. The way he grabbed the waitress' ass like he owned her.

'Are you not hungry? You've been picking over that steak like it did something to offend you. I'll get you a salad.' Milton waved the waiter over, but I stopped him.

'I'm so sorry Milton. I'm just not feeling too well. I've got a headache. I think I'll have to go up to the room and have a lie down. Sorry everyone.'

I smiled weakly as I got up from my seat and he grabbed my hand, holding so hard he was crushing my fingers.

'I'm sure you'll be feeling better once you've eaten something. Why don't you sit yourself back down?'

Milton was smiling at me, feigning concern, but I could see the rage simmering in his eyes. To him, this was an insult, leaving him alone for the night but having people around meant he couldn't explode the way he usually did. If I was going to rebel against him, this was the perfect time to do it even though I would pay for it later on. He enjoyed having me as a trophy at these sorts of events and my leaving meant he was without a broad to show off to the boys. But it didn't matter. 'Later on' would never happen as I'd be gone by then.

'I'm sorry, I can't stay. It's too bad. I'll sleep it off and come back down.'

Reluctantly, he let go of my hand.

By the time I got the elevator up to the room, it was already dark outside. I pulled my bag from the wardrobe and stuffed it with what clothes I had.

I thought about leaving one of the black dresses behind. The one he'd made me buy to replace the blue sequin one. I hated that dress as much as the blue one, but his words are buried so deep in my consciousness, like a maggot in an apple, that I was too scared not to take it! I hope one day I'll be brave enough to burn it.

The last thing I did was count through the money I'd hidden in my shoes. For months I've been saving it back at the mansion. All the times *he'd told me to buy me a little something for myself after an argument, I saved the change. It was like the Pearl from the past knew I would be needing it one day in my future. I'd smuggled it under the insoles of a pair of shoes I'd bought with me but had no intention of wearing.*

I left my keys on the table, next to the fruit bowl, took a deep breath and picked up my bag, relieved to be getting out of there.

On the way to the elevator, I felt a pang of fear seeing the young bellboy Nick standing next to the gate. He was on Milton's payroll. I didn't know what I would say if he asked me where I was going.

'Evening miss.'

Nick pulled back the lattice gate and I stepped into the elevator. Stepped into freedom. As we moved downwards it felt like my confidence was leaking out of me, only to be filled up with doubts. The elevator seemed to be slower than usual. With every floor we passed and ting of the bell, a new doubt crept in.

Ting.

Maybe I was overreacting like he always said I was. Was the relationship really that bad? I mean, sometimes Milton could be really sweet.

Ting.

He'd only hit me once or twice and I'd seen a lot of men do that at Grandmas when a woman had said something out of turn. I mean, he was generous. I never wanted for anything.

Ting.

He couldn't help losing his temper sometimes. He has a stressful job, and men just want a woman who will support them.

Ting.

I'm being selfish. Where would I go anyway? I have no family or friends. Not anymore.

Nick stood there smiling as he pulled back the gate.

'Here you go Miss. Ground floor.'

I stared my own freedom in the face. Felt it on my cheeks. Tasted it in the air. I stepped out of the cage and into the foyer to check it was real.

That was as far as I got. I just couldn't go through with it.

The rope that binds me and Milton is too tightly wound. I couldn't bear the thought of his reaction when he got up to the room and found me gone. I imagined him tearing the place apart to find me, worried the Abels had kidnapped me, or worse, shot me dead.

Milton might behave like a monster sometimes, but I knew he would still be crushed by my leaving him. He wasn't all bad. Just mostly bad.

'You know Nick, I think I've changed my mind. Do you think there's a spare set of keys to let me back in the room? I think I must have left mine on the table.'

I dare not look him in the eye but handed him a tip big enough for him not to say anything to anyone else.

I'm so sorry Grandma. I fear I've let you down.

I was so close to going through with it.

So close this time.

Love always
Pearl

46

SEPTEMBER 7TH 1927

❧ ⊢———•••———⊣ ❧

Dear Grandma,

I feel like such a fool not leaving when I had the chance.

Not least because I think I may know now whose blood was on Milton's hands and if my instincts are right then it means he really does have no morals, no scruples, no loyalty towards anyone, in any part of him.

To make things worse, Milton has been in an exceptionally good mood these last few days, armed with a bunch of red roses and a smile I haven't seen in weeks.

Today when he came home, he slid his arms around my waist and planted a kiss on my lips. It made me nervous. A storm often comes after the sunshine.

'You're in a good mood,' I said, and I was about to understand why.

Milton sat down at the table, waiting for me to serve him his dinner.

'That meeting the other night at the Marlborough went so well that the mayor has finally given me the go ahead to host the fall frolic and the pageant at Kings.'

With my own mind having been such a whirlwind, the pageant had completely slipped my mind.

'Well, that's fantastic,' I said, forcing a smile.

'He's feeling so swell about it in fact, I told him he'd make a perfect judge for the bathing beauties round.'

I had to stop myself from rolling my eyes. No wonder he'd had the go ahead. The opportunity for a strong powerful man to leer at young beautiful women in bathing suits would be enough to persuade him to say yes. It was one of the many reasons I hated the pageant.

Milton was beaming.

'I thought you might want to dust off that sequin dress of yours. You could have a float all to yourself to perform on.'

His suggestion caught me by surprise. I hadn't performed in months because he hadn't let me. The thought of wearing that sequin dress made me queasy. Funny how, when something was to his benefit, suddenly the rules he'd made no longer applied.

'I dunno honey,' I said sweetly, placing his plate down in front of him. 'I've not sang in front of anyone for some time. It's been a while since I've even rehearsed with the band. It's got to a point where I don't even miss it.'

'Oh, come on Pearl. You know you're my songbird.' He stood up from his chair and my muscles tensed.

Who knew if he was about to hit me or kiss me? He walked around and placed his hands on my shoulders, rubbing them gently.

'But you have such a sweet, beautiful voice. Don't you remember how I used to watch you up there on stage?' He lent down and kissed my neck, and my whole body involuntarily stiffened.

'What's up with you? Why so jumpy? Have you been off your powders again?'

I am, but I won't let him know that. I haven't taken a single sleeping pill for the last three days. Sure, it means my skin itches and my hands *shake, but it'll pass. And at least I know I can trust what I'm seeing and hearing late at night.*

There was a knock at the front door, and both of us froze.

'You expecting someone?' Milton immediately reached for his gun.

I shook my head and flinched back instinctively as he took out the shooter, thinking at first that it was the same gun from the other night. But it wasn't. This was Milton's usual revolver. The other one had been bigger than that.

The door knocked again. This time more frantic.

'Stay there,' Milton ordered.

My head was whirling. No one came knocking uninvited, especially not at this time of night. It wouldn't have been the coppers. They don't knock. The withdrawal from my sleeping powders made me twitchy. That, and the fact that the Abel brothers were no doubt still looking for revenge. It wasn't unheard of for someone to go to the door only to come face to face with the barrel of a gun. When Milton left the room, I ducked down under the table waiting for the gunfire to explode when he opened the door.

It was a woman's voice.

'Milton. It's me, Mrs. O'Malley.'

George's mother. Something bad must have happened. I came out from my hiding place and went out into the hallway. Poor Mrs. O'Malley stood there, face pale, hair and coat soaked by the pouring rain. Milton had flicked on the switch of charm he was so good at, standing there all smiles, and had invited her in. Champ ran over to her, wagging his tail.

'I'm so sorry to disturb you, Milton. And you Pearl. I just didn't know what else to do. I can't find George anywhere. He dropped Lou off this morning and never came back. I called at the drugstore. His house. No answer. No lights on.'

You could see the concern lined on her face, but Milton didn't move from where he was standing or react in any way to the news.

In my mind, I saw a flash of blood in the sink. Pink water gurgling down the drain.

This didn't look like news to Milton. He acted like he expected this news to come at some point.

A wave of heat moved over my body from my toes all the way up to the top of my head.

George.

The blood he'd been washing off the other night was George's.

'Perhaps you'd like to come in a moment and have a seat. Dry off properly.'

Milton opened the door wider to invite her in.

Mrs. O Malley shook her head. No, that's quite alright. I think I'll go straight to the police. Report him as missing.'

'Well, you can call them from here.'

He practically dragged her inside. I knew what he was doing. He was going to make the call for her. Call his old police buddy, Clyde. To Mrs. O Malley it would look like he was being helpful. It was the behavior of a concerned friend.

Milton stood next to her as she made the call, making out like he was doing her a favor having a direct line to Atlantic City's top law enforcement.

'Don't you worry, Mrs. O Malley, if anyone can find George, Clyde can.'

The sound of his sycophantic voice makes me feel sick.

He waited until the rain had stopped before seeing her out. Milton offered to drive her home, but she refused him. As she walked back down the path, a sly smile spread across Milton's face when he thought I wasn't looking.

Panic is rising in me again. Who is this person I'm living with? This isn't the Milton I used to know. He's long gone.

'I really hope she finds him,' I said.

'Me too,' he lied. He walked over to the coat stand and put his jacket on.

'Where are you going? It's raining cats and dogs out there.'

'To help find George,' he said. 'You don't think I'd leave my buddy out there in this weather, do you?'

Can you believe the audacity of the man?

Love always

Pearl

47

SEPTEMBER 8TH, 1927

※⊪━━━━⊪⊪━━⊪※

Dear Grandma,

It's the middle of the night, and I woke up parched with thirst.

Since avoiding my powders, I find it difficult to stay asleep. Usually, I'd go to the tap in the bathroom but every time I step in there, I see the scarlet horror in my mind's eye.

The sheets next to me were cold and empty and so I assumed Milton had stayed out, searching for George, or drinking at Kings.

There was no need to tiptoe anywhere with him gone so I went downstairs to get a drink and was about to switch on the light when I caught sight of a dark figure, hunched over at the kitchen table, bottle in hand.

I stepped back, startled.

It was Milton.

The wind taken out of me, I ducked down behind the banister and peered through at the man who sat there. The gas lamp he had on the table illuminated him from underneath, shadows flickering across his cheek as he sat talking to himself.

'It's not that I want to kill anyone,' he was saying. 'It's just that sometimes you find yourself in so deep, it's easier to keep on going than it is to turn back on yourself. You see what I'm saying don't you?'

He kept looking up at the chair opposite him. Who was he talking to? Had he invited someone back to the house? One of his buddies? He poured another glass of whiskey, and I tried to crane my neck round to see who it was in the chair opposite, but it was empty.

Either he was talking to himself or a hallucination because there was definitely no one else in the room with him. Goosepimples prickled my arms, all the way up.

'I'm sure when they find you, we'll all be able to rest again. Me. You. Your mother. Pearl. She thinks I don't know she's not been taking her powders but I'm not stupid. Something's wrong. She's planning to leave me or something. I can just feel it. Well, she can't go around just doing whatever she likes.'

He knew! He knew all of it.

Unsteady at the sound of my own name, I grabbed onto the banister. Turning slowly to go back upstairs, the floorboards gasped under my footsteps letting out a loud creak.

I heard the click of his revolver in the dark and I froze.

'Pearl. Is that you?'

I dare not turn around, heart pounding, palms sweating.

'Please God,' I silently prayed, 'don't let him kill me.'

Standing frozen on the stairs, not daring to breathe, I waited until I heard the clink of ice in the glass and the glugging of whiskey again, before tiptoeing back up the stairs. All the time, I could hear him rambling on, having a conversation with thin air.

Desperate times mean taking desperate measures and it's time for me to do the one thing I never thought I was capable of.

Grandma, please forgive me for what I'm about to do.

Love always

Pearl

48

SEPTEMBER 9TH, 1927

❧ ❧

Dear Grandma,

It is done.

I daren't make the call from home for fear the line was tapped. The only other place I knew I could make a call without being recognized was at one of those phone booths you find down on the boardwalk.

It was risky, I knew. Kings was barely a stone's throw away from where I stood and yet I knew all other cards were off the table. This call was my only hope of getting help to get out of there.

I paid my two cents; scarf wrapped tightly round my face to stop anyone from being able to give a full description of me. Time seemed to slow as I stood there waiting for the operator to connect me.

'Come on, come on, please pick up the damn phone.'

A moment of guilt and fear meant I was just about to put the receiver back down when the coin dropped, and a couple of pips later the operator answered.

'Hello. Atlantic City Police. Can I help you?'

Yes Grandma, I did call the police. You see, despite knowing what a betrayal of Milton's trust that would be, he has broken my faith in him so many times now that I have no other option.

Hearing such a soft woman's voice on the other end, eased my fear a little.

'I'd like to speak to Officer Simpson please.' I heard the tremor in my voice saying her name. You wouldn't know her, but she came to the house with another officer a few weeks ago when Milton came out of the hospital. When we were sat out on the patio she sensed straight away that something was wrong. She told me she understood what it was like to be with a man like Milton and that if I needed her to call.

Of course, I scoffed at the idea at the time, but now, now I think she might be able to help me.

The operator refused to put me through at first.

'I'm afraid she's not available to speak with personally, but perhaps I can help find which desk is best to put you through to?'

'No. It has to be Officer Simpson.' I was adamant. 'I won't speak to anyone else.'

Behind me a baby was crying. I turned to briefly take a look and caught the eye of the blonde mother standing right behind me as she cooed and cajoled the baby into being quiet. She had seen my face.

I was desperate.

'Look, my name is Zelda. She asked me to call.'

Zelda was the secret code word. She told me to use the name if I needed help.

'Okay Miss, wait a minute.'

There was a crackling sound as she put me through, and then Nancy's voice came on the line, sweet and homely as cherry pie.

'Hello, you're speaking to Officer Nancy Simpson.'

'It's me: the songbird from the Kelly place. You said to call if I ever needed help.'

'I'm glad you called,' her voice didn't waver. 'You know the Absecon lighthouse?'

'*Sure, I do.*'

'*Meet me there at one.*'

The lighthouse rises above the noise and gaudy pleasures of the board-walk, ignored by most of the vacationing revelers. As a meeting place it was an apt choice; a beacon that slices through the darkness to lead you into the light. The climb was arduous though, with every step my breath growing a little sharper with the altitude and the fear at the thought that I was betraying not just Milton, but you, Grandma. Betraying myself even, given the life we've led.

The wind whistled up the spiral stairs, rattling doors and portholes. I pulled my scarf back up around my face as I came out onto the viewing platform.

The gin soaked couple next to me were too busy gazing into one another's eyes to pay me any attention but as an unruly boy and his sister ran to the edge to look out, shouting boisterously, whilst their haggard mother came up behind, people felt compelled to look over to see what all the fuss was about.

Nancy sidled up to me, pretending to look out at the view, her rose perfume cloying. I thought my legs might give way. This wasn't what I'd pictured myself ending up doing when I met Milton but given recent events it felt like there wasn't much choice. I began to question whether I should do this at all, but as I went to turn back, Nancy instinctively placed her hand firmly on my arm to stop me.

'*Look, I know how hard it was for you to make that call and for you to be here. I know every fiber of your being wants to turn and go back but you've made the first step and that's often the hardest.*'

She let go of my arm and I made no attempt to bolt.

'*You know, I wasn't always a copper,*' *she said.* '*A few years ago, I was more likely to be drinking hooch than arresting those who made it. My*

Fred was a bad man. Always angry. Put me in the hospital one time. Broken ribs. Broken nose. Cut lip. Died in a bar fight. Left me penniless.'

I didn't say anything. I didn't know what to say to a confession like that.

'I stayed longer than I should have and if he'd have carried on living, I can't say for sure whether I would have left in a car, or a body bag. There are so many reasons they give to make you think that staying is the only option.'

I nodded. I think she really does understand the predicament I'm in.

'A woman can't live on fresh air. You know that as well as I do. So, when he was gone and I realized he'd drank all the money away, I signed up to do what I do now. Every time you have doubts about why you're doing this, just remember life gets better. And you don't want to end up stuck with Milton for the rest of your life.'

'I've met plenty of men like Milton,' I said. 'My own mother left when I was ten because of a man who had a pocketful of promises, gin and white powder.'

'I'm so sorry to hear that.'

'Don't be. I didn't miss her as much as you might think.' I looked out at the horizon and the sun burning in the sky. 'Grandma was the one to raise me right. When my mother left, she told me I was destined for greater things; not to live by the whims and wants of men like my mother had.'

'You like Atlantic City?'

'I liked it well enough at first. The bright lights of the stage are so blinding that for the length of a song you can imagine you're anywhere else. Don't get me wrong, I love the beach and the boardwalk but singing in speakeasies ain't so glamorous when almost everyone has their strings pulled by a local gangster. You're just a distraction from the scent of death that lingers on every owner's hands.

The punters are just as bad sometimes. You're just an alibi they can use when the law comes knocking. 'Oh yeah, that night I was watching some broad that night so it couldn't have been me officer.'

And as for the drink, well, the moonshine in these places is so raw you might as well be drinking poison for all the good lemon juice and soda does. And until you become a big enough draw for the crowds, being a singer don't pay too well neither. The man in charge is always offering to increase pay in exchange for certain 'favors.' I've known many women do it in order to be able to pay their bills. I'd rather live on bread and water, which for the most part I have, until Charlie and Milton of course. I guess when this is all over, I'll have to start the whole cycle all over again.'

I don't know what it was about her that made me want to talk the way I did opening up like a jewelry box to reveal the glittering truth. She hadn't even had to push me for information. I just felt comfortable in her company.

'Seems like we've both been struggling to shake the grip of men off our shoulders,' Nancy sighed. 'I thought when I joined the police I could make something of myself, but the truth is I'm seen as a novelty by the other fellas. To them a woman copper's as entertaining as a dog wearing a collar and walking on its hind legs.' She laughed.

'There's talk of getting rid of us. Us women prohis I mean. In San Francisco they banned women from going out in the field. Those agents are just living life behind a desk now while the men go and do the dangerous work.'

I turned to her. 'So, what's the catch in me coming to you?'

'I want to help you escape this Milton fella. I could see how scared of him were as soon as I met you and you clearly have no one else to help you otherwise you wouldn't be here now talking to a copper.'

I hated that she was right. She was the only person I had left to turn to, and she knew it.

'I thought we could both settle scores. You help me put Milton away and get promoted by giving me information, and I'll help you leave him. Not only will I help you leave him, but I'll also help you get out of this place for good. You'll be paid well so you've got the jack to move out, and you'll be protected. I can't say fairer than that.'

'You want me to be a rat?' I said it a little too loud. 'No. No way.'

I started to walk away but she pulled me right back. The two children who had been fighting with one another looked over at us.

'Will you quieten down. Look, don't be like most women. Don't end up tied to a man you can't leave because you think you have no way to survive. Who makes you feel small. Who dims your light until there's nothing of you left.'

I swallowed hard, tears welling up. She was right about that last bit. The way he looked at me just lately was more filled with hate than love. And then there was that hardened look he always had nowadays. I didn't even want to get started on what might have happened to George. I was going to have to tell her. I couldn't hold it in.

'I think he's murdered someone.' I just came right out and said it.'

'Oh?' Nancy's eyes widened.

I told her about the night I saw Milton cloaked in blood. About the missing gun. About the look on his face when George's mother told us he was missing.

'George? You think he's killed George O Malley?' The color drained from her face. 'Are you absolutely sure?'

She looked like she'd been socked in the guts, her eyes welling up with tears.

Why would she care? I thought. Then it dawned on me.

'Was George a rat?'

She didn't answer.

'Pearl, you're not listening to me. Are you sure it was George's blood?'

I sighed. 'I can't say for certain. I just get this feeling in my guts. Intuition I guess.'

'Well, we can't put anyone away on just intuition.'

'Look, if George was a rat, why do you think I would sign up to take his place, given he could be six foot under right now?'

Nancy shot me an incredulous look.

'Do you honestly think Milton would protect you if it came to it? If things turned sour you and I both know he'd sooner sacrifice you than hand himself over.'

I was beginning to hate her honesty. Every word was a blade to cut me deeper with.

'If I did agree, what would I have to do?' I asked her.

'It's simple. You just have to look, listen, remember names. Remember the details of deals done. Feed all this information back to me. You'll get paid a damn sight more doing that than you would singing songs for rich men and importantly you could save enough to leave Milton. If you're really lucky and we have enough evidence of this murder, we could put him away for good. You could start a new life for yourself where no one else knows you.'

Still, I couldn't quite bring myself to say yes.

'Look, it's a big decision. Go home and think about it. Just don't leave it too long.'

I started to walk away when she called out my name. I turned.

'Pearl, remember, this is your way out.'

Well Grandma, I have thought long and hard and I've realized that far from feeling dirty, doing this will be like washing my hands clean.

The more I've become embroiled with Milton, the more my own identity has melded with his and I hate myself for it. I hate how like my own mother's shadow I've become, manipulated, worn down by a man who pretends to have my best interests at heart but really, he couldn't give a damn about me.

And it isn't just about Milton. I'm just as much as a pawn in his game as he is in mine. I was going to do it alone but perhaps having someone else in on the game to a certain extent could work to my advantage.

There's something else too. Handing in those corrupt men will be like paying back all those girls I've seen sell themselves to owners when they couldn't make their own rents. I'll be doing it for all of the women who are trapped and can't get out.

I'd be doing it for you. For mom.

When Nancy has enough information on all the major players in this city, we'll bring it all crashing down.

Love always

Pearl

49

SEPTEMBER 10TH, 1927

✦⊪————⊪⊪———⊪✦

Dear Grandma,

These past few days, the name 'George O Malley' has been on every-one's lips. I heard it in the grocery store. The speakeasy. The hair parlor. You can't even switch on the wireless without hearing Mrs. O Malley's tearful voice:

'Please, if you have any information. Anything at all that might help find my boy and grandson, please go to Atlantic City police and ask for Officer Brooke or Officer Simpson.'

And if that wasn't enough George's face stares out from missing posters all along the boardwalk, his eyes following you down the length of the promenade. I'm sure Milton is counting on us never finding George. Usually search parties dwindle in numbers within a couple of days, rain-soaked missing posters get torn down and the missing person is forgotten about. But that isn't happening. Mrs. O Malley won't let it.

And the thing is she lacks the one thing, all of Milton's other adver-saries have: fear.

Without that, without knowing what Milton is really capable of, she continues to call the newspapers and talk on the wireless. She doesn't believe for a second that George has left town like Clyde suggested and she's wasted no time in telling the chief commissioner that. After only three days Clyde's been taken off the case, replaced by Jay and Nancy instead.

Incorruptible coppers. Milton has never met one of those before and I can sense that he's terrified. He senses all eyes on him so at the moment I feel the safest I've felt in long time. He knows he has to be kind to me because I've got so much dirt on him. One word from me and I could put him away. He doesn't know I've already spoken to Nancy about what I already know.

Each night as I button up my coat ready to join the search party, I can see the agitation in Milton's cold eyes. Officers join us with dogs and torches, and all the time Nancy and I have our eyes on Milton, waiting for him to do or say something that will lead us to where George lies but he remains stony faced, never hinting at where he knows George's body lies buried.

Tonight, Milton's own mother was there. She didn't even speak to him. Just walked right past like he was a stranger, which I guess he is now. Four months and he's not visited her once. Not since she told him she didn't like the ruthless man he'd become.

Seeing her, his body stiffened the way mine did when he tried to touch me. There was a flash of...something in his eyes. What was that? Terror? Guilt? Something else?

I stood at the top of the boardwalk, watching as Milton walked away from her and began searching in another direction. Nancy came and stood next to me, while Jay followed after Milton.

'I sure hope we find him soon.' Nancy said, but her voice was unconvincing.

'George is dead.' I said to her. 'You know it and so do I.'

She sighed. 'Well, it ain't looking good. No sign of a struggle at his home. No clothing missing out of his closet, so I don't buy the idea that he's skipped town, but we need more than a gut feeling Pearl. You know that. We need a body. A murder weapon. Evidence. And at the moment we have nothing. Milton maintains his story, that he didn't see George all the day he went missing. You haven't got anything for me?'

I shook my head. She looked disappointed.

'What if you don't find him?'

'We wait for a body to show up, I guess. One will eventually. I just hoped when it did, it would still be breathing. It just seems funny to me that Milton did a hit by himself. No Boss with sense gets his own hands dirty. You order someone else to do it for you. But if you're right, and Milton did kill him, it'll only be a matter of time before he cracks.'

But both Jay and Nancy are treating Milton like every other person who has a conscience. And I know that Milton doesn't have one.

After the search, me and Milton drove home. I was glad to go back to the roaring fire; the rain having soaked through my coat and sweater; right down to the button up shirt underneath. As we pulled into the driveway, Milton slammed on the brakes.

A Dodge had parked up in our usual spot.

'What the...who the hell is this guy?'

Milton took his revolver from the glovebox. Now my heart was racing. The door of the dodge opened, and Milton sat poised, ready to shoot. Jesse stepped out, hands up in surrender.

'It's Jesse, Jesus!'

Milton gave a nervous laugh and stepped out of the car.

'You gave us both a fright. Thought you were William Abel come to take me out. New wheels?'

There was a lot of backslapping and joviality between the two of them and as I got out of the car, Jesse looked my way and smiled, the scar on his forehead still raw salmon pink.

'It's good to see you Jesse,' I said.

Milton had already started off ahead of the both of us towards the house.

'Hey Milton, hang on a minute,' Jesse leaned into the car for his walking cane.

Grunting with every difficult step, but also insisting that neither of us offer help, Jesse followed behind us, up to the house.

Milton barely spoke at first. I assumed it was because he felt some responsibility for what had happened to Jesse, but now know that wasn't the reason. He was thinking about the best way to break bad news.

Inside, Milton gave Jesse the best seat in the parlor; the red leather chesterfield that sits next to the window with a perfect view of the sea on the horizon.

'It's good to see you both. Honestly, I hated being stuck in that hospital. I can't wait to come back. I know I might be a little slow, but I can still handle a tommy, and I swear when Thomas or William Abel comes for us, I'll be ready this time. Neither of them will even know what hit them.'

Milton shook his head.

'Slow down Jesse. Things have changed. The governor has given us the pageant on condition that there's no more bloodshed.'

'You're kidding, right?'

Jesse's smile faded and was replaced by raw anger.

'The Abels took Mickey's life and left me for dead and for what? So, you can pretend none of that happened? I can barely walk now because of what they did. The headaches I get from this thing they put in my head. Damn it, I couldn't even say Eveline's name when she first came to visit. Do you really expect me to forgive what they've done?'

Milton shifted uncomfortably in his seat.

'I'm not saying we should forget, just that we should lay low for a while, that's all. Until this pageant is over, you're not to lay a single finger on either of them, you understand?'

He spoke firmly. His decision was final.

'Besides, I have a new role for you now George has gone.'

This didn't have the mollifying effect Milton expected it to.

'So not only have they injured me beyond repair, you're demoting me, is that it? Sending me to the drugstore to be your shop boy?' Jesse spat the words out in disgust. He rose slowly to his feet, fist clenched, face red with fury.

Milton looked scared as Jesse towered over him. He knew he had no control over Jesse. Perhaps he never had.

'Come on Jesse, it's not for long. Just until I find someone else.'

Jesse didn't say another word, just took his cane and walked slowly with dignity to the door. He walked out leaving the door swinging on its hinges in the wind.

I got up to close it and when I returned, I found Milton, slumped down in his chair, head in hands.

'Well, that didn't go as well as I thought it might. Pearl, get me a whiskey, would you?'

Drinking again. It's a sign he's going to break any day, I'm sure of it.

And when he does, I'll be here to gather up every single shard of information.

Love always

Pearl

50

SEPTEMBER 11TH, 1927

✦ ⊶———•⊷———⊶ ✦

Dear Grandma,

Elmer is back and I'm glad because Milton has had me running around all

over town doing errands for the fall frolic. There's only a week to go until the pageant and as Jesse hasn't been back, it's just been the three of us getting things organized. Things are getting quieter in terms of news about George and I'm beginning to lose hope he'll ever be found. I'm no closer to getting Milton caught which means I'm no closer to leaving.

You'd think Milton would be in a good mood, but he seems to just get meaner as the day gets closer. I was stood out in front of Kings with Elmer today, decorating the float with paper streamers made to look like seaweed. Milton was trying to organize a pick-up of alcohol but no one was answering his calls and when Milton doesn't get his own way, he becomes bad tempered and a bully.

'Is that meant to be just hanging there like that?' He stood over me as I attached a streamer of shells to the back of the throne that will be his seat on the day, watching and criticizing my every move. If he was going to pick a fight, I would rather just get it over and done with.

'What's wrong with it?' I challenged him.

'What's right with it? This is meant to be a throne fit for a King and at the moment it just looks amateurish.'

To Elmer's credit, he tried to defend me.

'I don't think it looks so bad...'

I was done being his punch bag. I put the brush back in the glue pot and stood up.

'Well, if you think you can do any better Milton, be my guest?'

'Everything okay here?'

I looked up and there stood Jay smoking a cigarette. Milton bristled as the copper looked over our handiwork. The last thing Milton wanted was an unexpected visit from the law.

'Who's the throne for?' Jay smirked.

'Neptune.' Milton practically spat the name out at him.

'Really? Is this some local tradition?' Jay gave a puzzled look.

Milton loves an opportunity to show someone he is smarter than they are, so he relished being able to give an explanation.

'Neptune presides over the pageant, and the whole of the ocean if you're into the mythology. Whoever is Neptune presents the Golden Mermaid trophy to the winner and the winner takes the throne in Neptune's place.'

'And who is Neptune this year?'

Jay was just playing with him. He knew the answer. He just wanted to hear Milton say it out loud.

'I am.'

'Well, looks good.'

Jay nodded and with a flick of his wrist tossed his cigarette nub to the ground, landing it only inches away from the paper streamers. Milton's fury exploded and he walked right up to him, stopping with his face only inches away from Jay's.

'You fucking fool! You coulda burned the whole thing to the ground!'

Jay kept calm and shrugged.

'Sorry there Milton. I didn't think. Say, you weren't about to hit an officer of the law, were you?'

Of course, he was, and we all knew it. I would have throttled Jay myself if that cigarette had set it alight. All our hard work would have gone up in smoke.

Milton stood back to give him space and show him he wasn't threatening him in any way, but he had already dropped the mask and revealed his true self: a simmering pot of rage and hatred that threatened to boil over. Finally, someone else had seen a glimpse of it.

He wasn't about to let it take over the way it usually did. Milton spoke through gritted teeth.

'Of course not, Officer Brooke. It's good to see you taking an interest in local business. As you know, the governor of the town is also very excited for the event. Now, was there anything else that you wanted?'

Jay made like he was thinking hard about it.

'Oh yes, there was something else. William Abel was shot last night. Eating dinner with his family and a bullet came blasting in through the window. Looks like the shooter was aiming for his chest but missed and all William got was a bullet lodged in his right bicep. His ten-year-old daughter though, got a face full of broken glass where the bullet shattered the window. I sure wouldn't want to be the guy who ordered that hit, but I guess you wouldn't know anything about that now, would you?'

Jay must have seen the surprise in Milton's eyes as the news registered. The smirk on his face disappeared.

Milton looked at me and Elmer. 'You know anything about this?'

'What? Of course, I hadn't heard.' Elmer said to Milton. Then to Jay, 'is his daughter okay?'

Jay shook his head, 'She's at the hospital. Both of them are.'

It was time for Milton to take over.

'Do you have any idea who did it?'

'Well, it's funny you ask. One of my fellow officers pulled over your guy actually,' Jay looked at his notebook, pretending like he couldn't remember his name. 'That Jesse guy who works for you. He was pulled over only a block away with a gun in the car that matches the bullet lodged in William's arm. We've got him down at the station now.'

Milton didn't speak but I could tell by the fire in his eyes that he was furious. Jesse had deliberately disobeyed him. Now we are all in hot water, thanks to him.

We all know that Thomas Abel will not waste time getting revenge for what has happened to his brother and niece. He isn't going to let something like that go. It doesn't matter that Jesse had taken it upon himself to do this. The Abels will blame Milton. And Milton knows that.

Jay cleared his throat. 'So, Milton, if you wouldn't mind, I'd like to ask you a few questions down at the station.'

'Fine by me,' Milton eyeballed Jay, the aggressive tone of his voice, a base note underneath the top note of his words.

Milton nodded towards Elmer.

'You two okay to keep an eye on the place?'

Elmer nodded.

Jay cleared his throat and looked across at me.

'I'm afraid I have to ask for you to come along too Miss.'

'What?'

Jay was playing a dangerous game taking me along for the ride, but I had to hand it to him, at least the surprise in my voice was genuine.

Milton shrugged.

'Sure Officer Brooke, why don't you bring us all in? Me, my fiancé. What about her band? The cigarette girl? Bring them all, cause I got nothing to hide.'

Jay had him rattled and he was loving every second he got under Milton's skin.

Well Grandma, I played my part well. Shouting my mouth off that we weren't meant to be there. Causing fuss like I'd seen so many criminals do when they've been dragged in by the coppers, making them doubt themselves. And I must have done a good job; Jay's colleagues threatened to take a hand to me if I didn't shut up.

They left me and Milton sat on the wooden bench in the waiting room whilst they discussed us with the door ajar so we could overhear every word.

'Look,' I heard Jay say to Nancy. 'I'll handle Milton. You take Pearl.'

Milton leaned over to me, his voice a whisper.

'You see now why I kept you out of all this? You can't tell them what you don't know.'

What was that meant to mean? Milton kissed me on the cheek and stood up just as Jay and Nancy stepped out of the office.

Moments later I was sat in the fishbowl with Nancy, peering through the one-way glass into the small room they usually had the line up in. Behind the glass was Jesse; a giant bear of a man slumped in a wooden chair. The spatter of blood on his white shirt had dried to brown so it looked like mud.

'How long have you had him in there?' I asked.

'Not long. An hour maybe. You said he came to the house last night?' I nodded.

'He was waiting for us. He was upset. Milton wanted him to take over George's role at the drugstore and Jesse saw it as some sort of insult on account of his injuries. Like Milton was suggesting he wasn't up to the job anymore.'

'So, he was angry?' Nancy was writing it all down in her notebook.

'Fuming. Keep talking about getting revenge on the Abel brothers but Milton was very clear that he should do nothing. That he forbade it. Jesse did this by himself, not with Milton's blessing.'

Nancy nodded. 'Yeah, that's what he keeps on saying but I guess we just have to see what Jay gets out of him.'

Moments later the door burst open and in weighed Jay. I'd never seen this aggressiveness in him before, but I guess all men have it in them when pushed hard enough. He slammed down a photograph in front of him. I craned my neck to see it but couldn't. Jesse looked, moaned, and turned his head away.

'What's the matter? Ain't you proud? You did that. To a ten-year-old girl. Ten years old. Look at it, you piece of shit!'

Jay had his vicelike hands gripped either side of Jesse's head, forcing him to look at the photograph.

'I...I wasn't aiming for her,' Jesse cries. 'Just William.'

'Why him?'

'I already told you a million times. It was him that did this to me. Put this plate in my skull. Shattered my knee.'

Jay loosened his grip and Jesse collapsed onto the table in front of him, crying.

'Some mobster you are!' Jay is practically laughing at him.

'I should bring Milton in right now so he can see the sort of guy he actually has working for him. Some blubbering mess. A dumdum who can't even aim a gun right. You know if you ever get out of here, you'll be on everyone's hit list, don't you? Thomas Abel will hunt you down like the dog that you are. And Milton? You'll no longer be of any use to him. All you've done is put him in even more danger. What do you think he'll do?'

'I don't know. I just don't know.' Jesse is blubbering now, a bubble of snot peeping out of his right nostril.

I turned to Nancy.

'Do we really need to sit through all of this?'

Nancy nodded silently.

In the other room, Jay grabbed himself a chair and pulled it over and straddled it as someone might straddle a horse. He sat opposite Jesse, eye to eye. His voice softened.

'If Milton put you up to this Jesse, you can tell us. We'll offer you immunity. You know, the judge and jury ain't going to treat you too kindly, not when children are getting hurt. It don't look good. And in jail, the prisoners are even worse. They deal out their own punishments.'

Jesse shook his head. He sounded exasperated.

'I told you. I did it alone.'

Coppers and Christians, all drive like they couldn't care less if they live or die, and I guess that's because they don't. They're convinced they're on the right side of God and humanity, so why be afraid of death? Nancy is one of them and as we sped along dirt roads I gripped onto the car seat beneath me so hard that my knuckles were white. I was terrified we would crash at any moment.

'Where are we going? What about Milton?'

'Jay's going to keep him there a while longer. Keep asking questions; about Jesse, about George, about all of the pies he has his sticky fingers poked into. And while he does that, you and I can check out the drugstore; see if we can find anything that'll help us find out what happened to George. You might spot something I don't, what with you knowing the place. Here!'

She handed me a pistol.

'Keep this on you at all times from now on. Just don't tell anyone it came from me. I have to warn you that as we get closer to exposing Milton for who he really is, things could become more dangerous for you.'

I guess there's always been a part of me, even way back living with you, that I guessed I'd go out all ablaze in gun and hell fire. And right then, as Nancy handed me the gun, I knew I'd arrived. This was my path. The one that had always lay there, glistening in the dirt. I took the gun from her and put it in the roll top of my stocking. Nancy kept her eye on the road. Didn't even sneak a look to check, I wasn't about to point it at her.

'How do you know you can trust me with a loaded weapon?'

'I knew from the very first time I met you that you were just someone who wants to bring people to justice, just like the rest of us. What was that you talked about before? That was it: intuition.'

The rain was bouncing off the boardwalk as we pulled up outside the drugstore and I was glad of it, as at least the few revelers who hadn't yet ran for cover were too concerned about keeping dry than about Nancy and me taking a crowbar to the door of Kelly & Sons.

'You know, if you'd have asked, I probably could've got you a key,' I joked.

The door opened easily once the lock was off and when it did the scent of bleach and paint wafted out. Nancy and I looked at one another.

'Smells like our boy's been doing some decorating,' she said.

Inside, the floorboards were painted over in white, but the walls still had the same peeling wallpaper.

'Talk about a cover up,' she said. 'Who paints the floor and nothing else?'

'Someone who can't scrub the blood out of the floorboards because it's seeped into the wood if the corpse isn't taken away soon enough.'

Nancy nodded, But what I don't get is why Milton would leave it there for that long.'

'Either he didn't get a chance to dispose of the body straight away, or he was leaving it for someone else to deal with.'

I moved over to the shelves of medicine. For the first time I noticed how light the boxes were.

'You'd think Milton would try a little harder to not make it so obvious that this business is a front,' I said taking one of them off the shelf and opening it to show Nancy the empty space inside.

Nancy was busy rummaging through drawers and cupboards, not really sure what she was looking for. Milton wasn't stupid enough to leave any evidence of anything. Not of bootlegging, of murder. Of any wrongdoing at all.

'Maybe he never planned to kill George,' I said.

'What do you mean?'

'Just that, Milton is too smart to have someone killed on his own premises. If anyone was killed here, then that wasn't premeditated. George and Milton must have had some sort of disagreement and Milton was either too horrified to react rationally and clear away the body, or he wasn't able to. He didn't want to ask anyone else to do his dirty work for him because the others, if they knew, would turn against him. Everyone loves George.'

'You know, a secret as big as that: killing your best friend, could break a man,' Nancy said.

'Well, I guess we just need to put a little pressure on those hairline cracks.'

I opened one of the drawers and found the ledger.

'Hey Nancy. I found this. I doubt it'll have any of his real deals in it of course, but it might be worth a look.'

I handed the book to her and as she opened it to take a look, a piece of white paper slid out from between the pages and floated like a feather to the ground.

I bent down to pick it up.

'Madame Zelda's. All fortunes told. Palmistry, tarot and communications with the other realm.'

Nancy snorted and waved her hand dismissively.

'What a load of baloney. I wouldn't have had Milton or George down for this nonsense. Just throw it away.'

'Look, Nancy, I'd better get back to Kings soon. If I'm not there when Milton's released, he'll smell a rat.'

She nodded. 'Sure, I think we're done here anyway.'

She drove me back to Kings and I went back to decorating my parade float, adding the streamers Milton hated so much. Champ came bounding out, jumping up and licking me with such force I almost fell over.

'Easy boy!' I said.

He knows, Grandma. He knows Milton will get what's coming to him eventually.

Love always.

Pearl

51

September 12th, 1927

❖ ⊷────•◦•────⊶ ❖

Dear Grandma,

I've never seen Milton so crazed as he was this evening when Jay finally let him out. I was glad to be at Kings, because if we'd have been home alone, I would have been the first person for him to take it out on.

He was sinking whiskey after whiskey. Everyone else, his bartenders and bouncers all gave him a wide berth seeing the rage in his eyes.

'Fucking Jesse! I told him to hold off, but I should have known he would do something crazy like this.'

Only Elmer and I willingly sat at his table, trying to subdue him.

'What did you say to them?' he snarled at me.

'I didn't tell them anything,' I said.

'I don't believe you.'

He got up from his chair and helped himself to a new bottle of whiskey from behind the bar. I understood now why Nancy had given me that pistol.

Elmer leaned over to me and whispered.

'He's just scared the Abels will be coming for him. For all of us.'

As if Milton's rage wasn't enough to contend with. I was glad now that I could feel the weight of my pistol in my stockings, not just to defend myself against Milton but against the Abels too. Not that it would be much use against a tommy gun.

And then it dawned on me that in only a week's time, Milton will be sat on a throne as Neptune, parading through the streets of Atlantic City. Out in the open. A moving target, passing through crowds where anyone will be able to blend in and take their best shot. I couldn't help but smile a little Grandma.

Perhaps the bounty is big enough that more than one guy will try his luck.

But I remembered Milton wouldn't be the only one up on that float. Next to him, me and my band will be performing up on that float.

Now I'm scared spitless Grandma. I don't mind admitting it.

When Milton came back and sat down, Elmer tried to take the heat away from me.

'If you're looking to pay the bond for Jesse's bail, then I can give you a lift down to the station in the morning?' Elmer said, topping up his own glass with whiskey.

'For hurting a kid?' Milton shook his head and took a swig out of the bottle. 'Nah, he can wait in there a little longer.'

This isn't the way things are done. If one of your mob is taken in, you pay to get them out. Keep them sweet so they won't talk. Elmer and I looked at one another. What is Milton playing at?

'You know what Jesse has done? He thought he was doing me a favor by trying to take the Abels out, but what he's actually done is put me in the Abels' pocket. If we don't come to some agreement somehow, I'll always be on their hitlist. Not just me neither, Pearl, you; anyone who works for me.'

'So, what are you going to do Boss?' Elmer asked.

Milton thought for a moment. 'Do what Clarence should have done a long time ago. Negotiate. Get Clyde Thompson on the phone and down here right away. We're going to need him as a go-between.'

Elmer nodded and went to make the call.

To my surprise Milton leaned across the table and placed his hands on mine, his voice warm as he spoke.

'Don't you worry none, Sugar. I've got it all in hand. Everyone has their price. And it's not like anyone was actually killed on their side. They were just injured. It not the same as what they did to Jesse. Or poor Mickey. They have to understand that.'

But I doubt that they will understand anything but revenge. It's the only language you know when someone tries to hurt the one you love. And that has made us all a target. I stood up.

'Where are you going?'

I pointed up at the stage. 'You wanted me to practice, remember? Get a few performances in before the pageant.'

Too wound up in his own predicament, he barely batted an eyelid as I walked away between the tables of revelers towards backstage.

My hands were clammy and my breathing shallow as I pushed open the door and into the relative safety of the dressing room. After switching my everyday dress for a black tasseled one, I sat down in front of the mirror and spotted a vase of red roses Milton had left for me.

My thoughts drifted to you Grandma and the roses you had delivered to the house the last time I saw you. They were just like the ones in my dressing room. I leaned in and smelled their scent and with it my nerves calmed down.

I can do this. I just need to stay a little while longer and when Milton gets his comeuppance it will all be over, and I can go wherever I want.

Through the paper-thin walls I heard the tempo of the drums slowing down. It wasn't my band of course. Booker had left when Charlie did, taking most of the band with him. The clock said almost nine. My cue to go out there.

As the singer before me came back down the steps, riled up on gin and the buzz of the crowd, she stopped and smiled.

'Break a leg.'

I had forgotten what it felt like to feel the hum of the bass and beat of the drum beneath your feet as I walked up those steps and into the blinding spotlight. Looking out, I could barely make out the silhouettes of the audience sat at their tables dining on Oysters Rockefeller and drinking champagne, unaware of the mob warfare that was brewing around them.

For once I didn't find any comfort in not being able to see who was watching me. Any one of them could have been sent by the Abels.

'Good evening,' I leaned into the microphone, voice trembling. I took a deep breath and burst into a rendition of my signature song, 'It's a Sin to Tell a Lie.'

The glow of every match or every time someone stood up from their table or stepped through the front door, I expected it to be one of the Abel's goons toting a gun.

My voice quavered and quaked. I must get a grip again before the day of the pageant.

When Clyde walked in, I was relieved. Clyde and Milton greeted one another and after much whispered discussion, exchanged an envelope for a firm handshake.

I guess this means Clyde really is going to help Milton negotiate with the Abels but who knows at what price?

Milton and the audience whooped and cheered my performance when I got to the end of my set and at the end of the night when the cigarette smoke had dissipated and the leftover glasses and bottles had been cleared, and floors had been swept, Milton came over to where I sat waiting for him.

'We're going to stay at the Marlborough Hotel tonight, just to be on the safe side. My trust for Clyde only extends so far, and it's no secret to the Abels that we live at the Kelly Mansion so we can't go back there.'

He had me nervous now.

'Sure Milton, but if I can't even go back to get a change of clothes, what'll I do for something to wear? I can't live in this.'

I gestured to the black dress I'd just performed in.

'I'll sort something out tomorrow, but you're not to go back home. Not until I know that it's safe for both of us.'

'Do you really think Thomas Abel will agree to a ceasefire?'

Milton shrugged. 'Everyone has their price. I guess we'll find out if what I'm offering is enough.'

Back at the Marlborough Milton paced back and forth, his mouth and teeth wine stained from the glass of claret he'd been gulping down to calm his nerves. This was despite having Elmer guarding the door of the suite, gun loaded, ready to shoot at any moment, and Milton insisting on only one particular maid to tend to us.

The shrill scream of the phone made me jump in my seat. Milton got up and picked up the receiver.

'Yes. Well, what did he say?'

It must have been Clyde on the other end. Milton nodded a couple of times making agreeable sounds. He gave a lengthy sigh.

'Well, I guess I'll agree to that, if that's what must happen. Tell them, it's as good as done.'

He placed the receiver down and walked back to resume drinking.

'They've agreed,' he said picking his wine glass back up. 'A truce until after the fall frolic.'

For someone who had proverbially just dodged a bullet with his name on, he didn't look like a man who wanted to celebrate.

I can understand why. I wouldn't trust Clyde or the Abels to play their hand without keeping a few aces up their sleeves. I don't think there's anyone who hasn't got one or two extra cards in their pack.

Love always

Pearl

52

SEPTEMBER 13TH, 1927

❖⸺•●•⸺❖

Dear Grandma,

I'm writing this to distract me from the twisting feeling that something's not right. I'm sitting in Daphne's Coffee House opposite the police station, waiting for Eveline and Jesse to come out.

Milton asked me to make the drop of the bond money as he and Elmer have things to do for the pageant.

I didn't want to be the fly in the ointment of the reunion between Eveline and Jesse, so I handed Eveline the money and came here to Daphne's to wait for them both.

Daphne's is a swell place. I used to come here with Charlie sometimes as he loved the coffee and French croissants here. Of course, Daphne herself is just as fake as every other jewel in Atlantic City. Charlie nicknamed her 'the duchess' due to the air of arrogance she carries herself with, but she's no joke.

She serves coffee to every wife and mistress in town, all the time listening to them complain about their rich and powerful husbands and lovers, drinking in all of their secrets and confessions as they drink her coffee. If there's anyone who could make money being a rat, it's her.

Milton knows this so he warned me when I left the Marlborough.

'Not a word about the real reason why we're staying here,' he said.

As if I'd tell her. He seems to trust me less and less just lately.

And now I'm sitting with an empty cup, gazing through the window at the police station across the road where Jesse is still being held, his car sat outside waiting for him. The money comes with clear instructions for Jesse to drive both me and Eveline back home. If I'm too long gone, there'll be trouble.

I'm conscious of the clock ticking on the wall. It's almost midday and Daphne keeps staring, wondering when I'm going to pay my bill and leave, so she can change the table linen for the lunchtime crowd.

Oh, sometimes I'm so silly. I can see Eveline and Jesse walking down the steps now. They've just waved at me, so I've waved back and let them know that I'm coming right away.

The delighted way Jesse looks at his car, is almost the same look he gives Eveline when he...

53

THE ATLANTIC CITY TRIBUNE

✢ ⱶ⣿⣿ⱶ ✢

ATLANTIC CITY ROCKED BY CAR EXPLOSION.

5 DEAD, HUNDREDS INJURED.

A mysterious explosion, devastated a street in Atlantic City to-day, killing 5 people and injuring hundreds.

The clock had just struck twelve when the explosion happened. Witnesses described a jet of flame and a blast that shook the ground and whole panes of glass from street windows raining down upon them. It is believed the sound of the explosion could be heard several blocks away.

Hundreds of people fled the scene to safety whilst police have yet to confirm the number of deaths and injured persons. The blast is said to have been caused by explosives planted in a car parked just outside Atlantic City's police station. It was falling glass and not the explosion itself that caused the fatalities and injuries.

54

PART THREE: MILTON'S CONFESSION

❖ ▬▬▬ ▪▪ ▬▬▬ ❖

'Okay, so maybe I might have embellished the truth a little. Doesn't make me a murderer.

Unless of course you have evidence for that.'

Milton Costello, *The Atlantic City Tribune*, October 13th, 1927

55

Chapter Thirty-Nine

E verything had been going jake until Jesse ruined it all. Him acting the bimbo when he got out of the hospital did more damage than he realized.

The pressure I felt in those last few days too, to smooth everything out with the Abels before the pageant, made me sore. I recognized more of my father in the mirror than myself. The nasty curl of the lip when I smiled. The bloodshot eyes and trembling hands of a guy who needed liquor as much as he needed air to survive.

When did I become such a bruno? I don't know. It had happened so gradually I hadn't even noticed. All I knew was that when George disappeared, something shifted in me. Plates groaning, an earthquake of epic proportions was building beneath my feet and threating to topple everything, unless I took control.

I didn't expect the earthquake that arrived to wind up being Jesse.

Pearl kept spouting that Jesse was still a good guy and all, and that I should get him out of jail sooner rather than later, but that's the problem with Pearl. She sees the good in everyone.

Anyone could see Jesse was a brute for hurting that girl, accident or not. Poor kid would have scars on her face for the rest of her life. What he did made bad blood for everyone.

What he did also made me look a sap. What sort of big shot can't control his men? I can't have them go behind my back. No, the blow up on Jesse was the smartest thing anyone could have done.

I didn't have anything to do with it, of course, but I knew the hit was coming.

I didn't want details. Like I told Pearl, the less you know the less juice the law have to squeeze out of you.

Problem was because I insisted on knowing nothing, I also didn't know Pearl and Eveline would get caught up in the blow up. I mean, I was sweet on Pearl at the time. I would never hurt her deliberately. Sure, sometimes I told her straight if I didn't like something she wore, or if her friends said something I didn't think was right, but it was always to help her. To protect her.

I was at the hotel when the blast happened. The chandeliers above my head trembled. The floor shook like a tremor. When I saw black smoke floating across the horizon, I knew it was done.

Sirens rang out and people gawked in the street at the black cloud of smoke from two blocks away. I called Elmer to bring cigars and whiskey and we both sat down to talk about the final preparations for the fall frolic parade.

It didn't matter that the Abels had promised a truce in exchange for Jesse; I still felt this snake squirming in my guts, squeezing my intestines and lungs, choking the breath out of me even though I knew he'd been dealt with.

The whiskey Elmer bought dulled the fear a little.

'Hey Boss,' Elmer said, handing it to me. 'You sure you're, okay?'

'Sure,' I said.

But I was lying. He knew it and so did I. This whole thing with the Abela should have been dealt with; all packaged up in a box and tied with a neat, red bow, but something in me told me it wasn't over yet.

I stood up from my seat and stood by the window, checking my watch.

'Pearl should have been back by now. You don't think...'

My voice trailed off as Elmer got up and went to the phone.

'I'll get Clyde on the line.'

With sirens screaming outside, we waited for him to pick up. The squirming in my stomach got worse. It felt like the longest wait for him to pick up, but eventually he did.

Elmer passed me the phone.

'The good news is, she's not one of the dead bodies,' Clyde said. 'The bad news is we can't find her anywhere.'

56

CHAPTER FORTY

❖ ▬▬▬▬ ❖

I hadn't planned on making a habit of chinning with the law, particularly as I was still feeling sore about the grilling I'd had from Brooke with him trying to frame me for Jesse's mistakes. But when I bumped into him on his day off, he made sure I had no choice but to speak to him.

With Pearl missing, I had a head full of bees. I couldn't just sit around waiting for news so while Elmer checked the hospital for her, I took a walk along the boardwalk to see if I could find her. I wouldn't have been surprised if I'd found her watching the waves on the beach, oblivious to the chaos that was going on the other side of town she was so absent-minded sometimes.

'Milton?'

I looked up, and on the steps that led to the beach, there stood Jay Brooke. And worse than that, with him at his side was his small son, Jack. Jack looked so much like George's son Lou, it gave me the heebie jeebies.

'What are you doing down here, Milton? You don't look dressed for the beach, if you don't mind me saying so.'

I could have knocked that smirk of his from here to Timbuctoo. Say what you like about Brooke but he ain't no sap. His mind ticks like that bomb in Jesse's car, counting down the time till he can take a hold of you. The last thing I needed was him knowing Pearl was missing, as well as George. I weren't guilty of nothing, but the way he looked at me made me feel I'd committed a crime by existing. I acted like I had no kick in front of him, but underneath everything, my heart was pounding.

'I've come to see the 'Creatures of the Deep' show. Taking a break from organizing the pageant. It's that show where the fisherman goes out to sea and brings all these strange fish back. I don't imagine you have anything like that in the backwaters where you're from.'

I cast the line, but he didn't take the bait. He just nodded.

'Really? Well, that's where we're headed too. My boy loves it. Don't you, Jack? Me, I hate the sea. Can't even swim. Say, why don't you come along with us?'

I was trapped now. If I refused, I looked like a guy who had something to hide. If I went along talking to a flatfoot, I looked like I was some sort of rat. So, I didn't say anything. They walked close enough to talk to me, but not so close that we looked like friends.

'How you finding it at the Marlborough?' Brooke said. 'Seems kind of strange you staying there when you're living at the Kelly mansion.'

Boy Scout had been doing his homework again.

'Where'd you get the rumble about that?'

He shrugged, not giving anything away. And I sure as hell, wasn't about to give him anything.

'Well, you know how it is. Sometimes you just need a little breathing space away from home.'

He smiled. 'I mean, it's funny really, isn't it? Clarence Kelly is shot, and Clyde claims he doesn't know who it was who did it, despite being on everyone's payroll. Then Charlie Kelly goes away on vacation and just disappears into thin air just as you step into his shoes and get engaged to his ex-girl Pearl. George O Malley disappears, his body nowhere to be found. And now your associate Jesse is killed in an explosion, just as he was released out on bond, that you paid. Seems terribly unlucky to me. I mean, who could predict any of that?'

'I guess God moves in mysterious ways.'

What else was I to say?

'Have you ever seen an octopus?'

The sweet voice of Jack broke through the cold air between us.

I shook my head, and Jack filled the silence with mindless talk about sea horses and giant fish he'd seen at 'Creatures of The Deep.' I was too busy seething to really be listening. How did Brooke know I was at the Marlborough? Had he been following me?

The boat's crew were just pulling up the nets as we reached the end of the pier. The captain stood on the deck, addressing the gathered crowd like he was the ringmaster in a big top, not a guy in his fisherman's waders.

'What you're about to witness is a spectacle like no other. The sea is a lonesome place, full of strange and wonderful creatures just like this one...'

In the net there was something grey and squirming. Jack buried his face against his Da's leg as the captain pulled the creature out.

'Some say this eight-legged beast comes from the very depths of Hell...'

The crowd gasped at the sight of it writhing. What a bunch of saps. It was an octopus, nothing more than that and here this swindler had them believing it was the spawn of the devil.

When the show ended, I tried to walk away but Jack was eager to find out what I thought and so now I was stuck walking back along the boardwalk with them both, when all I wanted was to have peace and quiet.

'Oh look, a fortune teller!'

Jack stopped at the window of Madame Zelda's and my stomach twisted. I looked for anything to distract Jack away from the black drapes he was trying to peer through.

'Hey Jack, you fancy some taffy? My treat.' I pointed across the street at the Saltwater Taffy shop and Jack's eyes widened.

'Yeah, sure Sir. Thank you.'

Brooke stepped in to stop him.

'Its fine. I'll get it Milton. You get off to Kings if you want. I'm sure you have a lot to get done before you open today.'

This guy wouldn't even accept candy from me. Showing me right here and right now that he wasn't like Clyde or the rest of those coppers. So clean, he squeaked when he walked. He made me sick.

When Clarence was in charge, he taught me that if a powerful man offers you something, you made damn sure that you take it. Cause if you don't that man'll make you pay for your mistake. And here I was being openly disrespected by Brooke, and in front of Jack too. I could feel the rage building up inside me, but I didn't show it. Instead, I shook his hand, making sure to squeeze real tight.

I waited for the two of them to go into the taffy shop and once I was certain they were no longer looking in my direction I snuck into Zelda's, the bell above the door tinkling to announce my arrival.

CHAPTER FORTY-ONE

❧ ❧

I 'm not sure when I started believing in fate but when Jack called out Zelda's name it was like she was calling me to her.

Everything the girl had said would happen had happened: I had been promoted, I practically owned Kings and the write-up they'd given George in the paper certainly suggested he would be well remembered as 'the greatest' of the two of us. And with George out of the picture, so was his son Lou. His success she predicted could no longer affect me.

The last time I visited the girl had said there was something standing in my way and that once that block had been removed that I should go back to her. As sad as I was that George had gone, it made me wonder if he had been what had been holding me back all along. I wouldn't have to put up with his judgmental looks anymore and still feeling a little hinky about my relations with the Abels despite our truce, I wanted to be as prepared as I could be for anything I needed to do to survive.

I wasn't speaking to any assistant of Zeldas this time. The girl was small fry. I wanted the predictions to pour forth from the mouth of the oracle herself. I wanted to meet Zelda.

When I walked in, the girl from before was standing behind the counter in the exact same spot I left her in. Mists of patchouli incense swirled in the air. Even the people sitting around waiting for their appointments looked familiar. When she saw me standing there, the girl put the book she was reading to one side and smiled.

'I knew you'd be back.'

'I wanna see Zelda this time.' I was firm in my demand.

She looked bewildered. 'You can't. She's not here.'

'Well, I guess I'll just wait for her then.'

I sat down on one of the green sofas.

'Look mister, I already told you. She's not here.'

All of the frustration at being disrespected by everyone bubbled up and boiled over, and I snapped.

'Well, is she ever here? Every time I see you, you talk about her and yet I've never seen her. Not once. I'm beginning to think that you're a liar. Does she even exist?'

My voice was too loud. A couple waiting, got up and left. At least they had some respect for who I was.

Momentarily, I felt bad for the girl, her being on the receiving end of my frustration, but fair's fair.

'Look, its high time I got the truth from Zelda's mouth not some...conduit of hers.'

The smile disappeared from her pretty face. I hate to admit it, but it felt good to put her back in her box.

'Fine,' she said. 'Go and find her. She's down on the beach.'

'How will I know who she is?'

'She'll be wearing her black cape.'

***

Ten minutes later I was back on the beach, coattails blowing out behind me in the wind; brogues sinking into the sand.

Across the beach, a family was packing up their sand filled picnics up before the storm came. The wind swept their windbreaker up into the air and carried off down the beach, the two boys chasing after it like it was a kite. The beach was mostly deserted save for one broad at the shoreline watching the waves roar. Her cape blew out behind her like raven's wings. I knew it instinctively. This was her. This was Zelda.

As I walked towards her, without even turning to look at who was approaching, she raised her arm up and gestured for me to come in closer. I tried to see her face, but she kept pulling her hood up and turning away from me, just enough that I could never quite make her out.

'I knew you'd find me eventually. They always do.'

Her voice was unnaturally amplified over the crash of the waves and the wind, almost like she was transferring her thoughts from inside her head directly into mine.

'You want me to tell you about your future? You want to know if things have changed since I spoke through my sister? And now you have come to call for the spirits yourself.'

I nodded.

'Don't get me wrong. I'm grateful for the things she told me. All have come true except one. I wanted to check if there's anyone else that stands in my way.'

'Well, if you want to consult them, look at the waves and nature will tell you directly.'

I stood at the edge of the sand. For some reason I was reminded of the night of Clarence's party and how I had dived in to save Pearl when I wrongly thought she was drowning. Out at sea the waves rose up, swirling this way and that, before settling and forming a shape that looked almost human.

'What do you see?' she said.

The shape was unmistakable. A boy with short hair, and in his hands, he brandished a sword of flame.

'It's a boy with a flaming sword.'

'Truth and justice and very important to this person. If you are to succeed you must beware them.'

I shook my head. 'But it doesn't make sense. Are you trying to tell me that Lou is still going to take my place? That's impossible. He's four years old.'

She said nothing and it made me want to take hold of her round the throat and shake the answer out of her. She pointed at the grumbling grey clouds above.

'The clouds will tell us more,' she said, and they shapeshifted into a giant skull wearing a crown.

'That doesn't look like a great omen,' I said.

'To the contrary. It shows that you will still reign over the town despite the one planning your downfall. You will reign until the dead rise up.'

I laughed out loud.

'The dead can't rise. I'm safe.'

I would be hitting on all eight now and there was nothing anyone could do about it. She had given me what I wanted to hear.

'There's just one last thing,' she said. She bent down and picked up a long thread of seaweed and placed the slimy rope in my hands. 'You must bury this in the sand. That way the bond between you and your fate is set and can never be broken.'

I couldn't see anything that was bad about any of the things she'd said. I got down on my knees and dug with my hands, deep in the cold sand. She walked away from me without saying another word, leaving me there digging like a dog, the wind blowing sand in my face.

The dead couldn't rise.

I was invincible.

58

CHAPTER FORTY-TWO

❖━━━━━━❖

After Zelda's I drove back to Kings, keen to find out if Pearl was okay. We had gallons of medicinal alcohol to shift and punters that needed to know the fall frolic was going to be the bees. The blow up that had happened was just a stain on an otherwise starched white canvas. A canvas that was ready for them to paint with joyful memories of vibrant floats and pretty girls.

When I arrived, Clyde was already there with the liquor.

'You know, this pick-up nearly didn't happen at all,' Clyde said gravely.

He hadn't stopped smoking cigarettes since I'd got there. Once he'd smoked one down to the filter, he'd dash it to the floor and light another. I tried to keep my poker face as he unloaded the crates of booze from out of the car as I knew what would be coming next. A request for more money.

'I don't know what you're talking about Clyde,' I said.

This only made him suck even harder on the filter of his smoke.

Of course, I knew what he was talking about. Word had already gotten out about what happened to Jesse and his girl. So now the usual goons on Clyde's payroll had Jello for guts and were scared spitless to do anything that might upset Thomas Abel and put them on his hitlist.

That's why Clyde had bought a scrawny kid I'd never seen before with him. He was the best he could get, some jumped up sixteen-year-old called Frankie, with hair his mother cut for him in their front room. A boy who'd piss his pants if he came up against real trouble.

'You haven't heard?' Clyde snorted, incredulous. 'They think they might have found George O Malley. Well, his finger anyway. Guy was standing outside in his own back yard when some seagull flew down; George's finger in its beak.'

It was like the temperature dropped all around me. Finding a missing body part didn't bode well for finding the rest of him alive.

'How can they know it belongs to George if it's just a finger? Could be anyone's. Jesus, I know plenty of guys who done someone wrong and had their fingers chopped at the knuckle.'

'The commissioner is getting someone from New York to come and take his fingerprint. They say he's wearing a sovereign ring too. Just like those Clarence gave out. Just like the one he gave you.'

He pointed at the gold sovereign on my own finger.

'My point is that it was difficult to get someone to help with this tonight. People are getting scared. First Clarence dies. Then George disappears. Atlantic City is a dangerous place to be a bootlegger.'

I was beginning to lose my patience.

'If you're looking for a bigger tip Clyde, and I know you are,' I said, 'I'll give you one right now.'

His eyes lit up, astounded that persuasion had been so easy.

'You will?'

'Sure. I got this one from Clarence Kelly himself. You know the difference between loyalty and a tiger?'

Clyde shook his head.

'You should never turn your back on either of them.'

I looked him right in the eye as I said it and I handed him his envelope containing the same amount we'd already discussed.

'Now you just leave the crates to me and Elmer here and you worry about finding more men to protect me at the pageant.'

I patted him on the back, and he bristled. I had the upper hand now and he knew it. And I had made him look a sap in front of Frankie in the process. He stood pumping my tires with his words a little longer.

'Sure thing, Milton. I'll have officers round every corner, watching your back. If Thomas even thinks about making a move, my boys'll be on him. I've promised the mayor there'll be no trouble in Atlantic City.'

He thanked me for the money and stuffed it into his pocket and whistled to his boy to follow him.

'Come on Frankie, let's go.' And the two of them got into their car and drove away.

But now the question buzzed round me like a mosquito.

Just how loyal *was* Clyde?

59

CHAPTER FORTY-THREE

✣ ▮▮▮——————●●●——————▮▮ ✣

I hated the storehouse. The cold knifed your bones in the same way
it did in the one we'd had back home. My father would lay out
huge chunks of slaughtered cows in there.

No matter how many times I'd been into the storehouse at Kings, I
still always expected it to have that same animal and blood smell when
I opened the door, only for my nostrils to be surprised by the sweet
oak smell of bourbon.

I could have let Elmer stack the crates by himself, but I didn't
want him to have to go in alone. Loyalty works both ways. Elmer
understands that, even if Clyde doesn't.

The crates were stacked in columns. One false move and you could
knock a whole tower of them to the ground. And that would mean a
lot of wasted shine.

'Go grab us the ladder, will you? Must be round the front, near the
bunting.'

Elmer nodded. I could have waited for him to come back but how
could I explain the reasons for wanting to wait for him? No, if I did
that, I'd look weak. So, I went in without him.

The place was just as cold as I remembered. A cold that chilled your
body to its core. No amount of blowing on hands or rubbing them

would make them feel warm again. I carried my first crate down the aisle towards the gap I could see at the back of the room, but at the end of the crates, something moved.

My heart thudded in my chest. 'Hello. Anyone there?'

No reply.

Slowly I put the crate down and felt for my gun. Reassured to know it was still in my pocket, I walked, quietly as I could, to the end of the aisle and peered around the corner. No one there. Stepping out into the open, my own shadow rose up against me, a giant. The sheer size of it taunting me. It looked like Jesse. A reminder of a life extinguished.

My head swirled. My breathing shallow. This was like Clarence and George all over again. I closed my eyes hoping that when I opened them again the specter would be gone, but when I did, it was still there. So, I raised my gun, aimed it right between where its eyes would've been.

'Milton, you still in here?'

I swung round to see Elmer walking down the aisle towards me.

'It's just me. Put the shooter away.'

He was staring right at the blank wall, right where the shadow had been standing.

'Yeah,' I said. 'Everything's fine.'

I could see in his eyes that something else was wrong. He didn't have the ladder. In his hand was an envelope.

'For god's sake, what is it? It better be good news.'

But I could see from the turned down corners of his mouth, that it was anything but. He started to speak, stumbling over his words and having to restart a couple of times before he eventually spat out what was eating him.

'It's Pearl. She's gone.'

'What do you mean, gone?'

'She came in Kings all wide-eyed and shaky hands, you know. I offered her a drink, but she refused. Said this was goodbye and she weren't coming back. She left this.'

He handed me the envelope, my name on the front in her scrawl, the hotel watermark on the flap on the back.

For a moment I just stared at it, flipping it over in my hands, too incredulous to open it. If I did that, I would be admitting the truth to myself that I didn't want her to leave me, and I didn't have time for sentimentality over some broad who turned out to have been more trouble than she was worth.

Instead, I stuffed it into my trouser pocket, unopened.

'Ain't you even gonna read it?'

I shook my head.

'What else is there to know? Either she'll come back, or she won't.'

'There's something else. She took your dog Champ with her.'

Now that stung. The effort I'd gone to getting that dog. Truth was though, the damn mutt always seemed to like her better than me anyways.

'Look Elmer, all I know is that we got three days until the fall frolic, a trainload of tourists coming into town and a mayor that is going to be fretting over the fact a car has just been bombed. Quite frankly, I don't have the time to be sore about Pearl or Champ right now. I need to get this show up and running and rid of this booze before Officer Brooke comes sniffing back round here again.'

'Right you are, Boss.'

Elmer stubbed out his cigarette and stored what remained behind his ear for later.

'Now go and ring the press. Tell them this pageant is going to be the best damn thing they've ever seen.'

He nodded and walked inside but I lingered in the doorway for a moment longer. I took the envelope out of my pocket. Stroked its edges.

I wish I could have spoken to her in person before she went. I liked having her around. Maybe I'd have tried to make her stay. Now she was roaming around, God knows where, telling all sorts of secrets and lies for all I knew.

I would open the letter after the pageant. There would be time to patch things up with her then.

60

PART FOUR: PEARL'S LETTERS

61

SEPTEMBER 18TH, 1927

❖⊢────•◦•────⊣❖

You know what, Grandma? Houdini's greatest trick wasn't his escapes. It was getting his audience to believe that he was trapped in the first place.

Of course, I knew it was only a matter of time before Milton would turn against me and try to get rid of me.

I'd felt it that day as I'd sat waiting for Eveline and Jesse. That feeling in the pit of my stomach that something wasn't right. I wasn't watching when Jesse curled his fingers around the door handle of his car and pulled. I didn't see the balls of flame burst out from behind him as he pulled the doors open nor see his and Eveline's bodies thrust upwards into the air by the blast. I only heard the ringing in my ears and saw the horror spread across Daphne's face as she took hold of my arm and pulled me down to the ground with her.

From under the table, I saw through the window the plumes of black smoke. Black raindrops of debris fell from the sky onto the sidewalk.

And right then it dawned on me: the explosion hadn't just been for Jesse and Eveline. I should have been getting into that car with them. There's no way Milton could have sent me without knowing I would get caught up in it.

I've been so scared to leave, and he's been lying and plotting to kill me this whole time.

Leaning on the table for support, I pulled myself onto my feet. Daphne sat shaking glass shards from the layers of her dress, perplexed, not yet realizing the enormity of what had happened and that the windows had blown out.

I stood for a moment watching the cops running back and forth like ants to the charred skeleton that had once been Jesse's car.

With hands trembling, partly due to shock and partly due to the realization that Milton wanted me dead, I stepped over the broken glass and walked straight through the blasted window. There wasn't much point leaving through the doorway with most of the shop front having disappeared.

I guess in hindsight, I could have done a lot of things. I have gone straight to the cops, faked my own death or got a train out of there. Instead, I walked, legs like Jello, down the street back to the hotel. I wanted to see the look on Milton's face when I walked back in there, a charred ghost back to haunt him.

In the foyer, Nick the bellboy dashed over to me, 'Are you okay Miss Blanchet?'

I suppose the streaks of soot down my face and on my dress were a little alarming. I could feel the eyes of the patrons at the front desk staring at me.

'I'm fine,' I said calmly and with poise. 'Just call the elevator would you, please.'

When I walked in through the front door of our suite, Milton was gone. The rage I'd been saving up to unleash on him had nowhere to go. At first, I was furious. I'd wanted a final showdown with him before I left but then I realized that this made it the perfect time to leave. Quietly and without fuss.

I knew he wouldn't be back for hours and so I sat down at the dressing table and used the hotel stationary to channel all of my rage into a letter to give to Elmer to pass on.

Then I got changed, packed up my things, put a leash on Champ and left.

Finally, I did it! I am free.

I hope you're proud of me. Of course, the situation with Milton became way more complicated than it should have been, but it doesn't mean that I've forgotten what I came here to do.

I haven't forgotten my promise to you, and I will see it though.

In fact, I already have a plan.

Love always

Pearl

62

SEPTEMBER 20TH, 1927

❖━━━━━━━❖

The Fall Frolic is the highlight of Atlantic City's calendar. It lights the firework of every hedonist who comes in from out of town with its promise of a great time: jazz and cocktails, magicians and cabaret performers, jazz bands on street corners and of course the main highlight: the street parade and bathing beauties contest.

The crowds were already swarming in from the train station. Shoals of revelers pushed past me as I moved against the current, hiding among them with my overnight bag and Champ at my side. I wasn't staying around for the pageant.

I don't know when, or if I'll ever get chance to gather my jazz records and books from the Kelly Mansion. It's not safe to go back. Thankfully, I still have the money saved from the last time I planned to escape.

No matter how much Milton claims in the press that he had nothing to do with the bomb under Jesse's car, my guts tell me he meant to be rid of me that day and he wouldn't hesitate to try again.

I won't let him get the chance. I'll be hiding out for a few days in Princeton on my way home to New York.

Men talk about Princeton like it's the garden of Eden or something, all their talk about lush leafy trees and lofty noble ideals. But even paradise had its snake in the grass, and I'm counting on finding one there that can help me be rid of Milton once and for all.

I never once believed that baloney story of Milton and Clyde's; that Charlie Kelly left for Princeton, and they weren't able to track him down and bring him back. Either he hadn't gone there in the first place, or he didn't want to be found. I assume it's the latter.

I've been here now for two days searching for him. I've been to every college library, every fraternity house and not one person has heard of Charlie Kelly. I've sat at bars in speakeasies pretending I was after a singing gig, hoping to overhear someone talk about him. Kept my ears open in the grocery store. Charlie is nothing if not charismatic, so someone must know if he's here, but I've come away with no leads at all.

I've got to say it's beginning to make me nervous. I've no other plan to fall back on. I've placed all my chips on this one number.

It doesn't help that I'm missing Milton too. I hate to admit it, but the way my body aches for him is worse than any sleeping pill withdrawal. I lie awake at night feeling like I want to scratch my own skin off. I replay memories good and bad like a record on the gramophone. Every day I look in the mirror and remind myself that if I can just get through this one day, tomorrow they'll be another. I'm praying that one day I'll wake up and barely think about him at all.

I was starting to wonder if Charlie really had disappeared when I found a small café with rooms above. It was a quiet place where they don't ask questions. I left Champ in my room and headed downstairs.

I took my cigarette case from my bag and asked the owner, Walter, for a lemon soda and a match.

'I'm killing time before meeting a friend,' I lied.

I gestured to the one table where a young man and his beau were sat sipping drinks and staring into one another's eyes.

'Quiet in here. It always like this?'

He shook his head.

'I guess most have other plans for tonight.'

The vagueness of his answer and uncertainty in his voice begged for more questions.

'A party?'

He nodded.

'There's a blind tiger down the street that opened up in someone's basement. The locals nickname it The Wisteria Club because they say it's a place for social climbers.' He gave a wry smile. 'Looks to me like it's a bunch of boys and girls having a good time on Daddy's trust fund.'

I know in my guts that it's the right place. I gulped down my soda and thanked the man.

If I'm going to find Charlie anywhere in this town, it'll be there.

Love always

Pearl

63

SEPTEMBER 21ST, 1927

❖ ▪▪────•••────▪▪ ❖

Dear Grandma,

I don't know where to begin in telling you the story of what happened tonight.

The Wisteria Club looked more petting party than blind tiger to me. Two couples necking on the front porch.

One girl passed out on the lawn outside, her friend trying her best to bring her round. This was no sleek discreet operation like in Atlantic City. Whoever was running this show was brazen. They didn't care if they were caught. Probably friends and family in high places.

It wasn't difficult for me to get inside. A quick walk round the side of the building and I'd found the green door. The guy who was meant to be checking everyone in was too busy kissing the cute blonde next to him up against the wall. By the time he'd realized someone had slipped past him, I had already reached the bottom of the stairs and had disappeared through the mist of cigarette smoke.

This was no Kings. The furniture was a mix of hand me down sofas, worn tables and stools and used whiskey barrels. The candles in mason jars were the main source of light, shadows flickering against the walls. The worn plaster that had flaked off in places, revealed the bare damp brick underneath. Not that anyone seemed to mind about the state of the place. The jazz band playing in the corner of the room had everyone up and dancing.

I sat down next to a slip of a boy. He was freckle faced with red hair and looked to be barely out of school, let alone college. Behind the bar, a familiar face greeted me.

'Pearl!'

It was Booker.

'Oh, my goodness! What are you doing here? I wondered where you'd moved to.'

'Well, you know I own this place. Well, I'm one of the owners. Still get to tinkle the ivories sometimes too. Shall I get you your usual?'

'You remember it?'

'Of course. A Mayfair.'

I nodded and he turned away to make it.

I nodded at the red-haired boy who sat next to me and took my cigarette case from my bag.

'I'm Pearl. You here all alone?' I said offering him a cigarette. 'Smoke?'

He took one from me and popped it into his mouth, all the time not taking his gaze off Booker, even as he struck the match for us both. He took one long drag before breaking out into the cough of a non-smoker.

'Name's Frankie. I'm waiting for a friend,' he said.

Having used that line myself, I knew he was lying.

'Oh, I'm here hoping to get a gig. I'm a singer.' I said, trying to make conversation.

As Booker reached under the counter to get the bottle of gin, the boy reached into his suit jacket, and I spotted the glint of his handgun.

He looked pretty young to be a dry agent, but they seem to be recruiting them younger and younger nowadays. He was certainly one who was new to the game by the looks of him, or else he wouldn't be so stupid as to take a place down by himself.

As Booker shook my cocktail, oblivious, I snatched the boy's wrist with my hand before he had chance to curl his fingers round the gun.

'Unless you have an entire army of officers backing you up outside, I wouldn't even try it.'

His eyes widened, like he couldn't believe anyone would dare speak to him that way, but he remained frozen to his seat.

'Are you threatening me?' he hissed.

'I'm trying to keep you alive, is what I'm doing,' I said. 'You don't think places like this have guns? Look, I've seen the headlines all over the papers too, men like Moe Smith and Izzy Einstein all making these huge busts. Making all this money. Why wouldn't you want a part of it? I'm telling you; there's a good reason why they take down places in pairs.'

'What would you know about it,' he scoffed.

'Go ahead then,' I said. 'But if you open fire in here, it'll be your funeral.'

Booker had finished pouring my drink and as he turned to bring it over, the boy swigged the last of his drink tossed some notes onto the counter and got up to walk away,

'I think he was a prohi,' I said.

'Really? Oh shoot!'

Booker whistled two long notes and waved in the direction of the band. They nodded to someone in the crowd and the next moment the crowd parted and there he was, dressed in a blazer, his razor cut hair gone and replaced with his chestnut curls brushed forward. He no longer looked like a gangster's son, but he was still unmistakably Charlie Kelly.

So, he was alive! More than alive.

Despite the passion he stirred in me, I also remembered how it ended.

Milton had been pouring poison in my ear for so long, telling me Charlie was no good, that when Charlie walked away, I had no fight in me left. I made no attempt to get him to stay.

I know now everything Milton told me was lies. But it's no matter now. In Charlie's eyes, I'm the one who abandoned him.

I took a deep breath and took a swig of my drink to calm my racing heart as Booker made a gesture to Charlie that I assumed was the signal to say there was trouble. Charlie pushed his way past dancing couples towards the bar and as I swiveled on my stool to face him, his expression darkened.

'Charlie I...'

But before I could start to speak and tell him about the boy who had been there, a girl from the dance floor had broken through the crowd and was tugging at his sleeve.

'Aww Dickie, won't you come back and dance with me?'

He put his arm around her shoulder and steered her away, whispering something into her ear and her smile turned into a pout. She walked away back through the dancing couples and sat herself down at one of the cabaret tables where she sat glaring across at us.

Before I'd even had chance to say anything else, he had gripped my arm and was dragging me away across the room, his head down, ashamed to be seen with a ghost from the past.

'Charlie, look I'm not here to cause any trouble...'

I tried to explain but it was no use.

'Don't call me that name here.'

His voice was low and gruff and completely unlike the boy I had known at Kings. His hand pinched into the flesh at the top of my arm as he frog marched me up to the top of the steps. Once there, he nodded to the guy on the door, who stood back to let us pass through the green door.

Outside, Charlie let go of my arm like it was on fire, but he spoke softly.

'What are you doing here, Pearl? You can't just walk in here after leaving me for someone else and expect me to be all smiles.'

I wanted to tell him about the dry agent at the bar, but I could tell he wasn't about to give me much of his time for very long, so I decided that could wait.

'Look, I know I did wrong. I made some stupid choices and I'm sorry for that. Believe me, I'm so sorry. You've no idea what it's been like.'

I wanted to tell him everything. How I'd been fooled by Milton's charm. How it was all a ruse to take control of me. How I was hurting.

But I wasn't there to get Charlie back. I was there to get him to claim what was rightfully his and should have been as soon as his father passed away.

'I had to find you. I didn't know what else to do. You need to come back with me to Atlantic City.'

He gave a snort.

'You've got to be kidding me. I thought you made it pretty clear when you flaunted Milton in front of me, that we were over Pearl...'

His voice travelled across the lawns in the quiet of the evening so that over on the lawn, two girls turned to look. There were so many things I wanted to explain but I knew he just wouldn't understand.

'This isn't about you and me, Charlie,' I said.

Aware of the girls that were watching us, he took hold of my arm again and this time, more tenderly, he linked his arm through mine and led me across the lawn, away from the partygoers.

'I told you not to call me by that name.'

'Sorry Dickie.'

It sounded so ridiculous, the name he'd given himself. We walked under the rustling leaves of the trees, back towards the college square and its clock tower.

'Where are we going?'

'Somewhere we can talk. Alone. Somewhere no one will find us.'

'You mean see us together.' I could hear the bitterness in my own words.

'In case you'd forgotten, I'm meant to be missing. And the fact you keep calling me Charlie just might raise a few suspicions.'

'You've got Booker working with you. He knows who you are.'

'True. But I know I can trust him.'

Ouch.

He led me up the steps to the clock tower and led me inside, closing the door behind us so we were alone in the dark.

'Keep hold of my hand,' he said. We walked slowly up the stone steps until we reached the beams just below the viewing platform of the bell tower.

From here, the bell hung above us overlooking the whole of Princeton. The moonlight drifted in and fell across Charlie's face and for the first time I realized he wasn't angry after all. He was scared.

'Now do you want to tell me what this is all about?'

'It's about Milton.'

He sighed and shook his head.

Look, Milton can do whatever he likes. We made a deal, Pearl. He runs Kings. Does whatever he likes, takes his cut. And I get to live here. Live the life I always wanted for myself. The life my father didn't want me to have.'

'So, he knows you're here?' He hadn't run away after all. It had been his choice to disappear. No more than a business deal.

Charlie nodded.

'We paid off every cop in town to abandon the search. I didn't want anyone to come after me.'

I knew it. When Charlie left town, if I even spoke his name, Milton punished me with his silence. Sometimes for days.

Any question I asked was met with a smirk and a refusal to answer. If he did answer, it was never the answer I wanted to hear.

'Why would you care? Wherever he is, he obviously doesn't care about you.'

In the end I stopped talking about Charlie altogether.

We sat on the top step, and he pulled out a hip flask.

'Holy water?'

He offered it to me, and I took a gulp. The whiskey burned the back of my throat, and I coughed, the way I always used to when I drank liquor neat.

Charlie laughed. 'Still not got the hang of it I see. It's fresh off the boat, all the way from Canada.'

I handed the flask back to him.

'I don't get you Charlie. You say you don't want to be part of your father's business but you're smuggling whiskey and running speakeasies, just the way he did.'

Charlie shook his head.

'This is different. It's just a bit of fun. No one's dying here. I'm no gangster Pearl. Surely if anyone knows that it's you. Everyone else expects me to be just like my father. Well, my father wouldn't want a son who runs away at the first sign of trouble.'

'Oh, so that's what you're really doing here, running away?'

He stared hard at me. If he wasn't sore at me before, he was now.

'What?' I shrugged. 'They're your words, not mine. And like it or not, you are Charlie Kelly, your father's son. You can run as far as you like but you can't run away from that. And you're certainly not Dickie *or whatever it is you've decided to call yourself. The Kelly name runs through your blood.'*

He sighed. 'I don't want to be a Kelly. I just want to be like everyone else. Why is it, of all people, Milton is the only one who seems to understand that?'

'But don't you see? Milton doesn't care. He never did in the first place. You're a toy to him. Just like I was. And Milton never looks after his toys; he wants them to break. Because when you're broken, he can take everything from you, whilst simultaneously pretending to fix everything. While you're here with your head in the clouds, he's razing your birthright to the ground.'

'I was upset, Pearl. My father had just died. You'd left me. I wasn't thinking straight.'

I put my arm around his shoulders, and he nuzzled into me. I'd forgotten how good it felt to feel the warmth of a man who made you feel safe.

'There's no point dwelling on it. It can't be undone,' I said. 'But I'm sorry for everything. Just hear me out for a moment. You remember the feud between your father and the Abels? Well, Milton has made it ten times worse.'

He pulled away.

'You're not listening to me Pearl. I don't want gunfights and feuds. I don't want to turn into some greedy bitter angry old man.'

I took his hand in mine and gave it a reassuring squeeze.

'No one says you have to.'

We held one another close. Two broken toys convinced they could mend one another. I placed my lips on his and kissed him hard. His hand slid slowly up my dress and along my thigh, his breathing heavy and quick, my heart pounding in time with his.

Over in the distance, past the campus and across the lawns a cop car was pulling up at the Wisteria Club. The drunken girls on the lawn did their best to stand but they were handcuffed before they could toss their bottles into the bushes. The officers marched in single file through the green door, the doorman with the lipstick marked mouth pushed up against the wall whilst they tipped tables and smashed barrels.

But we couldn't hear anything except the beating of our own hearts, our bodies entangled, camouflaged by the shadow of the bell above us.

***

*'Y*ou know, the view from here really is something,' I said af-terwards, standing in the archway that overlooked the town, cigarette smoldering in my hand.*

'Yeah, it is.'

His answers were clipped, and I tried to figure out if it was out of shame, regret or something else, but he wasn't giving anything away.

I crushed the tip of my cigarette against the brick.

'So, I've been dying to ask, who's the girl?'

'What girl?' He took a swig from his hipflask.

'The one back at the club who was so keen to dance with you?'

'Annie? Oh, nobody.'

'She sure looked like somebody to me. And you know her name too so that's a step up from where you were in Atlantic City when I met you.'

He smiled then. The ice had thawed.

'She's just a girl who lives nearby. A judge's daughter, if you can believe it.'

Of course, she was. She was the embodiment of everything Charlie was trying so hard to be: wholesome, respectable, moral. I almost felt bad about being there persuading him to come back but if he thought he really belonged there, he was very much mistaken.

I used to see it all the time with you, Grandma. Those men in high places, their cookie cutter, ringlet wearing wives at home whilst they partied with whiskey drinking, bobbed haired starlets they claimed to find so morally offensive. The one who sat in stranger's rooms, talking late into the night; that was the real man, not the one back at home.

It was getting late. The bell would soon be sounding eleven. I laid it out plain for him.

'I meant what I said about Milton and the Abels. If you don't intervene and claim what's yours, the Abels will kill Milton and take Kings from under your nose. And when they do you can bet your bottom dollar, they won't be funding no basement speakeasy without you earning your keep. This 'lifestyle' of yours will be dust and you'll be in their pocket over your own birthright Charlie.'

Charlie shook his head. 'I told you, I ain't coming back there.'

'Suit yourself.' I turned to go and then remembered. 'Oh, you might want to know, George has gone missing.'

'He has?'

I nodded.

'There's no body yet but he's dead for sure. Jesse too.'

'Jesse? Who whacked Jesse?'

'I told you; Milton has all lost control. Of himself and of his...' I corrected myself, your family's business.'

He took a long gulp from his hipflask this time, mulling things over in his mind. I wasn't sure if it would make him come back or dissuade him even further.

Out across the horizon there were flashes of lightning cracking the sky, only there was no wind. No rain. Charlie came to stand next to me to get a better look and suddenly reality dawned on him.

'Oh god, that's my place. Its gunfire.'

He took the steps down two by two, stumbling down in the darkness.

'Wait for me!'

I called out after him but there was no holding hands on the way down. He was already running across the lawns by the time I made it to the bottom of the stairs. I chased after him.

The group of girls who'd been passed out on the lawn were headed towards us, all of them sobered up by the shock of their situation. One of them held a bloodied handkerchief to her brow and was shaking and crying as her friend put her arm around her to hold her up and keep her walking.

'What happened?' Charlie accosted them.

'The place got raided,' one of them said. 'Grace here, got caught up in the ruckus. The cops are arresting people.'

My stomach dropped.

'I'm so sorry, Charlie. I meant to tell you straight away at the club. Me and Booker caught this guy there who we thought was a prohi.'

'Why didn't you say something? Come on, let's go.'

He walked across the lawn so quickly that it was hard for me to keep up.

'Charlie, will you slow down? We can't just go busting in there. We don't even know if it is the cops in there. That could be anyone shooting the place up.'

He didn't answer. Just charged on ahead and I hung back a while pretending to fix my stocking while I removed my pistol from my garter and slipped it into my handbag. If it was the guy from the bar, I had already seen the pistol he had. And if it wasn't him? Well, I guessed we might need some protection.

The cops had gone by the time we arrived. Booker was nowhere to be seen. Someone said they'd seen him being taken away in handcuffs and the pool of blood across the bar suggested there had been quite a struggle.

'Damn fool,' Charlie said. 'He should have known better than to fight them.'

It looked like he wasn't the only one to have put up a fight. The place was a mess. Tables upturned. Stools broken. And importantly, bottles of gin and the barrels behind the bar confiscated and smashed up with axes and hammers, pools of alcohol seeping into the floorboards.

'Dickie! Where have you been?'

Annie came running over to us, her voice and hands trembling.

'Annie, are you okay? How many did the cops arrest?'

'Oh, these weren't cops,' Annie said. 'They said they wanted me to tell you that they were sent by Thomas Abel.'

The enormity of the situation hit him right between the eyes. I could read the fear on his face.

It had been a stupid idea to try and bring him back. Charlie was right: he's no gangster. He's too scared to fight for what is his. He doesn't want it anyway. He is exactly where he should be, and I should have left him well alone.

I'm the one who belongs in Atlantic City: tarnished gold, swept up in hedonism brights lights and bad men.

I walked away leaving him with Annie cradled in his arms, telling her everything would be alright, when I knew it was nothing of the sort.

Back in my hotel room, Champ lay on the bed while I dialed the number Nancy had given me. I had my whole speech planned out. How as much as I wanted to do good and lock Milton away, it wasn't safe for me to go back.

I wouldn't tell her about Charlie. If he wanted to stay in Princeton and live an anonymous life, the least I could do is respect his decision.

As fate would have it, no one picked up the phone. Not Nancy. Not Jay. Not even Clyde.

No one to warn about the trouble coming to Atlantic City.

Love always

Pearl

PART FIVE: MILTON'S CONFESSION

✣ ▮▬▬▮▮▬▬▮ ✣

'I mean, all I have to say is that in this game, there's never really anyone you can trust.'

Milton Costello, *The Atlantic City Tribune*, Sept 29th, 1927

CHAPTER FORTY-FOUR

The day of the pageant, the air practically fizzed with champagne and ritz. All the pretty broads dressed in their finest and lined up ready to promenade and wave at the gathered crowd. I almost wished Pearl had been there to see it.

It was two o'clock and the procession was about to start. I was walking up and down the float, rehearsing my speech and swishing my trident through the air. Only days ago, I'd been uncertain about, well everything, but now, I knew no one could hurt me and that I was invincible, I didn't worry about anything too much. I knew I would always come out on top.

When I heard the marching band clash their cymbal to signal the beginning of the parade, I took my position beside one of the wave shaped cut outs and looked back and nodded at Elmer. He was hidden amongst the scenery for protection purposes. He nodded back and gave me a flash of the gun he had inside his jacket, and I was reassured.

The marching band moved off with the first four contestants in their swimsuits and sashes walking delicately behind, waving to the gathered crowd.

The sun was out, everything was swell, and I knew the event would make the papers. I made sure to play my part, striding up and down the float, shaking my trident at the cheering crowd.

As I passed Clyde and his family, he waved at me a little too eagerly. I gave him a wink and a nod, but Clyde looked scared spitless. He pushed through the crowd to shout to me.

I shrugged at him. 'I can't hear you.'

Frustrated at me not being able to get his meaning, he left his family's side and ran alongside us.

'It's the Abel girl.' He shouted over the din. 'She's dead.'

He couldn't keep up with us and fell back, rejoining his wife and kids. His words slowly sunk in. If what he said was true and Thomas Abel's niece really had died, then the truce between me and the Abels would be null and void. They'd be coming for me.

I waved at the children in the crowd and posed as we passed by the newshawks and photographers, smiling a cardboard smile. Despite knowing I was invincible, my pulse quickened. Every spectator in the crowd that surged towards us had me itching to reach for my gun.

I tried to catch Elmer's eye to tell him the bad news, but he was too busy waving at the crowd.

'Elmer!' I yelled. 'Elmer, you chump!'

Next thing, someone in the crowd called my name.

'Milton! Give us a wave.'

The bulb flashed and standing next to the photographer, the girl from Zelda's grinned up at me, a bouquet of white lilies in her hands. A funeral posy.

Above the noise of the band someone shouted out.

'He's got a gun!'

The crowd dispersed, screaming and I knew straight away that the shooter was there for me. I dropped to the floor as shots rang through the air.

With blood buzzing in my ears, I rolled across to the opposite side of the float and jumped down onto the ground. The outline of the gunman disappeared into the crowd as he ran along the boardwalk. He was headed for the boat I could see coming in at the port at the other end.

Even with my leg the way it is, I still gave chase. Pulling my gun out, ready to take him out, I followed after him, pushing my way through the handful of tourists who remained. I heard a voice behind me and turned to see Elmer behind me. The shots had missed him too, thank God.

The boat was drawing in closer, and we both exchanged a look, knowing that we didn't have long before he would be on that boat and on the way out of there.

We both ran after him, people screaming as they spotted the shooters in our hands. When we reached the edge of the boardwalk the guy had taken a bunk.

I looked around frantically.

No sign of him anywhere.

Where was Clyde when you needed him? Where was the law? Something felt hinky about the whole thing.

'Elmer, I think we need to go. We need to get out of here. Now.'

'What?'

'I think it's a ruse. If he'd have wanted to hit us there, he would have. The shooter's just bait. They want to get us both up here, out in the open. They're coming for us.'

Panicked, I looked around and thought I saw a flash of William Abel's face in the crowd that remained.

Elmer saw him too and aimed his gun and shot him dead.

A woman screamed and the crowd scattered, revealing his brother Thomas standing there, gun raised back, face red with fury.

Thomas shot first but the bullet skimmed over us and flew overhead. The next part all happened so fast that neither me nor Elmer even saw which direction the second bullet came from but the next I knew there was a bullet tearing into Elmer's chest as he stood next to me.

The gun fell from his hands as his knee buckled beneath him.

There was no time to waste. No time for last words. I ran as fast as I could to the edge of the pier, all the time shots firing off around me like fourth of July firecrackers.

Using all my strength I lifted myself over the barrier and jumped. My legs and arms flailed, floppy as a ragdoll. The fall was over in seconds but felt like hours. When my body hit the hard surface of the sea, I thought my bones had shattered.

Whilst I was in the water, the papers said Thomas strolled over to Elmer calmly and that by some miracle, Elmer was still breathing, lying like a fish on his side gasping for air. As Thomas walked towards him, Elmer summoned the last bit of strength from inside of him and pulled out his gun. With the crack of a bullet and a flash of fire, Thomas Abel's last breath left his body, and he fell to the floor and died right next to Elmer.

Beneath the pier, I clung to one of the iron supports, coughing up sea water as Elmer and Thomas' blood dripped down between the slats of wood above. The air filled with sirens, and footsteps stampeded across the boardwalk above my head. I could hear the familiar voices of Officer Brooke and Officer Simpson.

'I swear we had Milton here a second ago. Where the hell did he go?'

66

CHAPTER FORTY-FIVE

❖ ▪▪───••───▪▪ ❖

T he problem with prohis (aside from the fact they want to arrest me for giving people what they want) is that they think they're different to us. They seem to think that they live by some sort of moral code superior to ours.

And sure, perhaps my idea of what's moral may differ to them somewhere along the line, but there's a whole lot of values that we share too: loyalty, family, justice to name just a few. When Jay Brooke came jumping in the sea, right after me that day of the pageant, I'm sure he thought he was doing it for all the right reasons, whatever those were.

His buddies weren't so quick to follow though. The law always think they have the upper hand, but the second Brooke left his buddies behind he made us more evenly matched. We both drank out of the same bottle now.

Then there's the issue of territory. He was swimming up into that cave under Kelly & Sons not thinking how this was my territory he was coming into. I know where every gun is hidden. Which barrel holds whiskey and which holds dynamite. And other things besides.

I guess it's kind of poetic thinking about it: how the beginning of my end started there, in the same place I first defended George O

Malley that time. How that one action of killing weasel had made me rise up to where I am now.

I sat behind one of the barrels, clothes dripping salt water all over the floor, peering between the gaps. Brooke lifted himself out of the water. As soon as he was on solid ground it was like he suddenly became aware of his naivety in the situation and took the gun from his holster, brandishing it at any corner where he heard a sound in the darkness.

A boy with a flaming sword.

I knelt in the dark, grinning from ear to ear like a cat watching a mouse walk towards its open jaws. I reached down for my own gun, but my holster was empty. What the hell? I patted down my pockets. Nothing. Searched the floor with my hand in the dark but it was gone.

I must have lost it when I jumped over the side of the pier.

Now I admit this did change the stakes a little. I was either going to have to disarm him or run. As he drew nearer to the barrel I was hiding behind, I took my chance and I lunged out and slugged him hard in the guts, knocking the wind out of him enough to bring him to his knees. Damn copper still kept a tight grip on that revolver though.

He aimed it in the dark and fired one shot that sped past my ear and ricocheted off the wall and into one of the barrels, whiskey pouring out all over the floor.

It wasn't worth trying to fight. I ran to the stairs as a second shot rang out. The next thing I felt was the searing pain of the bullet tearing into my bicep. I fell against the wall, clutching my bleeding arm whilst Brooke was getting on his feet.

Using the wall to support me I slid along, my arm leaving behind a pulpy trail along the bricks. I found the stairwell and with the last burst of energy I had in me I climbed those steps to the door I knew would lead to the drugstore. If I could just make it there, I might have a chance of surviving.

I pushed against the door once. Twice. A third time and it opened just as Brooke appeared at the bottom of the steps.

I stumbled over to the soda counter, fumbling for the rifle I knew was strapped underneath, but as I reached for it, my vision mottled yellow. My arm was bleeding profusely now and before I could take hold of the gun, everything went black.

67

CHAPTER FORTY-SIX

When I came round, Brooke was standing over me, gun barrel staring me right in the kisser.

'There's nowhere else to run Milton,' he said. 'The game's up. All your men are dead. It's just you and me.'

My arm hurt so bad I couldn't bring myself to answer back.

'You know, those barrels down there, there's not so many. If you want to talk, we could perhaps carve out a deal. You'd get a lesser sentence.'

I managed a laugh. 'A lesser sentence? And be a rat. No thanks.'

He took the safety off. 'I know you killed George O Malley. Your buddy Jesse and his girl. What makes you think I won't shoot you here and now?'

I managed a grin. 'Because you're a boy scout. You want the newshawks to take my picture to put in the papers alongside your name. You want the medals and the promotions. You want what you call justice but there's one problem with that.'

'What's that?'

'You have no evidence. Where's George's body? You don't have it. Everyone knows you coppers haven't a clue.'

'That doesn't matter. I have information. Someone who has a detailed knowledge of all of your business interests.'

A rat. A goddamned rat! He had to be yanking my chain, but I could see from his smug face that he wasn't. He was deadly serious and still talking.

'The informant doesn't matter so much now anyway. That scene you just pulled out on the pier is more than enough for me to take you in.'

'On what grounds? I didn't fire a single shot. You ask witnesses, Elmer was the one firing the gun. He shot Thomas Abel, not me.'

He thought about it for a moment and knew I was right.

Brooke's hopes for that medal were fading. He knew it and I knew it. All he had on me were a few barrels of whiskey. And most of those were classed as 'medicinal' thanks to George.

'But you know, I guess you're right. The game is up,' I said. 'For you.'

I leaned across and snatched the rifle, bringing it swinging upwards to crack him across the jaw. Whilst he was still reeling from the blow, I stood up and smacked him once more for good measure, forcing him to drop his revolver. I kicked it to one side as far out of reach as possible. Now it was me pointing the gun at his head.

'Get down on your knees.'

It's funny how all the bravado seeps out of someone when there's a gun pointing at their temple. Brooke knelt down, sniveling something about his wife and kids.

'I'm not interested in your family,' I said. 'But I am interested in who the rat is that claims I killed George.'

'I can't tell you,' Brooke shook his head.

'Oh, come on Brooke. You've got a gun pointing at your head. You're going to die here, with no chance of saying goodbye to Mrs.

Brooke and the little ones, unless you tell me that name. You don't want your kids to grow up without their daddy, do you?'

He shook his head. 'No, no of course not.'

'Well, then tell me. Who's the rat?'

I pulled back the safety catch to make it more real for him but I was shocked at how quickly he crumbled. I thought he was the untouchable one, but I was wrong.

'Okay, okay, I'll tell you. It's Pearl. It's Pearl.'

My heart was a furnace.

Not Pearl. Anyone but her.

The love of my life had betrayed me in the very worst way. Maybe it was the blood loss, maybe it was the shock, but the whole room lurched around me like I was trapped in the center of a fairground ride.

Brooke lay at my feet sniveling. As hurtful as it was, it was better knowing the truth. I nodded to show I understood.

'Thank you, Officer Brooke, that's all I needed to know.'

Then I pushed the barrel of the gun right against the bone of his temple and pulled the trigger.

68

Chapter Forty-Seven

❧ ⊷————•••————⊶ ❧

My ears still rang from the shot when the footsteps came towards me, unheard. They stopped next to where I lay slumped against the doorframe, the black leather shoes polished and shiny.

The pain of the bullet lodged in my arm caused me to drift in and out of consciousness, and at first when I heard him call my name, it sounded like his voice was floating above me, ethereal.

Only this weren't no angel. It was Clyde.

'Milton, can you hear me? Oh Jesus Christ!'

I don't know if the blasphemy was at the sight of my own shirt, soaked crimson or the sight of the crater in Brooke's brain and the blood that pooled beneath him.

In too much pain to speak, I grabbed the hem of his trousers, twisting the material in my hands to pull myself up from the ground. The blood loss meant I was just too weak to stand, and I collapsed back down again on the cold tiles.

In the distance, wagon sirens screamed. It wouldn't be long until the rest of the flatfoots turned up and when they did, I would really be behind the eight ball.

Clyde stared down at me, making no attempt to help me up.

'What the hell happened here, Milton?'

But there was no sense of urgency in his voice.

'Clyde, what are you doing just standing there? You got to help me!' I managed to croak.

Anyone else might think I was talking about getting a doctor or surgeon for my arm but not Clyde. He knew exactly what I meant. He could hear the slamming of car doors, and raised voices coming, just as well as I could.

'I mean, I don't know Milt. You know what they say about tigers and loyalty.'

So, this was what it was all about. He was throwing my own words at me, sore that I'd made him feel a chump. I swear he was smirking as he spoke.

'You've killed an officer of the law. A fine one at that. The cost of this, well, it's hard to put a number on it.'

Only Clyde could see this as an opportunity to get the jack he thought he was owed. The shadows of officers were outside now. I could see their silhouettes through the glass. Now one of them was slamming his body against the door, trying to bust it open.

'The money doesn't matter Clyde. Name your price.'

He grinned. He had me in the palm of his hand and we both knew it.

'George O Malley.'

'I don't know anything about George.'

Clyde shrugged. 'Suit yourself. But do you know what I've spent the last few months doing since they blocked me from that case? Patrolling the boardwalk. Reinforcing traffic laws. You give me George O Malley's dead body, and I'll be a hero. I'll get my old job back and I'll make sure you don't get the chair. I can't say fairer than that.'

The door burst open, and they all swarmed in, five or six officers; one of them was that woman Simpson who came to the house. She was another bluenosed cookie-making girl scout, just like Brooke had been. It was in the way she walked, hair pulled back into a bun, her lips pursed like she was sucking lemons.

One of the flatfoots spotted Brooke lying dead on the floor and that's when all hell broke loose as the great big bimbo came at me, face screwed up in anger, fists flying.

'Why you son of a bitch!'

Clyde didn't even try to stop him. He let him crack me one, right in the jaw.

I guess Clyde was making his point. He could protect me if I paid him. If I didn't, then this was the sort of treatment I'd get.

When the bimbo raised his fist to sock me another, Simpson barked the order for the others to drag him off me.

'That's enough.'

In the corner of the room, the coppers let go of the bimbo who'd hit me, leaving him pacing like a bear to calm down.

Simpson stood over me, hands on hips.

'I don't know if you remember me, Milton. Names Nancy Simpson. I've had my eye on you for some time. I always thought we'd lock you away on tax evasion or bootlegging though, not murder.'

She looked over at the body of her dead partner and swallowed hard. No wonder she didn't stop the guy from hitting me. Probably wanted to sock me herself.

Clyde's voice broke through.

'It was the girl.'

Simpson turned to look at him.

'Which girl? And what the hell are you doing here Wilson?'

She nodded towards his polo shirt and slacks.

'I was at the parade with my family, off duty. I followed Milton here after the shoot out on the pier, but I got here too late. There was a woman here too. Pearl Blanchet's her name. And when I arrived, she'd already shot Officer Brooke dead. Milton here, tried to stop her from getting away and got a bullet in the arm for his trouble.'

What was Clyde doing? Trying to frame Pearl now?

Simpson looked down at the brown patch growing through the material on my arm. He clearly wasn't lying about me being shot but getting her to believe Pearl was behind it all, well, that would be more difficult.

'And why would Pearl do something like that?'

Clyde kept quiet on this one. He looked at me for an answer. He wasn't going to frame her all by himself. Either I went along with his crazy story, or I sentenced myself to death.

'Because she had just found out that I had been double crossing her, that's why,' I said. 'I was Brooke's informant.'

She looked confused. 'He never mentioned anything about you that ever made me think...'

'Why would he?' I butted in before she had time to mull it over.

'I'd been informing Officer Brooke about the business interests she kept. It was never me running the show. It was all her. If you worked so closely with him, he must have mentioned he had someone?'

'He did but...it couldn't have been you.'

Coppers never tell anyone else they work with the names of their informants in case the information is leaked. Clyde once told me that, and now that seemingly useless bit of information was working in my favor.

'Who do you think double crossed me and set me up on the pier tonight, trying to get me killed?'

'He's lying!' the bimbo who socked me shouted from the corner of the room.

She shushed him quiet.

'It's rather convenient that the only person to verify that what you're saying is true, happens to be dead, don't you think?'

'I know you don't believe me, and that's fine, but why would Officer Wilson here, lie?'

She looked at Clyde and he nodded.

'Pearl told us both that she murdered George O Malley, isn't that right Milton?'

There it was. The golden egg Clyde had laid for himself. Now there was no going back.

'Well, take him in for questioning, I guess.' She gestured to Clyde, still suspicious.

Clyde leaned in, handcuffs at the ready, a twinkle in his eye. He must have been waiting his entire life to get me cornered like this.

I closed my eyes and leaned back against the doorframe as the cold metal bracelets snapped around my wrists. No one makes a fool of Milton Costello. No one.

The more I thought about it the more I grew to like Clyde's plan.

If Pearl had betrayed me by ratting me out to Brooke, what better way to get revenge than frame myself as the rat and her as the criminal. She wasn't ever coming back to Atlantic City because if she did, I would be waiting for her.

And even if she never came back, this idea of Clyde was a great way to get revenge. It was bloodless, clean and I wouldn't have to lay a finger on her.

As Clyde helped me into the back of the wagon I leant in and whispered.

'If we're going to do this, we need to do it properly. Search the house. They'll be her sleeping pills in the bathroom. Check the drawers in the desk in the dining room too for letters, diaries; anything we can leak to the press that frames her in a bad light.'

Did I feel bad about it, throwing her to the wolves? She was the one who lit the touch paper in me, the day she left.

Now I knew she was a rat too, and filthy lying rats deserve to be caught.

69

PART SIX: PEARL'S LETTERS

70

SEPTEMBER 27TH, 1927

Well Grandma, they say revenge is a dish best served cold, but I think we'd both agree its best served piping hot. You just have to be careful not to burn yourself.

And as I lay on the bed in my room, with Champ lay next to me I tried not to think about the scene I'd witnessed of Charlie with his arms wrapped around Annie. I had been careless. My own plans against Milton had failed and seeing Charlie with someone else scalded. I hadn't wanted anyone's heart to get caught in the crossfire. All I'd ever wanted was to get back at Milton.

If you'd have seen the look Annie shot me! I knew I'd outstayed my welcome. She was right, of course. No matter how much Charlie claimed she meant nothing to him, I could see in the way she held him that he meant the world to her. As usual I had strolled in where I wasn't wanted, leaving a trail of mess in my wake.

I'll get over losing Charlie. I know by now, I'm more comfortable with things ending this way. I was just going to have to face facts that I had failed in putting Milton behind bars, as hard as that was to admit to myself.

Next morning came and I must have tried calling Nancy fifteen times with no answer. Something was desperately wrong. I knew it. Dread curled in the pit of my stomach like a viper, biding its time before getting ready to strike.

I packed my case, put on my best coat and walked down the stairs with Champ to find Walter and his boys gathered around the wireless. When they saw me approach, Walter quickly switched it off.

'Oh, don't turn it off on account of me gentlemen. I'm just going to pay my way and go.'

Walter got up from the table.

'Forgive me Miss but it's not easy listening for a young lady such as yourself.'

I smiled. 'Honestly, don't mind me. Please switch it back on.'

One of the guys did as I asked, and Walter followed me to the counter whilst I counted out notes from my purse. The news announcement blared out:

'Atlantic City revelers are still reeling after yesterday's massacre at the annual Fall Frolic event. Four men were shot dead during the parade and were named as local businessmen Thomas and Wiliam Abel, Elmer Clinton and Officer Jay Brooke who was caught in the crossfire as he heroically gave chase....'

Jay was dead. It couldn't be true. And yet I heard it clear as a bell on the wireless.

'Are you okay Miss?

'I'm fine,' I said but I sat down anyway.

'I'll get you a brandy.'

As he poured my drink, there was more news to come.

'The annual fall frolic parade and bathing beauties pageant was cancelled and organizer of this year's pageant, Milton Costello, is being questioned by police on suspicion of murder...'

I swear Grandma, I didn't know whether to laugh or cry. I couldn't believe it. Milton was finally behind bars.

I downed my shot and left a pile of notes on the counter.

'Thanks for everything,' I said to Walter.

But Walter was looking over my shoulder.

'You here for the lady?'

I turned and there in the middle of the aisle between the rows of plastic tables and chairs stood Charlie, his chestnut hair unbrushed, shirt still on from the night before. All traces of 'Dickie' were gone. All that was left was authentic, flawed Charlie and I've never loved him as much as I did right then.

'I came to give you a ride to the station.'

He picked up my case, oblivious to the thoughts running through my mind.

'Have you heard? Milton's been arrested.'

He planted a kiss on my forehead and led me and Champ out of there, leaving the men to sit around the wireless blaring out dancehall music. We walked together to his car, and I noticed the boxes and clothes piled up on the backseat. It looked like Charlie was leaving town, but I didn't have the guts to ask him outright.

Charlie never drove slowly, but he did that day. Every now and then he opened his mouth slightly as if he was going to speak but then he thought better of it.

'If you got something to say Charlie, just spit it out, will you?'

'It's just I can't believe you were going to go without even saying goodbye.'

He shook his head, his ego bruised.

I shrugged.

'Well, seemed like you had your hands full already. Besides, looks to me like you have the same idea. Does Annie even know you've gone?'

He shook his head.

'I already told you there wasn't anything serious between me and her. I knew it wouldn't last. She saw a little bit of trouble last night and she's gone already. She left with the sunrise, if you must know.'

'Look, I'm sorry Charlie if I muddied the waters there. I didn't mean for anything to happen between us.'

He sighed.

'But it did. God damn it Pearl, it always does. Sometimes I think if things between us had ended differently; if Milton hadn't arrived and put a wedge between us, maybe things would have been different. Me leaving town, isn't about you or Annie. It's about me facing up to myself.'

I stopped him before he could go any further.

'Look Charlie, I made a lot of mistakes. I should have been there for you when your father died.'

'It's okay.'

'It's not. Thing is, when we were together you treated me just the same way as you treated Annie, back there. You made me feel like you always had one foot out of the door, looking for the next best thing. I know you hated me being a singer. I'm hardly marriage material. Not like a judge's daughter.'

'I never said I wanted marriage material.'

'Well, what about college? Have you just turned your back on that too?'

'I can't go back now. Not after last night now I know it wasn't the Abels.'

'But I thought Annie said it was?'

'You heard the news. The Abels were shot dead yesterday afternoon. How could they have given orders if they were already lying dead in the morgue?'

He had a point. And just as the realization hit me, we both said it out loud.

'It must have been Milton.'

Now I saw the quiet rage that had built in him in the way he gripped the steering wheel, overtaking recklessly. It was in his elongated silences. But this wasn't like Milton's silences that were dealt as punishments. Charlie's silences were to protect me from the fury that burned inside of him that he didn't want me to witness.

It had taken long enough but Charlie had finally realized that he'd been taken for a fool and that Milton had manipulated him just as he did with everyone he met. He'd thought the arrangement he'd gotten with Milton meant he'd got the cat's share of the cream, when in fact he'd been given a sour deal and kept out of the way so Milton could position himself to take over completely.

I put my hand on his thigh to reassure him and eventually he spoke.

'I've been thinking about what you said and about what happened last night. I'm going to stop running. I'm tired of it. I'm going back to Atlantic City to loosen Milton's grip on what's rightfully mine.'

I'm not sure why but the words of a confession were on the tip of my tongue. I was ready to tell him everything: about my past with you, Grandma. How me and George fed information to the coppers to blow the whole bootlegging business apart. He had a right to know if he was going to be picking up where Milton left off. I wasn't scared of showing him who I was anymore.

'Look Charlie. I have a confession to make. Truth is, I'm not who I say I am.'

But he didn't understand my meaning.

'Hell, are any of us who we say we are? Look Pearl, what's past is past. What matters is that despite everything, you still cared enough to find me and persuade me to step up, even when I didn't want to hear it. If

you don't want to come back to Atlantic City, then I'll accept that. That's your choice. I know you don't like to feel tied to anyone.'

Another silence hung in the air. I didn't know what to say. What to think.

I hadn't planned on returning but part of me wanted to see if this thing with Charlie could work this time. I also felt cheated that Milton had been locked up by someone else, not me, and I couldn't resist the idea of going to visit him in jail to see him one last time. Sometimes, the thirst for revenge makes you do things you know are going to hurt, but you do them anyway.

'Who said I wasn't coming back to Atlantic City?' I gave Charlie's leg a squeeze and he smiled.

'Well, if that's the case we're definitely going to need more gas.'

He gestured to the needle on the fuel gauge that hovered just above empty.

'There's a map in the glove compartment. See where the next gas station is.'

I took it out and opened it out across my lap.

'I guess there's Trenton.'

But Charlie wasn't listening. He wasn't even paying attention to where we were going, staring intently into the rear-view mirror.

'What is it?'

'It's nothing.'

But I could tell it wasn't nothing. I turned around in my seat to take a look. Behind us a Maroon Ford T took a right turn and disappeared down a side street.

'They've gone now,' Charlie said.

'Relax,' I said. 'The Abels and Milton are gone now. Who else could be possibly gunning for you?'

But words weave spells you don't ask for. And I he was certain someone was tailing us.

Trenton couldn't have been more different to Princeton. Gone were the lush, manicured gardens and the sweet tweeting of the birds. Instead, the air hummed with the rhythmic cacophony of rich languages spoken, the growl of the steelworks furnace and the repetitive beat of hammer on steel. Dust floated down in the air like dull fireflies, streaking the windows of grocery shops that lined the street. Through the gloom blinked the soft neon glow of the town's slogan: 'the world takes - Trenton makes.'

In the center of everything sat an old gas station, as though the town had sprung up around it and the building itself couldn't summon the energy to bother shutting up shop and closing down.

The attendant sat in his wicker chair, looking as old and weary as the gas station itself, one oil-stained hand holding an air trumpet towards the blaring wireless he had on the floor next to him. He was the sort of client you and the girls used to call a 'working man'; someone stinking of grease and sweat from working so hard to make ends meet, that they couldn't care anything about their own appearance.

As soon as we pulled up next to the pump he got up from his chair and ambled over.

'Well, ain't this the bee's knees?' he whistled at the car the way some men whistle approval at a woman. Yes, Sirree, she's a real beauty.'

He was practically shouting he was so deaf.

What with the old man yelling and the wireless blaring out, it was difficult to focus on what either one was saying. Charlie, eager to chat about cars to someone who actually cared, got out of the car to talk some more.

The voice came out of the wireless like an apparition at a seance.

'...the body found in the barrel beneath the boardwalk has been confirmed as that of George O Malley, found with one finger removed from his right hand...'

I looked at Charlie, who had drifted across the forecourt with his newly found friend to see the old man's car collection but he made no reaction. He hadn't heard the news.

I guess it's not so much of a surprise to hear George was dead. I'd half expected it. It just hurt to hear the words said out loud. What I didn't expect was the announcement that came next.

'...law enforcement officers would like to talk to Miss Pearl Blanchet in connection with his disappearance and are offering a substantial reward for any information on her whereabouts. It's believed she may be heading towards the town of Princeton. Members of the public are warned not to approach her but to contact Officer Clyde Wilson of the Atlantic City Police Department...'

At first, I thought I'd misheard. I mean, I'm innocent of killing George. Milton is the guilty one.

Thing is, if Clyde is in charge of the case, it already makes it an unfair fight. The whole thing reeks of the sort of corruption Milton would be only too happy to pay for. I'd embarrassed him by walking out, and I should have known he would want his revenge for that.

Hot or cold, he won't care how his revenge is served as long as it's my head on the plate and not his.

Love always

Pearl

71

THE ATLANTIC CITY TRIBUNE

ATLANTIC CITY SONGBIRD SNARED

'Ain't no sweetheart in the world worth going to the chair for.' So says Milton Costello upon hearing the news that his fiancé Pearl Blanchet has finally been caught by officers just outside Princeton, following a twenty-four-hour pursuit.

Both Milton Costello and his beau are accused of the murder of friend and business associate George O Malley, whose body was discovered beneath the Atlantic City Boardwalk only days ago.

Little is known about the sweet-faced songbird, struck dumb as she waits to be transferred to the county jail. Described by Milton Costello as a woman with loose morals and a love of sleeping pills and liquor, the two lovebirds are accusing one another of committing the murder. When asked if their impending marriage was likely to go ahead, Milton was adamant it would not.

'Why, course not? How could I sleep at night with a murderess lying next to me?'

72

SEPTEMBER 29TH, 1927

❦⸺••⸺❦

Dear Grandma,

I always dreamed of you seeing my name in the papers like you said you would one day, but I never dreamed it would be like this.

Back when I was with Milton, when days were tough, I used to think of you sitting in the parlor in your negligee, cigarette holder in one hand, and imagine you telling the punters all about your little songbird making it in Hollywoodland.

Now that name 'Songbird' haunts me.

I know if you were here, you'd tell me to stop crying, get up off the floor and fight back.

'Talk to the newshawks,' you'd say. But I haven't got the ritz like Beulah Annan, no matter what the papers say.

Milton must have found my letters and diaries back home and has been leaking details to the press in an effort to defame me. He thinks his quips about the songbird being caged are funny, but they say I'll be joining murderess row.

They've already made their minds up about me so what is there to say?

Milton won and I lost.

The sheriff bought me this paper and pen to write my confession whilst they wait for the authorities from Atlantic City to get here. He said I'll get a lesser sentence if I do that. He doesn't believe I'm innocent either.

I'm aware you don't know quite how I ended up here, so I'll explain to you exactly what happened in Trenton.

You'll remember that when I heard I was a wanted woman I was at the gas station with Charlie. He was talking to some old timer about carburetors, oblivious to the panic that was going on inside of me, having not heard the announcement on the wireless.

As I sat there, willing Charlie to turn around so I could gesture to him that we ought to get going, the Maroon Ford T that Charlie had been so paranoid about pulled upon the forecourt.

I recognized the driver immediately. It was Walter.

'Oh God!'

I cursed aloud for whilst there was no picture of me in circulation yet, this was a man who knew my name. If he had heard the news bulletin, I would have been in a lot of trouble.

I sank down as low as I could in the passenger seat, praying he wouldn't notice me. Thankfully, Charlie was walking over to the car now, the old man alongside him. The old guy began filling up the tank whilst Charlie opened the door and searched in the footwell.

'Damn shallow pockets, my wallet must have fallen out.'

He paid no attention to me, sliding down in the seat. Probably thought I was helping to look.

He found his wallet and walked round the back of the car to pay the old man.

I glanced across at Walter in the Ford T, but the car was empty.

At some point during the search for the wallet, he must have got out of the car. Now I couldn't see him anywhere.

The old man had finished filling the car by now, but Charlie insisted on standing there, talking.

'Come on Charlie,' I willed. 'Just get back in the car and we can get out of here.'

There was a tap on the window that startled me.

Right there, next to me, stood Walter.

'You didn't make it very far then?'

I couldn't tell if it was accusatory or not. His tone of voice didn't give much away.

'What do you mean?'

Walter laughed.

'I mean, Trenton ain't so far. You left about an hour ago with your fella and yet I've managed to catch up with you.'

'Yeah, the two guys are talking cars. Can't drag them away,' I gave a nervous laugh.

'Well, I guess I'll be seeing you. Good luck, wherever you're headed.'

What a relief! He didn't know a thing.

I smiled and waved, as he walked over to the old man to ask about getting some gas and Charlie realizing he was keeping the old man from a customer, finally said his goodbyes and got back into the car, nodding an acknowledgement at Walter. He started the engine and as it purred, the news came on the old man's wireless a second time.

'Law enforcement officers are on the hunt for singer Pearl Blanchet who is wanted in connection with the murder of a druggist George O Malley...'

I kept my gaze in my lap and held my breath, not daring to look in Charlie's direction but I could feel his eyes on me.

'Pearl, what the...'

'What Charlie? Which part do you want to discuss? The part where I'm wanted by the coppers or the part where I apparently murdered

George? Because I'd hoped you knew me well enough by now to see I've been framed.'

My voice was quiet but shrill. Panic was getting the better of me.

'It's okay Pearl, calm down. I believe you. We'll talk about it later. We'd better get out of here, people are looking.'

He looked across at Walter, who was staring back at us.

As we sped away, I couldn't resist turning my head to see Walter frantically pointing in our direction.

'That's her!' he was saying to the old man. 'The woman they're looking for.'

I turned back round to face the road.

'Drive Charlie. Just drive!'

***

I could tell by the erratic way Charlie was driving, swerving side to side, that he was too busy watching Walter in the rear-view mirror to keep his eyes fixed on the road.

'I don't get why he won't just quit,' Charlie said, 'You'd think knowing that a girl was a murderer might make you back off a little.'

'Charlie, I swear, I didn't kill him.'

'Relax Pearl. I know you didn't. Was a slip of the tongue, is all.'

He went quiet a moment, and I could tell he was weighing up whether he should say what he really wanted to or whether to keep it zipped. He chose the first option.

'Do you think I haven't met people who've killed others before? You seem to forget who my Dad was.'

He had a point.

'I used to think morality was straightforward. That there was a right and wrong and a line that divided the two of them that you didn't step over, but now I know different. Sometimes it isn't so clear cut. Take Milton for instance. If someone whacked Milton, are you telling me there isn't a little bit of you that would be glad?'

I didn't answer.

'Hold on!'

Charlie took a sharp right turn down an alleyway, throwing me sideways, almost into his lap.

We went racing past overflowing bins teaming with rats and pot wash boys smoking cigarettes on their break and pulled out onto the main road where I was able to pull myself back upright and brush my hair out of my face. This wasn't the time to criticize Charlie's driving.

'Looks like we lost him,' Charlie sighed, relieved.

'I guess I'm just going to have to leave town,' I said.

'Well, I am trying...'

'I don't mean out of Trenton, Charlie. I'm sorry but I can't go back to Atlantic City now. I mean, I might not even be able to stay in the country.'

He shook his head. 'That's nonsense.'

'Is it? You know I can't compete against Milton and expect to win. I bet he's got every copper in the state in his pocket. The papers too.'

'Where will you go?' His voice was somber.

I'm not sure what romantic notion he'd had in his head when I agreed to go back with him, but that illusion was fading fast.

I looked out of the window at the passing buildings, so I didn't have to meet his eye.

'I don't know yet, but I was thinking if I can make it to New York, I can get a boat out of here. Go to Paris. Dublin or London even.'

'What if there's another option?'

'If you have a better one, I'm all ears.'

'Well, you know I'm sure Milton's pissed off a lot of people. I'm sure for the right price his early demise could be easily arranged for the right price...'

I couldn't believe what I was hearing. This wasn't the Charlie I knew. I cut him off before he could finish.

'Well, you weren't lying were you, when you said you didn't mind stepping over the line anymore?'

'Pearl, look...'

'No, you look. I don't want to cause you any more trouble. I've already done enough of that. Just take me to the railway station and I'll find my way by myself.'

'Whatever you want.'

As the patches of land became longer between the buildings and the houses less frequent, I could tell we were finally leaving Trenton and heading for the open road. Or we would have been if Walter hadn't pulled up alongside us.

Charlie put his foot down, but the engine couldn't outrun Walter's. We were racing head-to-head with him now, Walter checking over at us every now and then, shouting at us to pull over.

'Pass me your gun,' I said to Charlie.

He handed it to me.

'You realize he probably has a gun in there too, don't you?'

I nodded and took it from him, cocked the pistol and aimed in Walter's direction. Walter's hand came up to cover his eyes and I don't know if it was the lack of visibility or the bullet I shot into his tire that made him lose control and go careering into a ditch. I didn't care. All I knew was that we'd definitely lost him now and I had to get to New York before they released a photo and people started recognizing me.

'Look I don't mind driving you there all the way to New York, if that's what you want,' Charlie said.

I got the sense he just wanted to keep me in his sights as long as possible but the longer I stayed with him, the harder it would be when I inevitably had to leave.

I shook my head.

'Thanks, but the train'll be faster. Besides, Walter's likely to be lying dazed in that ditch. When he comes round, it'll be your car they'll be looking out for, with me in it. I'm sorry about that, Charlie. I didn't mean to drag you into this.'

'Don't you worry about that.'

He drove as fast as he could without drawing attention to us. As we pulled into the station alongside a line of people queuing up at the ticket booth, there was an aching in my heart I hadn't expected to feel.

Charlie delved into his pocket and handed me a wad of notes.

'Here, take this.'

I pushed his hand away.

'I don't want it.'

I didn't want anything else that put me in his debt.

'This isn't the time to be proud. You're going to need a jack to get where you want to be and given that everyone will know who you are by this time tomorrow, it would be foolish to step into a bank to get some right now.'

He held it out again for me to take.

'Think of it as a gift. No strings attached.'

I hated taking it, but knew he was right.

'Thanks Charlie. Once I'm settled somewhere, I swear I'll pay every cent back.'

'I don't care if you don't.'

We both sat there for a moment, the silence growing as neither of us wanted me to get out of the car.

'Honestly, if I ever lay my hands on Milton again...' Charlie gritted his teeth.

'Well, there is one last thing I have to ask. Once I've found somewhere to stay, I might ask you to do something for me. If I send a package to you to pass on, could you promise me you'll do it.'

'I promise.'

'You'll have to take Champ off my hands too; He'll draw too much attention. You'll look after him for me, won't you?'

'Of course.'

I leaned over and kissed him letting it linger on my lips for a while, not knowing if this would be the last time we ever saw one another. Deep in my guts I felt it probably was.

'Good luck songbird. Knock em dead in Paris.'

'I will.'

I went round to hug Champ and kissed him on the top of his head. I lowered my cloche hat a little so I couldn't be recognized, while Charlie took my overnight bag out of the trunk, slipping in his flask of whiskey for me.

I took it from him and walked without looking back. I didn't want to make the mistake of making eye contact. If I did, he would see the tears streaming down my face. I wanted him to think I didn't care. That way it would be easier for the both of us.

Songbird.

Charlie had meant it affectionately, but little did he know how that pet name would come to haunt me.

As I took my seat on the train, I spotted the same phrase shouting out from the front pages like a bad omen.

MISSING SONGBIRD FLEW THE COOP.

POLICE ON LOOKOUT.

But that wasn't the worst part. Underneath the headline, my picture stared out. Me in that awful sequin dress.

The newsboy was still cutting through the string that held the paper brick of copies. If I was lucky, the train would pull away before anyone had chance to see it, but Trenton wasn't the only stop along the line. What if passengers picked up the paper at other stops along the way?

By the time we pulled into New York, my face would be known across the whole of New Jersey. I just had to pray to God, I could make it before anyone recognized me.

***

*Y*ou *always said that people were too busy with their heads buried in their own lives to care too much about anyone else's, and I tried to calm my pounding heart my repeating that over and over in my mind as I made my way through the passengers sat side by side in their wicker chairs in coach class.*

The floor shook as the engine roared awake and clouds of smoke billowed past the windows outside. Through the mist I could see the newsboy laying out the papers calling out, 'Killer songbird wanted. Read all about it.'

The crowd were gathering round, buying up the papers for something to read on the journey. I looked away.

If I could just get to my carriage before they filled up the steps, I would be okay but in the doorway of the second-class carriage, a family was blocking the aisle with their bags. The porter was trying to help them put their bags in the overhead luggage racks but the proud head of the family, seeing it as a criticism of his masculinity, loudly rebuffed him.

'I have you know, buddy, I was a heavyweight champion back in my day. I can assure you I don't require your help.'

The porter stepped back apologetically while the gentleman's wife said nothing. As her husband shoved the bag more aggressively into the rack, she pulled two children in closer to her. If ever there was a woman who was scared of upsetting her husband, it was her.

Meanwhile behind me, a queue was forming. Some of them were clutching the afternoon paper folded under their arms, the crease of the paper right down the center of my face so that only my eyes peeped out.

Up ahead, behind the family, I could see there were people sitting down and unfolding their papers to read the front page.

A wave of sickness washed over me. These people had more money than coach class so were more unlikely to shop me in purely for the money, but the idea that a female criminal was aboard with them, well that might offend their morals enough to want to see me locked away.

I took a deep breath and eventually, after some cursing and rearranging bags, the family had all their luggage safely stored in the racks and they all sat down, freeing up the aisle so I could walk through. I strolled past the row of papers propped up, an audience of my own face staring out at me.

Finally, I reached the carriage that was to be mine. I pulled the door tightly shut behind me, pulled down the blind and dropped my bag so that I could finally let my legs give way and collapse down on the seat, weeping.

I cried out of anger at the unfairness of it all. At the papers for their slander and character assignation. At Milton for framing me and getting away with murder.

But most of all I was angry at myself for being too scared to tell Charlie I loved him when I'd had the chance.

Love Always
Pearl

73

SEPTEMBER 30TH, 1927

❖━━━━━━━━❖

I tell you Grandma, my stomach ached all the way from Trenton to Penn station but visiting the dining car was way too risky. So instead, I smoked cigarette after cigarette hoping to dull the growling hunger.

The engine juddered as we slowed down to a junction. Up ahead, I could see the railway sign: Princeton. This was the very last place I wanted us to pull into having only been there hours earlier, for it meant more people being able to recognize me.

I got up from my seat to take a look at the station and saw a crowd gathered around the newsboy on the platform, all of them picking up papers with my face as front-page news.

Among them, a boy I recognized: the boy with red hair from Charlie's Wisteria Club. Frankie.

In a panic I yanked down the blind before he spotted me. If me and Charlie were right about the attack on his speakeasy, then Frankie wasn't a dry agent or a spy for the Abels. He took his orders from Milton.

The passengers mounted the steps, their footsteps filling the air in the corridor outside as they filed past my room, bags and tickets in hand. Dropping down below the viewing window, I crawled across on my hands and knees and reached up to draw the blind across the door.

I sat, back against the door, heart pounding, hands shaking as I hitched up my skirt and checked that my pistol was still tucked inside my garter. It was.

Outside my door, silhouettes paused and passed by, their idle chatter loud enough to hear from where I sat crouched behind the door. The floor shuddered and the engine roared as it started up again, shaking my overnight bag off the luggage rack and sending it whizzing past my cheek and crashing onto the floor next to me. The thing created such a thump that I reached for my pistol.

I gave the bag a swift kick as punishment for startling me, then proceeded to rummage through it to check the flask of whiskey Charlie had given me was still in one piece. Whilst I was there, I took a long swig to calm my nerves.

I must have fallen asleep as the next thing jolting me awake was a rap at the door and a huge shadow of a man looming over me.

He tried to push the door open, managing to open it with just a crack to call through.

'Tickets, Miss.'

It was the porter that had helped the family with their bags in second class. Whilst I knew he was harmless I had learned from my years with the mob, not to open the door unless absolutely necessary when you were wanted by someone. Milton had been full of stories of people shot dead by delivery boys and florists.

I called out to him in my weakest voice.

'I'm so sorry, I have such a headache. Could you be a doll and pop back later?'

He paused for a moment, thinking it through.

'Well Miss, I'm meant to collect your tickets right away...'

He tried to push the door again.

'It's just that my ticket's at the bottom of my bag and with this headache I can barely see straight. I'll tip you well.'

I passed a handful of dollar bills through the gap, so he knew I meant it.

The money disappeared out of my hand and the door closed shut, leaving me all alone again. I was safe for now.

I didn't know how long I'd been asleep, but my back ached, and it was twilight outside. I stretched and got up to switch on the lamps to illuminate the room.

I'd been travelling for hours by now and it was getting to the point where I needed to use the facilities. I opened the door a crack and peeped out. The corridor that had been so filled with the hustle and bustle of passengers was empty now.

I grabbed my purse, pushed my bag back up on the luggage rack and left the room to find the bathroom. The way I figured it, most people would be in the dining car, or their bellies so full of dinner that they were too busy sleeping it off in their own seats to notice me walking down the corridor.

I took care not to make eye contact with anyone and when I got to the bathroom, I washed the rouge from my lips and cheeks and kohl from my eyes.

Milton, in his pride, had foolishly provided the police and papers with a picture of me dressed up to the nines. No doubt he wanted people to think I looked wanton, but his vanity could also be my saving grace. His actions meant my plain face underneath would be my best disguise. If only I'd had time to buy myself a wig before leaving town.

When I was done, I pulled the chain and opened the door to come face to face with Frankie.

We locked eyes for just long enough for me to see the look on his face that suggested he recognized me but couldn't quite place where from. He *must have seen the horror in my gaze too and I knew I had only seconds to get back to my room before the memory registered.*

Walking with urgency and not daring to look behind I made it to my room. I fumbled with the door handle, so panicked my hands were shaking.

I finally yanked the door open but as I tried to close the door behind me, a boot wedged itself in the gap. My gaze moved upwards to meet Frankie's as he shoulder barged his way in, bursting the door open and flinging me backwards onto the floor.

'It is you. I knew it!' he said. 'You're that broad everyone's on the lookout for.'

He pulled the pistol from his jacket, just as I reached for mine, both of us aiming at the other.

'I didn't do it,' I said.

'Really? It's hard to claim innocence when you have a gun pointing at someone's face.'

'I could say the same thing about you.'

'You're Milton's girl. Or was. I'm not sure who'll pay more for you, Milton or the coppers.'

'If its money you want, I can arrange that. Put the gun down and we can talk about it.'

He shook his head.

'Nah, you put yours down first. Look I ain't going to shoot you. You're worth nothing dead. No one'll pay unless you're handed in alive.'

Now I knew two things. One: I was in no real danger. He had laid out his cards before even attempting to call my bluff and that was a foolish move.

Two: he had no idea what he was doing. He was what you'd call 'all mouth and no trousers' and that gave me an advantage.

I lowered my gun.

'Fine. Look you got me. I can accept that. I'll come quietly. Just help me up, won't you?' I held out my hand.

Unsure what to do now, he hesitated, glancing back at the open door. Still, he helped me to my feet, and I brushed myself off.

He looked uncomfortable now. He hadn't expected me to come quietly.

'Now you just stay where you are.'

He raised his gun again just as the door opened and the porter stepped in.

'Tickets?'

Seizing my chance, I barged past them both, sending the porter flying forward. There was a gunshot as the two of them landed together in a pile on the floor. I didn't stay to check if the porter was okay. I could hear the boy shouting at him that he was an idiot, which told me chances were, he was absolutely fine.

I wasted no time and ran along the carriage, heads turning as I passed. When I got to the dining car I slowed down, but it was easy to see that I was flustered and that I didn't belong. A waiter moved towards me.

'Can I find you a table, Miss?'

'No, no thank you.'

I walked quickly along, past the first-class folk stuffing their faces.

I didn't know what I would do when I got to the end of the carriage. There would be nowhere else to go except outside on the caboose and soon enough the porter and Frankie would come through the same carriages and question the same diners who would point them in my direction.

When someone pulled the emergency chord, I knew it was already too late, and my time was up.

Panicking now, I ran out of the door and onto the caboose where a couple stood uncomfortably close together and a gentleman stood smoking a *pipe. I lifted my petticoats and climbed over the railing, clinging onto the metal, skirt billowing out as the tracks blurred beneath me.*

The woman screamed out.

'Don't do it! Don't jump.'

Even with the train slowing, it was still moving much too fast for me to land safely, but what other chance did I have? I could hear the porter's voice shouting out behind me.

'Somebody stop that woman!'

There was no more time to ponder. It was either jump or be caught. I took a deep breath, closed my eyes and jumped.

***

My landing was not a smooth one. I landed awkwardly next to the track, a pain shooting through my ankle. I looked up to see the porter reach the end of the train as it moved away from me. The mustachioed gentleman taking a smoke break, pointed in my direction just as Frankie caught up and to my horror, began climbing over the railing.

With barely time to catch my breath after landing, I pulled myself up and onto my feet and started to run, my twisted ankle smarting with every single stride I took.

I dare not look behind, but I could sense Frankie getting closer and closer until he was so close I could hear him panting as he ran.

The verge that led away from the tracks and towards whatever small town lay on the other side was steep, and with my weak ankle I struggled to run. I fell and slid backwards, and Frankie reached out, grasping at my ankle as I kicked like a mule. But fighting back was no use. He pulled me back down through the mud and I managed to roll onto my back, kicking out just as he stepped towards me and straight into my foot.

Hitting him in the weak spot of his groin he crumpled like a paper bag, groaning as he fell to his knees.

As the two of us grappled in the dirt a gunshot rang out.

The mustachioed gentleman from the train was brandishing a shotgun, flanked by the porter and a couple of other men with their sleeves rolled to the elbows.

'It's no use fighting, Miss. The best thing would be for you to hand yourself in. Let us take you to the sheriff.'

I didn't have the fight in me no more. I was outnumbered. And now the train had come to a standstill, there were more passengers climbing over the railing and running towards us to come and help them contain me.

I raised my arms in the air in an act of surrender.

Love Always
Pearl

74

OCTOBER 1ST, 1927

❖ ▒▒ ───── ▒▒ ───── ▒▒ ❖

So, Grandma,

That's the long and short of it. Now there's nothing for me to do but wait for Clyde to take me in.

Goodness knows how I've managed to fall asleep lying on this cold wooden bench in the cell. Damn deputy, won't even give me a blanket. No burlap sacking. Nothing. Told me I can go sing for it. Thinks he's a comedian.

This must be the most excitement they've had round these parts for some time. Holding a known felon has got their names in the papers and on the wireless. The sheriff keeps on combing his hair in case the newshawks and photographers turn up. I've heard the two of them talking, plotting ways they can make money out of me. Even planning to take the reward from Frankie and share it between the pair of them. Is there any law enforcement that you can trust?

'I'll call the guys at Atlantic City.'

The sheriff was gleeful as he made the call to Clyde. I've got no chance of a fair hearing now. Not that I would if I stayed here either.

At one point I asked for a glass of water.

'You don't deserve anything after what you did to that O'Malley boy,' the sheriff said. *'The way I heard it, the two of you had been making whoopie all over town for months before you had him killed.'*

Milton's words coming out of his mouth.

'Where did you hear that?'

'Everyone knows it. It's in the papers. On the wireless. Everywhere.'

Milton must be calling in favors from all of his buddies. The same newshawks who praise Milton for his community work and bury news of his shortcomings lower down in the columns. The ones who did the same for Clarence Kelly before him. The ones who refused to report on the fire we had at our place all those months ago. Everyone has a price, and powerful men can afford to pay whether in bribes or in kind.

The sheriff put down the phone receiver and swaggered over.

'Well, I'm sorry to say we'll be parting ways soon once the law from Atlantic City gets here. I just spoke to Officer Thompson just now.'

I'm going to lie facing the wall, so I don't have to talk to them and wait for Clyde.

I don't see how this will end well for me, Grandma. I'm just sorry you didn't get the revenge I promised you would.

***

I'm writing this as quickly as I can. I don't know how long I've been lay here but believe me when I say a miracle could be about to happen. I didn't pay much attention to the door opening and light flooding in the room until I heard the Sheriff scrape his chair on the tiles in his rush to stand. When he spoke, his voice was a mixture of surprise and disappointment.

'Can I help you, Miss?'

'I'm here for the prisoner.'

I rolled over to see the back of a woman in her skirt suit, hair scraped back into a bun, flashing her badge at two of them.

They inspected it like it was some rare artefact. The sheriff read her name aloud.

'Officer Nancy Simpson.'

Love Always
Pearl

75

OCTOBER 3RD, 1927

❖ ▪▪──────•••──────▪▪ ❖

Dear Grandma,

Firstly, I should tell you that even though Nancy took me away, I'm safe. When she walked in the Sherrif and his Deputy were falling over themselves to help her so they could get us both out of there.

'You know, I expected someone different,' the sheriff said.

The deputy looked past her and through the door like he expected someone else to step in and help her at any moment.

Nancy didn't shy away from the elephant she'd brought into the room.

'You were expecting a man, you mean? The officer you spoke to on the phone, no doubt. Well, I'm sorry to disappoint.'

'Pearl's over here.'

The sheriff led her over to my cell and unlocked the door.

She watched my movements closely, not saying anything. She put on a set of handcuffs and led me out to the wagon in the parking lot. She opened the door for me, shoving me onto the back seat. As she did, I heard the sheriff complaining loudly to his deputy.

'Well, that's what's going wrong with the world, son. A woman federal agent. We're all going to hell in a handcart.'

Most of the journey was spent in silence. You once told me when you were still alive that when the law take you in, the worst you can do is talk too much.

I looked out the window as the day turned to night, and the fields to brightly lit buildings, and eventually I didn't know where we were headed but it didn't look like Atlantic City. I leaned forward to ask her.

'What jailhouse are you taking me to?'

'We're not going to the jailhouse.

She kept her eyes on the road ahead.

'What do you mean?'

'It's okay, Pearl. You're safe with me. You were on your way to New York I believe when they picked you up. That right?'

'Yeah, that's right.'

'Headed for the ferry, I'd bet. Starting a new life?'

She glanced back at me in the rear-view mirror.

I nodded. To think I'd really thought I could escape. It seemed so foolish.

'Well, you should know that right now there are officers in Atlantic City surrounding Milton Costello's home. I've never believed the story that him and Clyde concocted. I've been investigating his business relations with Clyde Thompson for a long time. I know Clyde's been simultaneously helping Milton with his rumrunning whilst also turning a blind eye to his wrongdoing for a price.'

This was nothing new to me, even if it was to her.

'Well, now Clyde has grown a conscience all of a sudden. Been keeping a ledger of all of the illegal transactions Costello has been doing for some time. Fancies himself as an informer of sorts. I think he's hoping it'll raise him up the ranks. He's claiming it's the ranks of the law he has his eye on, but I don't believe that for a second.

Until we exposed him for the corrupt copper he is, it looked like he was planning to keep Milton locked up to leave himself a little opening in the bootlegging business. After all, without Milton, who else is there to take over as kingpin?'

Charlie hadn't even crossed her mind, and I wasn't about to remind her.

'So not only will we have stopped Milton from doing you any more harm, we'll have stopped Clyde too.'

'So, you believe my side of the story?'

My voice croaked as I spoke. There was a lump in my throat and tears welling that I was trying my best to stop.

'Thing is, both of us know Milton will go free.'

My stomach dropped.

'Free? No. No,' I shook my head. 'That can't happen. He'll hunt me down and kill me.'

She spoke bluntly. 'I'm sorry Pearl but it can, and it will. You know how it goes: Milton will pay those on his good side to defend him and crush your reputation into dust. Others he'll pay to keep quiet. He might do some jail time for the bootlegging, sure. Maybe there'll even be talk of the death penalty if he's found guilty of killing Jay or George, but pretty soon, given his influence with congressman, judges, journalists, those witnesses will fall and the case against him collapse and he'll go on with his life just the same as he did before. You however...'

'Will be condemned.'

I hated finishing her sentence, but I knew she spoke the truth.

'Oh God, I think I'm going to be sick.'

But she still wasn't done.

'I hate to say it, but even if you're not found guilty, you'll live with the words of those news reports around your neck. And if not that, you'll

be known as a rat, the price on your head paid for by Milton and his associates.'

I put my head in my hands.

'I thought you said when you picked me up, that I was safe.'

'And you are now. Back at the lighthouse I said I'll help you escape, and I will.'

I let her words sink in. She wasn't just going to let me go, she was going to help me get to New York so I could catch a boat across the water.

'I don't understand. What's in this for you?'

'Remember at the lighthouse I told you about what happened to the women officers in San Francisco? Well, they're trying to do the same to us. They say women distract from the job at hand. Don't like our methods. Say our boots are getting too big. If they're going to get rid of us anyway, I might as well go out with a bang and helping you escape would be a small victory for all of us,' she said.

I thought of what she'd told me about her life before. The life of drinking and bad relationships. Her job had been her escape. Her own way out. I wasn't sure what she'd do if that was taken away from her.

If you were here now Grandma, I know you'd understand.

I haven't forgotten my promises to you, and I swear I have a new plan for revenge, but I don't think I need to write to you anymore.

I love and miss you.

Love always

Pearl.

76

NOVEMBER 11TH, 1927

To my beloved Milton,

It's been months since we last saw one another and I bet you thought I'd never come back into your life. After all, I'm still a wanted woman, following your outstanding manipulation of the press and the authorities in making them believe I murdered George.

Officer Simpson warned me you would be acquitted, and I see from the headlines that she was right.

Which brings me to the real reason I'm writing to you, as I'm sure you are confident there is nothing else anyone can take you down for.

But I know better.

Let me cast your memory back to one day in August 1925 and the hot roasting Summer we had that year. You must have barely been out of the cheap oversized wool suit you used to wear, eager to do anything to rise up in the ranks. The turf war between the Kellys and Abels was only in its infancy and when Clarence asked you to do a favor you executed it beautifully and without question.

That favor was to visit a brothel in New York, said to be under the Abel's control that you also knew was frequented by a guy named Joe that you and George had had a previous altercation with.

All you had to do was light the match that would set the place alight. It was simple. Easy.

Only that place wasn't just a bawd house.

That place was my home.

Known locally as 'Grandma's House,' it was the place where I was born and where I grew up. My mother's love of the white powder was stronger than her love for me and when she left when I was ten, my makeshift mother, 'Grandma,' took care of me, treating me like the child she never had.

It wasn't as sordid an upbringing as you might expect. I was protected from the everyday business and taught to read and sing. As I got older, Grandma had me perform for the punters whilst they waited in the parlor, but she always encouraged me to leave that life behind and chase after my dreams of performing on Broadway or on movies in Hollywoodland. Of course, I never made it there, but it wasn't for lack of trying. The night you soaked that rag with alcohol and set my home alight, I was away at an audition.

It took three days for the flames to die down and when they eventually did, all that was left was a pile of bones and ash. They had to identify Grandma by her teeth.

Everyone spoke of the perpetrator being one of Clarence Kelly's men, but the law did nothing to find him. Of course, they didn't! Clarence would have paid them for their silence.

I heard your name whispered by those at Grandma's funeral and I swore to her right then that I would find those responsible one day and get my revenge.

Finding Clarence was easy. Always courting the press, it wasn't hard to follow him to Atlantic City. They were always looking for performers at Kings, so it wasn't difficult to introduce myself to Charlie and get a gig there.

Finding you was purely by chance. You might have gotten away with it if it hadn't been for you stealing Champ as you left the scene of the fire. That was how I knew it had to have been you, when you brought my dog into Kings. You always seemed so surprised to find that Champ liked me so much more than he did you, and now you know the reason why.

I had anticipated having to find a way to kill Clarence but meeting you meant you did the hard work for me. It was so easy for me to suggest his death to you and your greed and ambition took care of the rest. I hadn't counted on your slow unravelling after Clarence was out of the picture. I guess you could just call that lucky.

I didn't intend on becoming involved with you romantically, but I knew I would have to sacrifice my affection for Charlie to make things right. In the same way a prisoner can fall in love with their torturer, I guess that's what happened to us. It was like the light in me found the dark in you and together we became whole.

Whilst I was playing a role for the most part, my attachment to you was very real. At times I wanted to believe there was good inside of you and sometimes I did see glimpses of it. In those times, I would forget my real purpose of why I was there. I guess it was the death of George that made me see there was no other way to end this. There was nothing else anyone could do to save you from yourself.

You see, as you read this standing in your office at Kings, coffee in hand, I'm sitting at a table at a cafe in Paris eating breakfast. The sun is beaming down on me as you read this like God has given me his blessing for final retribution.

Perhaps you're looking about nervously or reaching for your gun, wondering who it is that is coming to take you out, but you don't have to worry about that. Revenge is already ticking.

I like to think that your hand is trembling, the paper shaking, as you summon the courage to look deeper into the box this letter was attached to. Perhaps you won't even get to finish this letter before the box ignites.

And with the realization that you only have moments of your life left, maybe you'll repent for the fiery hell you unleashed upon my family all those months ago. Perhaps even think of the bomb you planted to take out Jesse and Eveline.

As Kings goes up in flames and this letter shrivels and burns to ash, leaving no trace, I will sit back, sip my champagne and smile to myself in the knowledge that I kept my promise to Grandma, and got my revenge after all.

Forever yours

Pearl.

THE END

ACKNOWLEDGEMENTS

A book, whilst often written as a solo activity, is rarely edited as one. As such, I have a few people I'd like to thank.

Firstly, two separate writing groups, based in Leamington Spa. Many thanks in particular to Harriet Cummings who read through the original version of Milton's story and pointed out that whilst writing in 1920's slang was clever, it also made it very difficult to read! I'm glad I listened to your advice.

Thanks also to Poppy Sall, Dan Purdue, Cassie Ledham, Patrick Kincaid, Susan Stokes Chapman and Kathy Hoyle for the encouragement throughout. A heartfelt thanks to Andrew Barker for regularly reminding me to 'outrun the doubt.'

To the writing group at Temperance, thanks to Michael Moser for keeping a keen eye out for plot inconsistences and British idioms whilst also reminding me that every good villain needs a heartbeat, and every heartbeat deserves a story.

Thank you to fellow indie authors Lisa Brace and Jay Darkmoore who have been so generous with their knowledge and who answered so many of my questions about indie publishing. A huge thanks to cover artist Samantha Kelly who listened to my vision for the cover and breathed life into it.

Thanks to my parents who have always encouraged my writing, long before I ever dreamed of publishing anything.

And lastly, thank you to my husband Nathan who believed in my writing from the very start. Your presence is a daily reminder that love can be slow, steady and safe, yet still set the heart alight.

ABOUT THE AUTHOR

J.L. Flannery is a lecturer in Digital Marketing and Content Creation. She has an MA in Shakespeare Studies and has had work adapted for podcast Pseudopod. Her short horror fiction has been featured in Cosmic Horror Monthly. She also organizes writing events in inspiring locations as the founder of Secret Writing Retreats. This is her first Historical Crime Thriller.

You can find her on social media at
Instagram @JLFLANNERY
and Tiktok @JLFLANNERYWRITER

Printed in Dunstable, United Kingdom

66561638R00188